LONG
DISTANCE
LIFE

Also by the Author

Migrations of the Heart
A Woman's Place

LONG
DISTANCE
LIFE

MARITA GOLDEN

DOUBLEDAY   New York   London   Toronto   Sydney   Auckland

⚓

PUBLISHED BY DOUBLEDAY

a division of Bantam Doubleday Dell Publishing Group, Inc.
666 Fifth Avenue, New York, NY 10103

DOUBLEDAY and the portrayal of an anchor with a dolphin
are trademarks of Doubleday,
a division of Bantam Doubleday Dell Publishing Group, Inc.

LIBRARY OF CONGRESS CATALOGING-IN-PUBLICATION DATA

Golden, Marita.
    Long distance life / Marita Golden.—1st ed.
      p.   cm.
    ISBN 0-385-19455-2
    I. Title.
PS3557.03593L66   1989
813'.54—dc20   53 2 9 0   89-32939
                                                    CIP

ISBN 0-385-19455-2
Copyright © 1989 by Marita Golden

BOOK DESIGN BY GUENET ABRAHAM

All Rights Reserved
Printed in the United States of America
October 1989

FIRST EDITION

BG

For my mama, who showed me the way

Acknowledgments

A project of this scope required assistance and encouragement from a host of people and "forces," whom I gratefully thank. The list is long and I know there are folks who will not be mentioned, but please know that you are not forgotten. I want to thank Joseph Jordan and the Institute for the Preservation and Study of African-American Writing for offering me a way to write *and* pay the rent at a point when I wondered if I would ever have the time to write again in this life. Carol Mann for continuing to believe in me and becoming a friend and agent par excellence. Marie Brown for her ever-reliable advice. Elizabeth Clarke-Lewis for sharing with me her research on the lives of Black women migrants from the South. Eloise Greenfield for her memories of Washington in the forties. Brett Williams for telling me to look up Jim Daniels. Jim Daniels for helping me to "place" this story exactly where it needed to be. My surrogate mom Thelbert Hines for her memories of life in Washington, D.C., in the fifties. Coco Farrow, Karen Spelman, Tina Smith and Karen Wilson for recounting their work in the "movement." Cuthbert Simpkins for taking a scalpel to the manuscript in the early drafts and convincing me to make Washington a character in this story as well. The D.C. Commission on the Arts and Humanities for financial support. My eleven-year-old son for listening to Naomi and helping me to shape her voice. Nancy Evans for asking me what I wanted from Doubleday and then giving it to me. Loretta Barrett for accepting nothing less than the best I could do, for waiting when that was required and cheering me on when that's what I needed. The Library of Congress, where I almost lived for eight months in 1988. My mama for "living" once again through Naomi. My daddy, who, like Rayford Johnson, "didn't go nowhere" but stayed in my heart.

Except the Lord build the house,
they labor in vain that build it;
except the Lord keep the city, the
watchman waketh but in vain.

It is vain for you to rise up early, to
sit up late, to eat the bread of sorrows;
for so he giveth his beloved sleep.

Lo, children are an heritage of the Lord; and the fruit
of the womb is his reward.

As arrows are in the hand of a mighty man;
so are children of the youth.

Happy is the man that hath his quiver full
of them; they shall not be ashamed, but they
shall speak with the enemies in the gate.

—Psalm 127

LONG DISTANCE LIFE

N A O M I

The story of my family's no different, really, than the story of yours. I'm so old now, every day I live is a surprise to people who think old folks die on some kinda schedule. I wish I could say I'd accumulated a whole lot of wisdom from all I've been through. I probably got a little more sense than you, just 'cause I'm so old. But even *that* depends on who *you* are. I will say this, though, and it took me getting this old to understand why old folks said it all the time: I'd do it all the same. 'Cause I know changing one thing changes it all. And you not gonna get but so much of it right—you gonna get your share of sorrow, no matter what.

There's no secret to living so long like I have, nothing you can bottle and sell. I just tried to do right by folks and that took me a long way. There was a old woman down South where I come from. She was the woman everybody went to with their troubles. They called her Granny Eyes, 'cause she could see so good what would happen to you if you did this or if you didn't do that. She worked roots and healed folks through faith. Today she'd be making a load of money, but back then folks just brought her whatever they had. And people always asked Granny Eyes, when she looked them in the face real hard, to explain what was ailing them; or when she'd start to deciphering them cards she used, or fixing up some potion, folks would start asking, "What it look like, Granny Eyes? What it look like?" And she'd just say, "It look like *life* to me."

The earth embraced them all that day. Showers had preceded and heralded their arrival. The sprawling acreage of the cemetery was reticent, as patient as death itself. Rain-soaked and sodden, the ground trembled with the desire to relieve and release. Small streams of red clay oozed from the mounds of dirt piled around the open gravesite. Rainwater carried the clay in flashes past their eyes, like a reprise of everything they had forgotten and all that mattered most. The clay seeped into the dark soil that was fragile and swollen by the rain.

There had been a moment, brief and therefore terrible, when the sun had carved an opening in the sky, as Nathaniel's body was lowered into the earth. Logan Spenser had turned to gaze at the intruding rays as if he would see his brother's face, grinning as he often did, his laughter a spit in the eye, assuring them that his death was, after all, an elaborate joke.

Logan turned and watched the faces of his brother's friends. They were still so young they thought all they were was men. They did not know they were men and children of God. Yet tears stained their bearded cheeks. Disbelief was a flame blazing in their eyes. Trudy Bronson, the young mother of Nathaniel's child, stood amongst the throng of Nathaniel's friends. Her youthful woman-child face was shadowed by a thin veil. Trudy gazed ahead, sobs convulsing her slender shoulders, not daring a glance at the casket.

The sound of the earth landing on the casket punctured Logan's ears and he saw his mother Esther fall gently onto her knees. Two of the pallbearers lifted her from the ground and carried her to Logan's nearby car.

To survive this moment, Logan convinced himself it was a dream and Esther's fall and departure unreal. His grandmother stood beside him. Her broad, lined forehead introduced a face of weathered skin, supple and strong. Naomi's eyes had longed to see everything. They were eyes that had healed all who looked into them that day. Logan felt Naomi's hand reach for his and he knew that what he stood witnessing was not a dream.

The casket was covered with soil and the mourners began to drift away. The family and friends who had hovered around them, protective, strong in their numbers, hugged Logan and Naomi uncertainly, and walked, their backs relieved, toward their cars.

Logan told his wife Felicia to walk with Naomi to his car.

He would join them shortly. Standing before his brother's grave, Logan closed his eyes and thought how much easier death suddenly seemed than life. For it was life that had crushed his brother. Nathaniel Spenser had turned twenty-one, become a father and been murdered in the space of three months. Logan had nearly forgotten the ongoing terrors of that age. But this summer on his brother's taut face, Logan had caught glimpses of who he had once been. And in Nathaniel's presence he could almost smell the scent of life unlived and so desired that the longing for it could stop the heart.

Logan was suddenly dizzy, his mind pulsing so hard and fast that only a series of deep breaths restored his equilibrium. The scenes rushed on anyway, a jumble at first, a mass, then he saw clearly the day a few months earlier when they had played basketball at the Y.

It was just the two of them, one-on-one. That day the game had meant everything. They had played not to win but to rekindle a synchronism they had lost. Nathaniel was deft, possessive with the ball, bouncing it against the gleaming polished wood of the gym floor with the ease of someone who thinks the ball is his by right. He stalked Logan, surrounding him, faking him as effectively as an entire five-man team. Nathaniel's hunger spurred Logan to find a language of his own—resilient, workmanlike—simple enough to get the job done. Three times Nathaniel arched his lean body in the air, as he jumped high for a one-handed dunk. Each time Logan carefully, quietly defeated the ball, blocking it with a nick-of-time use of hands that he timed to Nathaniel's movements. And after a while Nathaniel knew in advance each shot his brother would make and yet he still could not stop him. After an hour of play, they nearly limped off the floor, high-fiving their way into the locker room.

"Little brother, you're all style and no substance," Logan had teased.

"Just what the world loves," Nathaniel laughed, peeling off his shorts. In the shower Logan felt a tinge of envy watching the sturdiness, the muscularity of Nathaniel's body, the thick calves and thighs and his chest, a little too wide and heavy for the lower half of his body. Nathaniel had been working out with weights and his muscles bulged, overconfident and strong. Logan watched the soap slide down his own chest and over his protruding paunch. He scrubbed his arms, solid but not as muscular as his brother's, and wondered what he would do with a twenty-one-year-old body. Nathaniel turned to Logan and, over the noise of the water, shouted, "Good game, man. You're not as old as I thought."

"It's all in the mind," Logan said, watching Nathaniel's eyes—the right eye noticeably larger than the left, both hard and determined—those eyes watching him and, Logan knew, wondering what in the hell it felt like to be almost forty. The small map of freckles beneath his eyes and along the bulge of Nathaniel's nose softened the hardness of his eyes. Still, the flintlike quality of Nathaniel's gaze always returned and made it hard to look into his eyes too long.

Nathaniel had seemed confident that day, but his laughter was brittle. His wide assured gait struck Logan as a camouflage and Logan knew that his brother possessed a secret, one that strangled the words Logan clumsily sculpted to discover the truth. What horrified Logan as much as the secret was its power. For in the face of the unknown, Logan realized that he preferred ignorance to knowledge that would test his will, his strength, his love. And so he was reduced to asking Nathaniel as they dressed after the shower, "So what's going on?"

"Same old thing." Nathaniel shrugged.

"No, I mean really," Logan insisted, daring to look deep into Nathaniel's unwelcoming eyes.

Nathaniel stood, silently buttoning his shirt, his thick brows furrowed, considering his answer with the utmost care.

Then he told Logan with a crooked, icy smile, "Nothing you need to know."

Rarely had Logan felt that he truly knew his brother. Logan was the child of Esther's youth, born of passion and the confusion of impending womanhood. Nathaniel was conceived in the season of Esther's radiant adulthood—the child she finally knew how to love.

Logan had known their father and forged a union with the man who had never denied him as a son yet never married Esther. Randolph Spenser died as Nathaniel lay in Esther's womb and his absence, Logan knew, had crippled Nathaniel, robbing some of the boy's resilience and strength.

So Logan had asked Nathaniel, as they stood in the gym dressing room, "Why don't I need to know?"

"Because your knowing wouldn't change a thing."

And Logan had wanted, in that moment, to slap his brother, to grab him and slam him against the metal lockers and to demand full disclosure.

Nathaniel had sliced through Logan's thoughts by saying, "Logan, you're my brother. Stop trying to be my old man. I never knew him. It's too late now."

"Not knowing him doesn't mean you owe me nothing."

"I never knew him so I've got to figure out what I owe myself."

"But you owe something to more than just yourself," Logan warned. "You always will. Don't forget that."

In response, Nathaniel had gazed at Logan with sullen disinterest, his lips pursed, his eyes filled with contempt. And Logan shivered inside beneath the blast of his gaze, remembering that this seemed to be the only way Nathaniel looked at everything and everyone now.

They had finished dressing in silence and walked out of the Y, parting in front of Logan's car with the formality of strangers. And as Logan watched Nathaniel walk away from him with an odd jauntiness, he imagined running to his brother, throwing an arm around his shoulder and retrieving what they had never had.

And there was another memory washing over Logan as he stood, unable to leave the grave site, the memory of the day Nathaniel became a father. When Logan entered the visitors' lounge of Washington Hospital Center, Nathaniel hugged him, composing himself quickly when they sat down together. Nathaniel had spent several months trying to persuade his girlfriend to have an abortion. Yet when Logan sat beside his brother, Nathaniel said in an awestruck whisper, "Did you see her? Man, she's beautiful. It's like a miracle or something." He paused. "I didn't want Trudy to have the baby. I told you that. But I just couldn't imagine . . ."

"You'll handle it," Logan said.

"I'm still scared."

"You should be."

"You know, she loves me," Nathaniel said incredulously.

"Does that surprise you?"

"I don't know," Nathaniel said haltingly, as if considering the possibility that he did not deserve to be loved. "Maybe it does. I had dropped her. Until today I hadn't seen her in six weeks."

"You don't owe her your life. You owe your baby a father," Logan said. But moments later he felt strangely dissatisfied by the neatness of the equation he had offered his brother. He thought of his wife and his ex-wife and the children he had fathered with both women. Logan knew, despite the confident platitude he had offered, that love exacts an asking price. His brother knew this too and it turned Nathaniel suddenly gloomy.

"You saw Trudy?" Logan asked.

"Yeah. I saw her first, in fact, then the baby." Nathaniel lit a cigarette as he spoke and Logan noticed the trembling of his brother's hands. "There wasn't much to say. She just kept crying. I stood at the foot of the bed, watching her, letting her make me feel like a dog. Then I put the flowers I'd brought on the table next to her bed and walked out. But when I saw the baby I almost forgot everything else."

Nathaniel took several puffs on the cigarette. Logan watched his brother's face unfold and then retreat.

"I feel that baby weighing on me like I've never felt anything else before." Nathaniel stood, his body tense, poised, Logan thought, for flight. He paced the floor, shaking his head in sorrow and disbelief.

"Nate, what do you think Trudy feels?"

Nathaniel let the cigarette dangle from his lips as he stared at the television monitor perched near the ceiling. "I don't know, big brother. Hell, I don't even care."

Logan could have offered advice in response to Nathaniel's sullen admission. But he chose silence, trusting it much more than anything he might say. He and his brother were men and so they spoke in ellipses, marching up to the edge of confession and then turning back.

They walked to the nursery and stood before the window that displayed the newborns like row after row of priceless objects. "There she is," Nathaniel exclaimed, pointing to a calm, tiny brown face wrapped in a pink blanket in the middle of the second row. "I don't even know if Trudy's given her a name yet."

"Why don't you ask her?" Nathaniel stood rooted to the spot, gazing at the infants with yearning and fear. But Logan watched as Nathaniel's face curdled into a mask of distrust as he said bitterly, "It's all a game, that's all, just a game."

"I'll be damned," Logan said.

"Sure it is," Nathaniel insisted.

"I'll tell you why it's not," Logan said. "If it was just a game, you could make up any rules, you could do anything to win."

"Tell me how what's in the street's any different? Or the bedroom, wherever?"

"In a game you don't pay dues," Logan said. "Not real ones anyway. It feels like a game to you because you're not ready to face up to how serious it is."

Seeking a conciliation that he felt was nearly impossible, Logan placed his hand on Nathaniel's shoulder and steered him down the corridor. "I've got a patient to see in Intensive Care," he told Nathaniel as they arrived outside the door to Trudy's room.

"What do I say to her?" Nathaniel asked, terror tightening in his eyes.

"Tell her how proud you are of the baby. Tell her how proud you are of her. Then ask her what she wants to name your child. Ask Trudy who she wants your baby to be."

Logan woke from these memories as from a deep yet unsatisfying sleep. The rain, despite the day's awful heat, landed cold and refreshing on his skin. The thin petals of the roses and lilies on Nathaniel's grave bobbed bravely against the weight of the raindrops. The canopy that covered the grave site shook in the wind.

Lincoln Cemetery sprawled over one hundred and thirty-five acres. It was here in this cemetery that Logan's grandfather was buried, on a sloping crowded hill a five-minute drive from where he stood. His father lay a mile's distance from Nathaniel, the son he had not lived to see. Drenched in the rain rapidly changing from downpour to storm, Logan felt a loneliness so deep he was afraid he would retch. But he was a man, as his father had been; a man like his grandfather, who Naomi said died fighting for his people; a man like his brother, who had assumed the prize was to be captured rather than bestowed. The rain had soaked through his suit and Logan shivered as it chilled his skin. Every muscle in his body was cramped and aching. He slowly turned to walk to his car, fighting the urge to stand before the grave the rest of his life or unearth Nathaniel and ask him, as he had not done when he lived, "Why, Nate, why?"

Nearing the car, Logan saw Felicia, Esther and Naomi watching him through the rain-streaked windows, their faces etched with the love that he, like Nathaniel, secretly feared he did not deserve. Logan hunched his shoulders and walked faster through the mud toward the women. They had gazed at him, enduring and faithful. Logan remembered that he was a man restored and completed by women such as these, so he would find a way. Even into October, the punishing heat of that August day lingered. It was called Indian summer, but Logan knew it was the tail end of a summer that had witnessed forty-five days of ninety-eight-degree heat. A summer during which he had visited his elderly patients in their homes, so fearful were they of sunstroke. The summer he made love to his wife at 3 A.M. on the grass at Hains Points because the heat made it impossible to sleep or to keep their hands off each other. The summer his brother died.

Logan had seen thirty patients today and he was exhausted. But he had promised Esther that he would stop by to see her and to check on Naomi, who had been in bed for over a week.

Behind the wheel of his Chrysler New Yorker, Logan scanned the street. He had come full circle. His offices were located in the same neighborhood where he had grown up, where he had lived with his mother, where his grandmother had periodically raised him. Fourteenth and Park Road was not far from what had once been the heartbeat of Black Washington. As a child, there were Saturday afternoon double features at the Savoy Theater, games of tag in stately Meridian Hill Park. It was a Black world in which a wonderful democracy of conditions prevailed—waitresses, doctors, preachers, winos, teachers, numbers runners and funeral directors, prostitutes and housewives, cabdrivers and laborers all lived as neighbors. The white world sat despised, irrelevant beyond the boundaries imposed by this community of grace. And yet Logan knew, even as a child, that Washington, D.C., did not belong to him or anyone who looked like the people he knew.

The White House, Capitol HIll—white men with power lived and worked there and drew the lines that checked the perimeters of Black hopes. And although the other world was off-limits, the universe that was home nurtured and saved him, made Logan think that the other world simple didn't matter.

Yet several blocks from where his office stood, the night Martin Luther King, Jr., was killed, he had joined an anguished angry mob and hurled stones, rocks and bottles at police. Fire and looting had ravaged the commercial zone of the neighborhood. Twenty years later, squat, efficient, charmless apartment buildings stood where bakeries and record stores once gave the area a hublike activity.

Logan often studied the neighborhood as he drove into it in the morning and out of it in the evening. Parts of the area had "recovered," but the fires had gutted the soul of the world these streets had made for him. Now drug sales took place in broad daylight before once eloquent Victorian houses.

When his father died he had left Logan a house in the neighborhood. The structure was in considerable disrepair, yet Randolph Spenser had made the receipt of a large sum of money by Logan dependent on his refurbishing the property. So when Logan returned to Washington, he decided to open his office in his father's house.

More than anything else, Logan Spenser had wanted to be safe. Courting the conventional, he had become a doctor because he had been seduced by the unequivocal goodness of the profession's aims. He had wanted to be filled with a nobility resistant to his own smallness.

It had been a good life. He had not allowed the skepticism of whites or the doubts of Blacks—and he had learned the difference—to hold him back. He had survived medical school and his internship, the closest he had come to war or hell.

Once, if someone were to ask Logan Spenser if he was happy, he would have said yes, although he did not believe in happiness as a goal or a state of mind. A neat balancing of the books would be enough, a tallying of the score that showed him at least coming in even with the forces out to get him. He had thought just a few months ago that his life had reached a plateau (even in his practice, certain types of misery and suffering had become routine). Soon he knew there must come the detonation of the tranquillity. The bursting of it into lethal shards, as a way of reminding him that he was alive.

And Logan Spenser thought he had done nothing in his life more courageous than remarry. Two years earlier he had suffered a heart attack, his second. He knew, had known for years, that that would be the manner of his death. Congenital heart defects had killed his father and one of his father's other sons. Knowing with this much certainty how he would die did not sadden Logan, nor did it inspire him to live with more passion. Logan Spenser lived his life the way everybody did, as though he had all the time in the world.

He had come full circle and there were days when the circle felt like a noose. Each time he drove away from the area Logan felt that he was, in fact, leaving nothing behind, that he would take these streets with him through his front door, that he would be walking them as they had been, as they were now, no matter where he went. When he arrived at his mother's house, Logan knocked several times and then noticed that the door was slightly ajar. He opened the door and found Esther sitting on the sofa, watching television with the sound off. She sat on the sofa surrounded by a pile of sympathy cards and photos of Nathaniel. The room was flushed with the odor of dying flowers, obtrusive in vases on the mantelpiece, the coffee table, even atop the floor-model television set. The daisies and carnations drooped lifelessly in shallow pools of stale water.

"Oh, Logan, I didn't hear you knock," Esther said vacantly, looking up from the pictures.

"Why's the door open?"

"I went outside to talk to Mrs. Sanders across the street and I guess I forgot to lock it when I came back." Logan sat down across from his mother, noticing immediately that she continued to gain weight. Since Nathaniel's death Esther had been on Valium and she possessed the somnolent air of the drugged. Her face was bloated by the effects of too much sleep. His mother's hair was as dark and full as it had been when Logan was a child. He vaguely remembered loving the resilient feel of the coarse and thick mass when Esther held him in her arms.

"How are you?" he finally asked.

Esther did not answer. Instead she continued to look at the pictures of Nathaniel, as if searching his frozen smile for something she had missed before. Words had never served them well. And yet Logan and his mother were bound more by the unspoken than anything they had ever said. Between mother and son words sparked confusion, set old wounds to howling. So they tiptoed around one another, only by accident stumbling upon revelation, careening full-tilt into honesty.

Two months after his death, Nathaniel's murder remained unsolved. Esther had told Logan this fact hurt her as much as if Nathaniel had been lost at sea and there had been no body on which to focus her grief.

Suddenly Esther looked up from the pictures, redeemed by what she had found on Nathaniel's face. "All this drug business, they're not talking about my son," she announced indignantly. "He wouldn't have been involved in such filth. He couldn't have been. He was *my* son, *your* brother, that's all either of us needs to know." Esther's voice was singed with a palpable pain, her eyes glistened with tears.

"You'll never accept Nate's death," Logan said gently, "unless you accept the truth."

"Well, I'll never accept either," Esther screamed, pushing the pictures aside and storming into the kitchen. "Never!" she screamed, slamming the kitchen door so hard that several miniature glass animals fell from the shelf on the living room wall.

Behind the door Logan heard his mother's angry sobs. Esther wailed and called Nathaniel's name and asked between the rhythm of her tears, "Why Nate, oh God, why?"

Logan went into the kitchen and lifted Esther from the floor where she was huddled before the stove, clutching her stomach. He led her back to the sofa and helped her to lie down. Esther sat up and reached for the bottle of Valium on the coffee table.

"Mom, try not to. Try to sleep without it."

"I know I won't. I'll just lay awake thinking about him, wondering why him and not me."

Logan brought a glass of water and watched Esther take the pill. As she lay on the sofa, easing into sleep, Logan asked, "What's wrong with Grandma?"

"She just won't get out of bed," Esther mumbled. "Feels fine, but says she's just tired."

Logan touched his mother's hair and looked into her face and saw how afraid she was. "Did I give him too much or not enough?" Esther asked. "You did good, Mom," Logan said and then, inspired by his mother's face to say the necessary this time—before it was too late—he told her, "You didn't kill Nathaniel. Nothing you did put him in harm's way. He loved you then. I love you now."

Upstairs, on the way to see Naomi, Logan stopped and

looked in Nathaniel's room. Esther had made his bed, swept, put everything in order after the nearly surgical search by the police during which a cache of four dozen cellophane bags of cocaine were found under a loose floorboard. It would be months before Esther would be strong enough to dispose of Nathaniel's clothes and other possessions. Logan knew he would have to urge her to do it and wondered how he would find the courage himself. He closed the door behind him and walked to his grandmother's room.

Naomi sat up in bed against several pillows, eating dinner from a tray, and stared with disinterest at the television on the bureau. "Do you feel bad?" Logan asked, hugging her gently.

"No worse than usual."

"Mom says you haven't been out of bed in a week."

"She didn't lie."

Logan rolled up the sleeve of Naomi's gown and, removing the stethoscope from his jacket pocket, took her blood pressure, then listened to her heart, the old woman bearing the examination with polite disinterest.

"You sound fine."

"I told you wasn't nothing wrong."

"Is it Nathaniel?"

"The boy's gone," Naomi told him, as if he did not know this, and turned to look at Logan significantly, her face determined, sure as she said, "But like I told your mama, we'll all meet up again."

"Then what is it? Why won't you get out of bed?"

"I want to rest. I'm tired. More tired than I've ever been in my life." Naomi reached for Logan's hand with a pitying glance that forgave Logan's inability to understand. "You think I'm ready to die. Not yet. I'm just resting." Her voice quieted his curiosity, though it did not soothe as she had obviously intended. They watched a few minutes of a game show where contestants dressed in ridiculous costumes and submitted themselves to various forms of physical humiliation to win a new car or furniture for their home. Then Naomi said, "You know, since I come up here, I never buried no one this young. I found Rayford, and your mama. There was bad times, but all those years I felt like I was charmed. Yes, Lord, I felt like I was charmed till now."

THE

WAY OF THE NEW

WORLD

Chapter Three

N A O M I

When I saw Washington, D.C., for the first time in 1926, I thought I'd never seen a prettier place. Down where I come from, Spring Hope, North Carolina, there wasn't nothing, not a single thing, to compare with what I saw here. The big government office buildings, the White House, the Washington Monument . . . and this is where I saw my first streetcar. And the way some colored folks lived! Had colored professors at Howard University and colored folks had houses sometimes just as good as white folks. Some people called it "up South," but it was far enough away from where I come to be North to me.

I'd come to join my cousin Cora, who'd come up the year before to keep house for the son of the family she'd worked for in Raleigh. Their boy had just got a big job as a judge and they let Cora go to come up here and work for him and his family. Cora didn't have husband nor child and she'd lost her mama and daddy back in 1918 when that influenza killed so many people. So when her white folks said they'd buy her ticket North and see to it that their son paid her a few more dollars a month, she just up and went.

Soon as Cora got up here, I started getting letters all about what a good time she was having going to the Howard Theater, how she'd joined a penny-savers' club, and one night on U Street had seen Bessie Smith, who she said was prettier in person than in any of her pictures. And how there was a whole bunch of folks from North Carolina in Washington, how it seemed like damn near every colored person in North Carolina was living in Washington, D.C. She stayed with that judge for a little while, but got sick of "living in," couldn't have no freedom or do what she wanted when she wanted, only had one day off. She wrote in one letter, "Sure they pay me a few dollars more and I got my own room, but the running never stops and they act like I don't never get tired. And his wife like to almost have a stroke if she sees me sitting down. You s'posed to be grateful for the chance to wait on them from six in the morning to whenever at night. They think I come North to work for them. I come North to be free." Then, sooner than you could say Jack Johnson, Cora wrote me saying she had quit her white folks and was working two jobs—at Bergmann's laundry and doing day's work. "I'd be working a third job if I hadn't met me a real nice man from Richmond who I spends my Saturday nights with and who takes me to church on Sunday morning," she said.

Sometimes young people ask why we all left down there. Well, I think folks just got tired. Tired of saying *Yessuh* and being ground down into nothing by crackers or hard work and sometimes both at the same time. And in those days the whites'd lynch you as soon as look at you. It's a shame young folks today don't know nothing about how we were treated then. It's too bad we were so ashamed, we figured it was best to forget and our children not to know. I had a cousin lynched in Florida, a boy—just fourteen years old. He'd been playing with some little po' white trash children and one of the girls said he touched her in her private parts. The white men got together, just rode up to Jimmy's folks' cabin and took him away while his daddy was out in the fields. They lynched Jimmy that night. And his daddy had to cut him down from that tree the next day and bury him. The daddy just went crazy little bit by little bit after that and rode into town one day a coupla months later, walked into the general store and shot the man who'd lynched his boy, then shot himself before they could grab him. Oh, and if you worked hard and made something of yourself, got a little store or some land, the white folks seem like they couldn't sleep nor rest easy till they took that away from you. Maybe they'd burn your store down or run you out of town. Colored folks just got tired. That don't sound like much of a reason, but it's the best one I can think of.

Now my folks, Beatrice and Jameson Reeves, were share-croppers. We lived in one of them shotgun houses, 'bout one room wide and three or four rooms deep. To tell the truth, it wasn't no house at all, it was a shack, but it was the first home I ever knew. We raised tobacco, 'bacca's what we called it then. All I ever saw my daddy do was work and I might have heard him speak ten words a month to us kids and my mama combined. He worked hard. But not never seeing noth-

ing for all his labor kinda took something out of him. There
was many a year my daddy never saw a dollar to hold in his
hand. By the time old man Cartwright, who Daddy rented
the land from, charged us for all them molasses, grits, fatback
and syrup'd been sold on credit, the sale of the 'bacca almost
wasn't worth it. And 'cause Daddy couldn't read or figger,
Cartwright's word was law. I think my daddy was so beat
down by the life he had he didn't even know *what* to say.
And I watched my daddy get old before he should've.

Now my mama, you couldn't shut her up! No matter what
she was doing—stripping 'bacca, cooking, washing clothes,
you'd find her either talking to the Lord or singing some song
or talking with herself. My daddy didn't as a rule say much,
but he did say he didn't want Mama working in no white
folks' homes. It was funny, they always wanted to get the
colored woman up in their kitchen, or cleaning up the house,
but scared to let the colored man within a mile, 'less he
crawled all the way. No, Mama wasn't allowed to work in
no white folks' house. So she did wash for the white families
and helped on the farm.

Washing clothes meant boilin' them over a fire. Washing
clothes meant using lye soap that eat up your hands like acid.
Sometimes, at the end of the day, my mama would look at
her hands and just sit there and cry. And she'd say, "I used
to have such pretty hands, such pretty hands." And Daddy
would start hollerin', "You worried 'bout your hands, I'm
worried 'bout getting food for y'all to eat." And Mama'd
tell him, "A woman wants to be proud of something she
came in the world with, wants to think some part of her is
beautiful. Even a colored woman wants that." And Daddy'd
look all ashamed and confused and suck harder on his pipe
and get up and go on the front porch. My mama was like
all the women I ever saw down there—they worked and
worked like dogs, with no thought that there was no other

way to live. And we *all* worked, every one of us. There was Jackson, my older brother, then me and after me come my sister Ruby that died of TB and my youngest brother Jesse. By the time I was three I'd been trained up to bring wood for the stove, stack logs, even carry small buckets of water. When I was nine I was washing, ironing, cooking. And there wasn't no such thing as free time. Every one of your spare minutes you were finishing up that day's work or getting ready for the next day's. Humph, many's the time I walked a half a mile to a neighbor's farm to milk their cow so we could have milk. By the time I was thirteen, I was a woman.

And don't even talk about 'bacca. You never got through with it. The whole year long you were either getting ready to plant it, harvest it or cure it. My daddy was just a "hanging on" farmer with five acres and two mules. All of us helped with the 'bacca. No matter how small we was, there was something we could do. You'd start planting the seedlings in the wintertime and while the seeds were growing you'd be cutting the wood to use for curing in July and August. Whole families'd get together and cut enough wood for all of us—oak, sweetgum, poplar. In the spring Daddy'd pull out our two mules, Nat Turner and Frederick Douglass—my mama named them that 'cause they were so strong—and he'd start breaking the ground. Then you had to transplant the 'bacca. We'd use spoons to put them little baby plants in the ground. Then once it start growing you had to top it, sucker it and prime it and cure it.

With 'bacca you worked from can't see till can't see. Mama'd get up at four o'clock to fix the dinner we was gonna eat at noontime. Dew'd still be on the 'bacca when you'd go out to the fields. And if you were priming, picking off the ripe leaves, well, you could be in the fields all morning.

One time one of our barns caught on fire when Daddy was curing. All it took was one old leaf that fell into the flute, caught fire and burnt up that whole crop. Daddy liked to had a fit. When the fire was finally out, he went to town and was gone a week, come back so full of whiskey we could smell him coming home a mile away.

We were poor, but it was the kind of poor where the Lord provides just enough and surprises you now and then with some extra. Mama washed those white folks' clothes so good, the women were all the time giving her old clothes and cast-off things they didn't want no more just 'cause they wasn't new. We got a pair of shoes once a year and had to make them last, and they were mostly for Sundays. Mama dragged us to church every Sunday and we stayed all day. But there were times it seemed like the Lord forgot all about us. We was poor and so I know how it feels to be hungry. *Real* hungry. I've gone days just eating a thin slice of fatback and a hunk of bread and was so grateful that the hunger pains in my stomach . . . I just went on working at whatever I was doing and just put the pains outta my mind.

I got me a little schooling now and then when we could spare time from the farm, so I didn't learn regular like. My daddy couldn't read at all. But Mama could and she was all the time tutoring us and teaching the ABC's and such. I wasn't never interested in no books, I'll tell you that right now. But that didn't mean I didn't have no imagination. One time I heard a carnival show was coming to town. Mama said the show was bad, had fancy women, dangerous men and city slickers. She complained so long and hard about how awful the carnival was, I knew I had to go see it. Didn't have a penny to my name, but I sneaked off from the fields one day and went on to town.

Now, we didn't usually go to town but two or three times a year. And when I got there I saw all the posters advertising the carnival. Since I didn't have no money, I stood out in front of the tent and set to wailing and crying for my life.

Just boo-hooed something awful. Pretty soon a old white man come along and asked me what I was crying for. I told him I'd lost the money my daddy give me for the carnival. You know that old man reached in his pocket and gimme a dime! Tapped me on the behind and told me to get along. Well, once I got in that tent, I saw more things than I knew God had ever made—a fat lady, must've weighed three hundred pounds, a dwarf couple, a man eating fire. Even had brought a tiger and I almost fell over when the man put his head in that tiger's mouth. And looking at all those amazing things gave me a powerful appetite. I'd spent a nickel on cotton candy and needed money for some soda pop and ice cream. Don't you know I used that crying number two more times and got folks to feeling so sorry for me I had money left over.

Well, naturally, I paid for my fun. Got home that night and got beat from sundown to sunup. Mama and Daddy were so mad they took turns beating me. I couldn't sit down too good for a coupla days, but every night for a long time I sure had some powerful interesting dreams. And I entertained Jackson and Jesse and Ruby a mighty long time with stories about what I'd seen. I wouldn't have missed that carnival for nothing.

Mama and Daddy were always telling me I thought I was grown, thought I was big and how I was headed for trouble if I didn't watch out. I think they thought that would scare me, but it just made me get excited about what kind of trouble they meant and what it would be like. And I didn't see nothing wrong with wanting to be big. Hell, Spring Hope, North Carolina, was so small it didn't take much to get bigger than that.

I got married the first time when I was seventeen. And I'm gonna tell you the truth, I got married mostly to get away from home. His name was Isaiah Matthews and he was a real nice boy. His daddy was a real farmer, not a sharecropper like mine, and he had twenty-five acres of land. He grew a little bit of everything—'bacca, corn—and he even had other colored folks working for him.

Isaiah was tall and skinny and he was one of those boys that everybody's mama likes—the kind that's all *Yes, ma'ams* and *Please* and *Thank you* and tipping his hat and opening doors. To this day, I swear I don't really know what Isaiah saw in me. Mama'd tease me about my big eyes, said with eyes as big as mine I'd always find what I was looking for. We'd have these church socials in the spring and summer and he was always asking me to dance and wanting to take me for a walk. I went along with it 'cause I didn't see no reason not to and he seemed like a nice enough fella. Now, I can talk up a storm most of the time, but Isaiah couldn't get a word outta me the first times we danced or walked by ourselves. Then he commenced to coming by our place. And Mama and Daddy were always so glad to see him, I felt like I had to say something. Isaiah'd talk to me about what he knew best—his daddy's farm—and I couldn't stand hearing that, but didn't want to tell him. And the more I listened to Isaiah talk about that farm and the work he and his daddy and their hands did on it, and not just about how much they made on their crops, but the smell and feel of the soil and what having land meant, the more I got to know him. The land he and his daddy had was theirs and they was doing good enough so that it gave them a good life. So Isaiah could tell me things about farming I'd never seen or felt—what it feels like to look at land and know it's yours, how it feels to harvest your crop and know *you* can set *your* price, about how it feels to be master of the land instead of slave to it. The land never gave me and my family no real bounty, so I never saw its beauty. But Isaiah made me think about things different.

▌ ▌ ▌

We courted for a while and then got married in the same church we'd both been christened in and met each other. We moved into a little house Isaiah had built with his daddy for us, and Isaiah started farming his own acreage. I helped out around the farm, but 'cause Isaiah had field hands, there wasn't much for me to do. Pretty soon I got tired of talking about crops and I wanted to talk about something else, but I didn't know what. Then I started wishing I'd paid attention in school 'cause at least I'd have been able to read some books better than I could. At night Isaiah'd come to bed, the smell of soil and fertilizer still on him, despite a bath, and he'd reach for me with those big old hands and get on top of me like he was mounting a horse. And Oh Lord! I'd cry all the way through it, but silent, like, so he wouldn't hear. And not never nary a kiss. That hurt more than anything, I think. I got more affection from the little boys I'd played house with in the fields. But he was happy. His daddy'd come by in the evenings sometimes, just pop in on us, and Isaiah'd hold me and slap me on my butt, playful like, and squeeze me and go on and on about what a lucky man he was.

I used to ride over to talk to Mama. She'd be in the back-yard standing over a big tub of clothes, humming "Precious Lord" or some other hymn, when I'd come up on her and she'd act surprised to see me, like, now that I had my own home, I couldn't never come back to my first. And one day I went back home in this new dress Isaiah'd bought me, he'd ordered it from the Sears catalogue, and, not saying a word, I just commenced to washing clothes with Mama, stuck my hands in that water and stood there with her, rubbing and scrubbing and wringing till my wrists felt like they were gonna fall off.

When we got through, I just plopped down on top of a

upturned basket and said, "Mama, I just don't feel a thing."
Mama touched my cheek with her hands, those old wrinkled-
up raw hands that made her cry, and said, "Honey, go on
back to your house and your husband. People do the best
they can. Remember that. People can't be nothin' that ain't
in 'em, or do what they think is impossible. You'd be surprised how a little love can go a long way."

I stood up and she hugged me and then told me to go on
home. I figured then, maybe if I had a baby, I'd be happy.
But six months after the baby was born, we woke up one
morning and she was dead. Just lay there in the crib Isaiah's
father had gone all the way to Charlotte for, her little face
turned almost gray, no breathing, no life. These days they
got a name for what killed my baby—sudden infant death—
but back then, we didn't know what had happened or why.
And I could tell Isaiah thought somehow I'd failed Martha,
been a bad mother, neglected her somehow. He never said
nothing, not direct like, but I could feel what he was thinking,
and that's all I needed to know. And I was hurting and
grieving and just tore up inside and whenever I'd mention
Martha's name he'd just walk away.

And that's when Cora started writing me. And the more
letters I got, the more I knew I had to go North. But Isaiah
didn't want to hear nothing about going North. "What I'm
a go up there for?" he'd ask me. "They ain't got no land for
no niggers up there. I got family been up there and come
back, say there's no room, no space, the crackers got you
penned in, just as tight up there as down here. What I'm a
go work in a factory for when I got my own land?"

But the more letters I got from Cora, the more I realized
I wanted to go North, but mostly I wanted to get away from
seeing my daddy sharecropping with a mule and a hoe and
my sister laying on the bed on the back porch, little bit by
little bit dying of tuberculosis. And I wanted to leave the
memory of my dead baby. Got so me and Isaiah didn't have

hardly nothing to say no more. Martha's ghost was still in the house with us. And since we couldn't talk about her, seemed like nothing else made no sense.

Then one night Isaiah told me I could leave. Said I could go on North, since North meant more to me than him. I didn't say a word. But that night he come to bed and held me real tight, but real gentle like, and we made love like I'd given up hoping we ever would. And he kissed me all over my body that night. But when we finished, he lay next to me and said, "Naomi, you can go North, but if you do, don't look back 'cause there won't be nothin' here no more that belongs to you."

Cora had wrote me in one of her letters that soon as she got on the train to leave North Carolina she felt free. Said she felt like she was being born all over again. Sure she was sitting in the Jim Crow section, up front where all the coal, smoke and dust rose up, got in the windows and ruined your clothes. But she said the chugging of that train couldn't hardly keep up with her heart, she was so excited. I wish it'd been like that for me when I left. Pretty soon I left Isaiah and moved back home. Daddy stopped speaking to me altogether when he found out I was going North. And Mama took me out in the yard one day and we stooped down on our knees underneath of a big old juniper tree we had and she commenced to digging. Next thing I knew, she was pulling a cigar box out the ground. She rubbed the dirt off the top of it and opened the lid and inside I saw a pile of coins and paper money.

"This here is the little extra I been making over the years, setting aside for the worst times and the special times," she said. I don't think there coulda been more than thirty dollars in that box. But Mama reached in that box and gave me everything in it. She wrapped the money in a small rag and stuffed it down the front of my dress. And before I could say a word, she said, "Now, when you get settled up there, maybe

Jackson can come up too. Your daddy don't want him to go, but you and Jackson's the strongest ones the Lord give us. You got to get away from here."

A few days later Mama and Jackson and Jesse rode over to the train station with me. And before I got on the train, Mama said, "Girl, you better write us every two weeks." "Mama, you know I ain't one for sitting still that long, or puttin' that many words on paper." "Well, now's the time to learn," she says. She hugged me and I thought how I'd never seen her look so pretty and sad at the same time. She had on her Sunday dress, you'd have thought she was going instead of me—she was so excited. Jackson hugged me and while I was holding on to him, I looked over his shoulder and I saw Daddy standing way off near the ticket booth, looking like he'd just come out the fields. He just stood there and held up his hand like he was waving at me, but not really waving goodbye.

Cora was living in a rooming house on Ninth and O streets. Room wasn't no bigger than a minute, but it seemed like a palace to me. She had a Victrola and had cut out pictures of Josephine Baker, Ma Rainey and Louis Armstrong and put them all over her mirror and the walls. Cora was what we used to call a good-time girl. Even down home, she was always the one knew where the fun was and if there was no fun happening she could make some.

First thing I wanted to do was get a job so I could start sending money back home. But Cora wouldn't even let me talk about a job that first week. And all we did was party. The woman that run the rooming house was a big old Black woman named Blue. All you had to do was look at her and you'd know how she got that name. And seemed like the downstairs where Blue lived was always filled with folks coming in all hours of the day and night. And it was always liquor flowing and cardplaying.

We'd go over to the O Street Market and you could get

pigs' feet and chitlins and fresh geens as good as down home. And Cora seemed to never run outta money. I figured that had to do with her never running outta men.

We were having a good time, then one night when we were getting ready to go to a party, I noticed Cora putting this cream all over herself. I asked her what it was and she showed it to me. It was bleaching cream. Now, Cora's about the color of half-done toast, so I was confused. "What you using this stuff for?" I asked.

"Everybody uses it, men and women," she told me, snapping her stocking tops into her garter. "Girl, there ain't no such thing as a brown beauty in this here town. You either yellow or you ain't mellow." Cora was just rubbing the cream in her skin, all over her face and arms, as she told me this, like she was trying to get it down into her bones.

"Well, I'm gonna take my chances," I told her. "I sure ain't gonna use no mess like this. Besides ain't you heard 'the blacker the berry, the sweeter the juice'?"

But Cora had to have the last word, saying "Naomi, I ain't heard *nobody* say that since I come up here and I'll bet money you won't neither."

Finally I started working. I lived in with a Jewish family for a while, but living in didn't suit my style. The madam worried me to death, all day long talking and complaining 'bout her husband, scared he didn't love her, scared he was running around with somebody else, scared she was getting old. That was 'bout the loneliest woman I ever knew. I could hardly do my work for her bending my ear. But the worst thing was I couldn't go when and where I wanted. Nighttime I'd be so tired, all I wanted to do was go to bed. And so then I started doing day's work, had three or four families I cleaned up for and I got my own room in Blue's house and started sending money home regular like.

Now, day's work wasn't no celebration either. And I had every kinda woman for a madam you could think of—the kind that went behind you checking corners for dust and dirt, the kind that run her fingers over the furniture you just got through dusting, the kind that just got a thrill outta giving orders, the kind that asked more questions 'bout my personal business than anybody got a right to, the kind that tried to cheat me outta some of my pay. But in those days there wasn't much else a colored woman could do. Hell, even some of the college girls—the dinkty, saditty ones—cleaned up for white folks in the summertime.

For the longest time I just worked and saved and worked and saved. Then one evening I come in and Blue was sitting in the dining room. For a change, she was by herself. Seemed like Blue wasn't happy unless there was a crowd of people around her. But this night she was by herself. I'd been having this same dream over and over about somebody named Macon and I figured I might bet a few pennies on the dream's number. So I asked her to look up Macon in her dream book. She looked it up and said the number was 301. "I think I'll put fifteen cents on it," I told her, reaching into my pocketbook. I thought Blue was gonna laugh me right outta that room. "Fifteen cents?" she hollered. "Fifteen cents?" And she commenced to laughing so hard she was shaking all over and tears came into her eyes and start to rolling down her fat old Black cheeks. She wiped her face with a handkerchief and says, "Girl, what you waiting for? I been watching you going out here day after day, cleaning up the white folks' houses. That all you want to do with yourself?"

Now nobody'd ever asked that—what I wanted to do— the whole time I'd been North. Cora was so busy partying and I was so busy struggling I hadn't had time to think further than the day I was in. So I didn't quite know what to say at first. "Well," Blue said, folding her arms in front of her, looking at me like the schoolmarm in that one-room schoolhouse I went to did, when she knew I wasn't ready to give the right answer. And that look in Blue's eyes and her laughing at me made me pull up something I'd been carrying around since I moved in her house. And I just said it all of a sudden. "I want what you got. I want a house. And I want plenty money." And just saying it like that set me trembling so hard I dropped my pocketbook on the floor and my feet kicked over the bag of clothes one of my madams had give me that day instead of my regular pay.

"Well, tell me how you aim to get it? Lessen you got some book education or your folks gonna *leave* you some money, there ain't no legal way for you to get either one. You gonna have to start gambling with everything you got."

"But I ain't got nothing," I cried.

"You got more than you think. You got dreams, like the one you come to me with just now, and, honey, they worth more than you think. They sho 'nuff worth more than fifteen cents. You got sense and deep-down feelings. Listen to 'em. They'll tell you what to do. You think the Rockefellers got to be Rockefellers playing it straight? And if all you gonna put on 301 is fifteen cents, I won't even write it up."

I put a quarter on 301 and it come out the next day. I give Blue a cut and that was how it started.

I got to playing the number pretty regular then and soon I was playing every day. To be honest about the thing, though, most folks never won nothing. But seemed like I had some kinda gift. Numbers were about the only thing I paid attention to in that one-room schoolhouse in Spring Hope. That first year I hit two times for small change. Then I played a number that come to me the night one of my madams accused me of stealing. I played that number and hit for enough to start me on the way to saving for a house.

My first house was over on R Street. I rented out the top two floors to decent folks, respectable people who'd come up from the South like me. But where Blue'd let anybody live in her house, I'd only let families or married couples or single folks I thought wouldn't give me no trouble live in my place. Folks who went to church on Sunday and went to bed at night 'cause they had to work the next day. Now, that don't mean I was a saint, but I sure didn't want to live amongst a whole buncha sinners.

I found out I couldn't live in a whole house like I lived in one room. Cora took me downtown and bought me the kinda clothes that said I was a lady and just putting those clothes on made me feel different, made me feel *big* like Mama and Daddy'd always said I wanted to be. Then Cora told me I couldn't have a house without a car and her and her boyfriend took me to this place where I bought a big black Chevrolet.

When I got settled good in the house, I sent for Mama and Daddy and Jackson and Jesse to come up and spend some time with me. Mama had a time getting Daddy to come, even after I sent them all train fare. But finally they came. And seeing that house through Mama's eyes was like seeing it for the first time. I'd planted a Carolina garden out in the back-yard of squash, tomatoes and peas, just like I'd have done back home and Mama sat on the back porch when she saw it, shaking her head and smiling. I'd put a big mirror with gilt framing over the fireplace and seemed like every time I looked up Mama was staring at herself in that mirror, almost like she'd never seen herself before. She took off her shoes in the house and walked barefoot on the carpeting I'd put all on the first floor. And she had me take a bunch of pictures of her sitting in my car. And the big bathtub with running hot water, humph, I thought Mama was gonna live in it, she found a excuse to take a bath three times a day.

But Daddy, seemed like the house just made him mad. Mama was all the time pointing something out to him and he'd just go on out on my porch like he did on the porch back home, and sit there sucking on his pipe and not saying a thing. Daddy and one of my roomers, Mr. Chavis, would sit out there talking about down home. He talked to Mr. Chavis more than he talked to me. And so one night I just went outside and butt into their conversation, told Mr. Chavis I wanted to talk to my daddy. "Now, you ain't said hardly nothin' to me since y'all got here," I told him. "Not even *Congratulations* or *Good job*. I worked hard for what I got, Daddy, and I want you to be proud."

He took the pipe outta his mouth and said, "I am proud of you, Naomi. Real proud. But you got to understand. I've worked another man's land for over twenty years and just barely kept my family from starvin'. My daughter comes North and gets so much it puts me to shame. Tell me how I'm s'posed to feel about me. Sure I'm proud of you. So proud I'm damn near ready to bust. But I look at all you done and feel like all my life's been a waste. You a landlord. I'm your daddy and I'm still a tenant."

"Why don't y'all just stay on up here? You don't have to go back."

"I got to go back 'cause of the land. That farm, little as it is, is all I know. I ain't got much longer. I'm too old to learn a new way of living. 'Sides, they can't run us all out. That land's got more of our blood in it than theirs. Not all us s'posed to leave. Some of us got to stay, so y'all have a place to come back to."

Well, ended up Jackson stayed on and I gave him a room in the house and he got a job as janitor at the post office.

Now, in all this, I hadn't really had me no romancing. There'd been one or two men, but if they'd been worth remembering, I woulda told you about them. And most times I was working so hard to get something, make some money, I didn't have time to be courtin' nobody. The truth is, I didn't make no time. So when Mama and Daddy went back home, I went with them and filed my papers and got my divorce from Isaiah.

Well, with Cora's help, I finally found me a sweetheart. It was 1929. Now, whenever you say 1929 to folks, first thing they think of is the Depression. Well, I think white folks were hurt most by those bad times. Colored folks were born in a Depression, everything just about that they knowed was Depression. Yeah, times got tough. But then, they'd always been tough for us, weren't no big thing, so we knew how to get through it.

Folks down home were hit real hard. I was sending home not just money but clothes and food. And going down three or four times a year just to check for good measure. But lots of folks just gave up and that made it easier for folks like me who wanted to get going!

I was renting out my second house by then, over on P Street, and Cora was living in it, collecting rents for me. One night we had a fish fry. I was hitting numbers pretty good and was even a bag lady now and then, what they call a courier, taking folks' numbers and their money and delivering it to a old Italian guy downtown. The coloreds was the front men, but it was the whites that really controlled the numbers game. I was figuring to get outta that end of things 'cause that old Italian couldn't take the money without putting his hands on me, no matter what I said.

So we had this fish fry and the house was packed. I can't remember now the exact reason we had that party, but in those days didn't always *need* a reason. That night me and Cora was frying up the fish when her boyfriend Harold walked in with the handsomest man I'd ever seen. Now, I don't mean handsome in the way he looked so much, but the way he stood and carried himself. It was just something kinglike about him. He stood up so tall and straight and looked at you like you'd be a fool not to like him. And when him and Harold come in the kitchen out there in the living room somebody had put a Alberta Hunter record on. The song was "Gimme All the Love You Got" and Alberta was singing.

I was standing at the table, my hands covered in cornmeal,

dipping porgies in batter, and Rayford Johnson looked at me like he didn't plan to never look nowhere else. He was half bald and the top of his head was real shiny. And he had a mustache and the Lord knows I'm a fool for a man with hair on his face.

Harold introduced Rayford to me and Cora and since I couldn't shake his hand I gave Rayford Johnson the biggest, brightest smile I could muster. Then him and Harold went on into the parlor, where folks were dancing and laughing and Alberta was singing, "I want all your loving 'cause I can stand a lot." Dipping some fish in a frying pan of oil, Cora says, "Harold told me Rayford's a teacher over at Dunbar."

"Well, I wouldn't mind studying with him sometimes." I laughed.

Well, all the while we were cooking those fish, Rayford was hanging around near the kitchen, peeking in now and then, like what we were doing was the most interesting thing. I had a houseful of liquor, music, fast and pretty women and he wanted to watch us cook fish, so I told him to come on in and pull up a chair. He had a bottle of beer, looked like he hadn't took a single sip from it. Soon as he got settled in a chair, though, Cora took off her apron and said, "I'm going to dance."

He watched Cora leave us alone, like he was glad to see her gone, and I went on frying the fish, just like he wasn't even there. "So all this belongs to you?" he asked me.

"What you mean?"

"This house."

"Yessir, I guess it does," I said, kinda cold and suspicious-like, wondering if he was after my money.

"You should be proud of what you've achieved."

"I am."

"I can look at you and if you don't mind my saying, I can tell you believe in dreams *and* hard work."

I didn't know what to say. Hadn't too many folks been

able to read me so fast and especially not saying it like he did.

"Our race needs women like you if we're ever to progress. Our men do too."

I had gone to the sink and was washing my hands and his words just felt like a warm welcome cloak all around me. I'd gone to the sink 'cause he was looking at me so open like and yet so friendly and trusting I could hardly stand it.

"Miss Naomi, I can look at you and tell you're a good woman, somebody I'd like to know."

And you know, all those words didn't sound like jive to me. He had the sincerest way of saying things. Rayford made you feel like he wasn't the kind of man who'd lie to you that you wasn't the kind of person anybody'd want to lie to.

So with all those noise going on in the living room and fish frying on the stove, Rayford Johsnon acted like he didn't care about neither. And I sat down at the table with a plate of porgies in front of me and I asked him, "You sound like one of those race men."

"And proud to be," he said, real serious. And he kept looking at me like he was trying to figure me out. He looked just like a schoolteacher. But I knew I could make him crack a smile if I wanted to. He took a big swiggle from his beer and then he says, "What do you think the Negro's got to do to progress in this country?"

Now, I'll tell you, I wasn't expecting no question like that right then. I was thinking he'd tell me how good I looked or ask me to go out and dance. Politics and all that—well, the folks I run with, we didn't get too concerned about all that. But after I got over being surprised I felt kind of special. He must've thought I could answer the question or he wouldn't have asked it. So I said, clearing my throat real good before I started to speak, "Well, I think the colored, I mean the

Negro, has got to depend on himself and develop something of his own before anybody will respect him."

"You're a very astute observer," he said, smiling at me like I was one of his students who'd done him proud.

"Well, I don't know about all that." I said, getting up to turn over the fish. "But I do know we won't make no progress unless we all make it together."

"So you don't subscribe to Du Bois's Talented Tenth theory?"

Now, I hadn't heard nothing about this man Du Bois or his theory, but I asked Rayford, just guessing, "What happens to the other ninety percent?" And don't you know he smiled and then laughed and I could see the part of him he tried to hide. He took a swig of his beer and just said, "Miss Naomi, you got real good sense, real good."

When I sat down I asked him, "You don't sound like you from the South, where you from orignial?"

"Oklahoma. An all-Negro town called Langston. My folks were some of the first Negroes to go to the West in the 1880s. They left Tennessee, looking for land and a better life than they had in the South."

"Did they find it?"

"Took them some time, but they did. My daddy's a undertaker and my mother teaches music."

Now, with all that behind him, coming from those kinda folks, I'd have figured Rayford to be stuck on himself, but all he was telling me didn't seem to phase him one bit.

"How come you left Oklahoma?"

"Well, I'd been teaching school and then I heard about Marcus Garvey."

"You mean that little old Black man from the West Indies? The one always talking about Black this and Black that?"

"Well, I wouldn't describe him quite that way. He was and is a prophet. A man ahead of his times."

"Ain't he in jail now?"

"Unfortunately, yes. But that's where most prophets end up at some point in their career. He was a Moses, a *Black* Moses for his people."

"What did you do with him?"

"I was business manager of the *Negro World*, the paper of the Universal Negro Improvement Association. Worked for him three years. That was the best time of my life."

"Why you say that?"

"The man's vision, his accomplishments. And for a period of my life I was part of it all, helping to make a difference in the lot of the Negro." Rayford got real sad when he said that, like he was remembering something so special he didn't know how to put a value on it. "I mean, do you know what the man and the organization did?" he asked me. "The UNIA set up groccery stores, had a chain of laundries in cities all over the country, a publishing company. We had members in the Caribbean and Africa. And, of course, the Black Star Line."

"I heard that ship almost sunk," I said, sucking in my jaws.

"The white men that sold it to us took advantage of our inexperience, sold us a piece of junk, a ship that wasn't seaworthy. But had there ever been a shipping line owned by the Black man in America before?"

I felt ashamed for saying what I did. Then Rayford reached in his pocket and pulled out his wallet and in a little side compartment he pulled out a cigar ring and shows it to me and it's got Garvey's picture on it. As he handed the paper ring to me he says, "The best years of my life, bar none."

Well, by the time Rayford got through talking about Garvey, I didn't feel like eating no fish. But me and Cora set everything out. And I didn't feel like dancing neither. I just felt like sitting there, looking at Rayford Johnson.

We sat in the kitchen till two o'clock in the morning, just telling each other stories about what we'd done. Until I met Rayford, I didn't think I had much to tell that anybody'd be interested in. When I told him about my parents sharecropping, he talked about all the poor Black folks down South, when I told him how bad I felt for my daddy and what he'd said about my house, Rayford talked about all Negro men, and when I told him how Jackson had settled into his job cleaning over at the post office, he wondered if the North was really gonna be much better. When Rayford Johnson left my house that night, I knew I had found me a sweetheart.

Now, imagine that, me, who hated the thought of the inside of a schoolhouse, courting a teacher!

Well, me and Rayford became a pretty hot item. And 'cause of the kind of man he was, I kinda cut back on so much partying and almost turned into a homebody. In the summertime, we'd go over to Griffith Stadium and see one of the Negro League teams play and one time Rayford took me to the Jungle Inn to see Jelly Roll Morton. But Rayford could turn a evening just having dinner and listening to the radio into something special. But he was the seriousest man I ever met. He was renting a room and all in the corners and under the bed he had stacks and stacks of those "race" magazines, *The Crisis* and *Opportunity*. It was 'cause of Rayford that I started reading more than the comics and the obituaries in the paper. I had to keep up with him so I started reading the news too.

One day I went over to Dunbar and watched Rayford teach a class. He had those kids eating out of the palm of his hand. He lectured them about everybody from Hannibal to Herbert Hoover and Mrs. Bethune. The thing I liked was, he talked about folks living right then and slowed the kids how they were making history. I'd grown up thinking education was studying folks that were dead. Rayford let me know education was just about everything you did or thought, no matter when it happened.

I felt pretty good. Had a sweetheart and no more empty bed blues. And serious as he was, Rayford Johnson knew how to please a woman. Some mornings I'd get outta bed when we'd been together and feel like I could tear up the house and put it back together again. He wasn't making no whole lotta money as a teacher but he never asked me for a dime. He had a old Ford somebody gave him and when we went out we went in his car, not mine. He had pride and I think that's what won my heart more than anything else.

Well, we'd been going together almost a year and I knew what I wanted. So one night he came to see me. I'd fixed pork chops, rice, gravy, collard greens and biscuits. He coulda took one look at that meal and knew I meant business. We listened to some Louis Armstrong records he'd brought over and then we got in the bed. Oh, he fixed me real good that night! And afterwards, we're laying there, him smoking them Chester-field cigarettes he'd been smoking, he told me once, since he was sixteen, and I'm feeling all soft and warm and happy and I just asked him, just like that, to marry me. I hadn't never seen a man blush before, but Rayford laid there, looking like what I'd said had made his day.

When he got himself composed, he says, "You don't leave nothing to chance, do you, *Miss* Naomi Reeves?"

And I told him, "Only way I'm gonna get what I want is to ask for it. I always figure on hearing yes. And no don't scare me 'cause I heard no all my life and it ain't never stopped me yet. But smart as you are, I knew you'd have sense enough to say yes."

Now, once I become Mrs. Rayford Johnson, I was happy as a fox in a henhouse. I turned over the running of my two houses to Rayford, let him collect all the rents, cut him in on everything. I've heard women talk about *Never let the left hand know what the right hand is doing* and you know who the left hand is. But you can't keep secrets in a marriage. Not a real marriage anyway. And I'd waited too long to share my blessings with a man to play hide-and-seek once I got him.

I was twenty-four when me and Rayford got married. And I felt like I had already lived a lifetime. In those days wasn't no such thing as waiting till you grew up, life just come along and dragged you into it. Yeah, I was young, but had already had one husband, lost a child, been divorced, been dirt-poor, left home, worked like a dog, cleaned up other folks' homes, played the numbers, got a house and decided I could have the kind of life I wanted. I was young, but only in age. And where I had come from, age didn't mean nothing no way.

When I got pregnant, then I had everything I'd always wanted. I went back home to Spring Hope to have my baby. Back then, no matter where you lived—in New York, Chicago, Philadelphia, wherever—*home* was where you come from, and it was just natural to go home to do something as important as having your child.

Mama and Dadddy was still inching along on the farm, but the money I was sending made a difference. They'd bought some new furniture and Daddy'd bought a car, but it sat in the yard half the time, 'cause he ran out of money for tags or repairs. I went home in April to have Esther and maybe 'cause I was gonna give birth, or 'cause I was so happy—whatever—seemed like home was the most beautiful place. I just took it easy till my time come, sitting on the porch in the day, doing little chores around the house, going for a walk with Mama sometimes in the afternoon, staring at the stars at night. No place else smells like the South in springtime—the azaleas, the flowering dogwood just bust out and you can't hardly smell nothing else. And waiting for Esther to come, I realized that it was the beauty and the feel of the South that I missed, living in the North.

Well, Esther start coming about two o'clock one morning. They say a child that comes early in the morning won't have trouble finding their way through life. Mama told Daddy to go on over and get the midwife, Aunt Gin, but when he went out to start that old car, the engine was dead. So Jesse got on the old mule, Nat Turner, to ride the two miles to Aunt Gin's. Daddy's out in the yard in his long johns, cussing at the car and kicking it. And my water's broke and the pains are coming so fast I can't hardly breathe. Well, don't you know, Mama's just holding my hand and praying real hard, trying to drown out Daddy's cussing and telling me to push, to push real hard, and I'm moaning and screaming for God and Rayford and by the time Aunt Gin gets there Esther's come on out.

About the only thing Aunt Gin was good for by the time she got there was to give me some of that special root tea they give to women after they give birth. I'd lost one baby in Spring Hope and now I had come home and had another one and I'd decided that this child was gonna live.

About a week after Esther was born, I'm still taking it easy and waiting for Rayford to come and drive us back to Washington and Mama comes in the bedroom while I'm nursing Esther and tells me Isaiah had come to see me. Now, you know how it is when somebody is on your mind and you just can't shake them and next thing you know, there they are, well, there was Isaiah.

I finished nursing Esther and put her down to sleep and I combed my hair and put on a pretty dress Rayford had bought me and then Isaiah comes in the room.

"Howdy, Naomi," he says, fumbling with his hat. He's dressed in a suit and I could smell he'd just shaved before he come.

"Howdy, Isaiah." He'd filled out some and looked like a man, not the boy I married. He sits down in a chair beside the bed and says, "I see the North's been good to you."

"You could say that."

"That's a pretty little baby you got there. What you name her?"

"Esther."

"I got two boys, Gregory and William," he says. Then he takes out a picture of them and shows me. And they look just like him.

"Mama told me you and Vera Robinson had got married. She's a good woman," I said.

"Sure is. Don't take a lot to satisfy her."

"You satisfied me, Isaiah, as far as you could. I was just s'posed to leave, that's all."

"And I was s'posed to stay."

We sat there talking a pretty good time, about crops and the land, some of the things we used to talk about and about some new things. I told him about Rayford and then he told me all about Vera. Just felt like I was talking to a friend, not somebody who I'd hurt real bad one time. Then Mama comes in and invites Isaiah to stay to dinner, but he says no, he's late getting home already. And then he tells me to bring Rayford to the house when he comes and not to be a stranger. And I feel real good when he leaves 'cause I know Isaiah just like I'd never left him and I know he meant every word he said.

Being a daddy don't change Rayford much, except he spoiled Esther and got even more serious than ever, worried about the world and the Negro's place in it. Then those nine boys down in Scottsboro got accused of raping two white women on a train and the white folks tried them in lickety-split time and wanted to send them to the electric chair. I felt pretty bad about those boys. All you had to do was read the story and know the women made the whole thing up. And one of the boys wasn't but twelve years old, still a child. Rayford got involved with a bunch of folks raising money for the defense of the boys. Although he didn't cotton much to the NAACP, he attended their rallies and even wrote a couple of articles for the *Chicago Defender* about the case. Then in '33, he took me and Esther down to a big protest in front of the White House to try to get Roosevelt to get those boys out of jail. Now, I've never been one for raising Cain in the streets and I'll tell you I didn't want to go, but Rayford said I had to bear witness, had to put myself on the line. Said if all those white folks, the Communists and the socialists, if they could come from all over and march for nine Negro men, why couldn't I? Well, I did and carried Esther too, although Mama woulda had a fit if she had known that. Roosevelt not in office a good three months and us knocking on his door about the Scottsboro Boys.

That demonstration didn't set them free, but I did feel good being part of it. And to this day, one of my favorite pictures is one Rayford took of me standing in front of the White House gate, holding Esther, and she's got a sign in her hand that reads:

ROOSEVELT ENFORCE FULL RIGHTS FOR NEGROES.

When it come to Esther, Rayford told her everything he knew, and I give her everything I never had. She had her daddy's walk, come into a room just like a queen coming into a court, and she had my spirit. I wanted her to have everything I never did, so I gave her tap dance and piano lessons. And Esther had the prettiest room in the house. But she was my daughter so I couldn't raise her to be useless. I trained her to help me around the house and in the summertime she'd go to Spring Hope for a few weeks and help Mama and Daddy on the farm, same way I did.

Rayford was all the time reading to her. He didn't believe in fairy tales and such and at bedtime he'd tell Esther stories about folks like Harriet Tubman and Sojourner Truth. I asked him once why he was always pounding all that stuff in Esther's head all the time, why he couldn't just let her be a little girl. "She'll find out she's a Negro soon enough," I told him. And he just said, "But we got to let her know what it means."

Those were good years. Roosevelt had set up a whole bunch of agencies—the NRA, the "ABC" and the this-that-and-the-other—to turn the Depression around and we were doing OK. I felt like my life was set—you know how it is when you finally get everything in place, just the way you want it and everything you touch, near 'bout, turns to gold. Well, we had a coupla years like that. Then, the same year that fool Hitler got the white folks to killing themselves in every country they lived in, my world turned upside down too.

Rayford had been feeling poorly for some time, had been coughing a lot and having trouble breathing. Finally he got to feeling so bad he went to the doctor. Turned out he had a cancer of the lungs. Now, back then, if you had cancer they just wrote you off and started digging your grave. Folks didn't even like to say the word in public, that's how much it scared them. The doctor gave Rayford six months to live, but he held on for two years.

Rayford fought that cancer the way he fought everything, like he couldn't think of not winning. Mostly, he just decided not to give up, and he threw away those Chesterfields and never smoked another one. We found a doctor that put him on a special diet and we thought we had it licked, but it come back and come back strong. He started losing weight and got so sick he had to be put in Freedmen's Hospital. The doctors there said it'd be a waste of time to operate. Well, I just about moved in the hospital with him. Slept on the floor beside him every night and I'd hear him wheezing and rasping and his breath coming so hard and slow it sounded like every breath was his last one. He couldn't breathe good and he couldn't sleep. He was too proud to let them shoot him full of morphine, so the pain was always there. He'd lost so much weight he was down to damn near nothing, cheeks all sunk, and his hair had got gray.

And I'd get up from the pallet on the floor and let him know I was there for him. Help him struggle to get a sip of water and just hold his hand. And he'd whisper sometimes, when he could muster a breath, "Tell me a story, Naomi. Tell me a story." And I'd tell him about Spring Hope or the time I ran away to the carnival or how Blue shamed me into playing the numbers. I'd tell him, real slow like, to make the time last and it wouldn't be until I was finished with the story that I'd feel the tears on my face.

One night Rayford opened his eyes while I was talking to him and he saw me crying and he says, "Dying is the most frightening thing I ever had to do and, Naomi, I'm so scared." And then we both started crying and somehow us crying together like that gave me strength.

Rayford died in his sleep one night with my laying there on the floor beside his bed. I woke up the next morning and loved Rayford Johnson so much I was glad his misery was finally over. Then I saw a piece of paper on the bedstand next to his medicine. He'd scribbled on the paper in a handwriting that looked like something Esther would write: "I had all the time that belonged to me and I found you."

Esther didn't speak a word for a year after Rayford died. And I wore black so long my friends had to talk me out of it. I wish'd I'd been a child so I could've just shut out everybody and closed in on myself. I birthed Esther, so I knew she hadn't gone crazy or got retarded like folks was saying, telling me to take her to the doctors. Hell, my baby missed her daddy and she just didn't have the words to say how bad she felt. And when she did start talking, the first thing Esther says over dinner one night is, "Mama, he's coming back. He told me." And I said to her, "Baby, he didn't go nowhere. I got him right here in my heart."

SINS
O F   T H E
FATHERS

The second summer Jackie Robinson played for the Brooklyn Dodgers, Esther decided to become a woman. That was the summer she spent her evenings listening to baseball games on the radio, reading *Ebony* magazine, where all the women looked like Dorothy Dandridge, and falling in love with a man she wanted mostly because he already belonged to someone else.

Sitting next to Naomi in a middle pew

at Greater Faith Baptist Church on Sundays, Esther even heard Reverend Samuels, a tiny bantam rooster of a man, preach about Jackie Robinson. "White folks spitting at him, calling him *nigger*, and the man still plays the game like God made him to do nothing else." The reverend whispered the words conspiratorially, as if sharing knowledge too sad and precious to be spoken aloud. The paper fans ceased to rustle the air and even the children, squirming and irritable in the heat of the church, were stilled by the reverend's eyes, traveling laserlike and sure among them. "But what they don't know is, Jackie Robinson's got *God* on his side," he shouted, joyously pounding the pulpit. "They think he's playing a game," the reverend squealed. "And I bet some of you think that's all Jackie Robinson's doing too." The reverend's hands swept the hall in a broad mock accusation that made every member of the congregation wonder momentarily if they were indeed guilty as the reverend charged. "Naw naw. He's one of the chosen. And he's setting us free. Setting white folks free too, though they don't know it. Free! Free from hatred! Free! Free from fear! Free! Free from blaspheming!" the reverend screamed. "Freedom's a heavy burden, that's why they hate him! That's why they throw rocks and bottles and cans, trying to hit him." Beneath a huge painting of a blond blue-eyed Jesus whose eyes bled a long-suffering, unreal patience, Reverend Samuels's tiny body shivered in quakelike spasms within the folds of his sable robes. "They used to being blind and they know Jackie Robinson's gonna make 'em see." As the sermon wound down, rhythmic and explosive as the tail end of a tornado, Reverend Samuels led the congregation in a prayer for Jackie Robinson and the covetous bitter soul of America.

Obediently bowing her head, Esther prayed for her own freedom. She prayed for the man she loved. Esther prayed not to return to Howard University, where she had been a student for two years. And she asked the Lord to allow Naomi to let her go, to free her from the cloistered existence Naomi forced on her daughter like an inappropriate, unwanted gift.

This was the summer that Naomi conscientiously steered Esther out of the grasp of the young men who hovered around their door at night as bold and insistent as fireflies. And so, the second summer Jackie Robinson played for the Brooklyn Dodgers, Esther ached for the knowledge her mother was determined, out of love, to deny her.

Reverend Samuels's prayer was blistering and sonorous, full of praise, riddled with fear of the Lord, amazed by the smallness of man. The congregation's prayer both overshadowed and inspired Esther's own humble yet fervent supplication.

In the pew in front of her sat Aunt Sally James, the oldest woman in the congregation, born in slavery. She regularly frightened the children in Sunday school with accounts of how she got the whelps on her back, then broke into a black-gummed, toothless grin and pushed a Mary Jane into each child's expectant palm. In the midst of the prayer, jolted by possession, Aunt Sally rose from her seat and danced for the Lord, her flimsy body arching in grandeur, tossed by an unseen force. Aunt Sally moaned for the Lord, shouting, "Jesus! Jesus! Jesus!" Aunt Sally spoke, her tongue twisted and articulate, breaking the sacred code. Aunt Sally danced and spoke, her pleas jagged, her body jerked and soothed. Aunt Sally danced for the Lord until she was through.

The choir snatched the moment of silence that engulfed them when Reverend Samuels said "Amen" and Aunt Sally sank, replenished and consumed, back into her seat, the women on either side of her engulfing her trembling, slight body with their arms. And when Esther opened her eyes and lifted her head, she felt the tears that had arrived in a sudden startling moment of transcendence as she glimpsed the freedom she sat yearning for. The sight whirled, dervishlike, before her, evaporating as soon as she felt its touch. She lifted her head and felt the tears and Naomi pressed a tissue into Esther's white-gloved hand and rose to sing "Amazing Grace," pulling her daughter up beside her.

When Esther told Naomi that she wanted to work that summer, Naomi told her she could get a job, as long as she wasn't cleaning anybody's house or watching someone's babies. Even though those jobs were considered respectable, sought after and the classifieds were filled with ads for COLORED GIRL WANTED, FAMILY NEEDS LIGHT-SKINNED COLORED GIRL or COLORED DOMESTIC SOUGHT, Naomi admonished Esther, "If you want to work so bad, go on, but get a job where nobody can treat you like a mule or a slave. I swallowed enough pride for every woman in my family. I swore I'd save you from that. Stand behind a counter, but don't stand behind nobody's stove but your own."

And so Esther worked in the record store owned by her uncle Jackson. It was the summer that Esther thought if she could be anybody in the world, she would be Sarah Vaughan, young and pretty, possessed of a catlike sensuality. Sarah Vaughan sounded, Esther was sure, like a lily would, if a lily could sing. Young people from the neighborhood came in the store to buy records and men came to sit in the back room with Jackson, who'd lost an eye in World War II in Italy and had brought the store with money he'd saved working three jobs before he was drafted. Before he was drafted, Jackson had dinner with Esther and Naomi one night and told them he had three thousand dollars saved up. "I didn't know they paid those kind of salaries at the post office." Naomi laughed.

"Don't you worry about how I got it, just be glad I got it," Jackson said pointedly. He was a rough-hewn, broadly built, solitary man, who had never married and who worked as though labor was a sacrament.

"What you gonna do with that much money?" Naomi asked.

"I don't know, but I got a feeling things gonna be different when the war's over and I want to be ready."

"They said that after the *last* war," Naomi told him.

"They say that after *every* war."

"Things *will* be different for us after this one," Jackson assured her. "Not just here, but everywhere—Africa, Asia."

"What's Africa and Asia got to do with us?"

"Same thing England and Germany's got to do with *them*."

"You sound like Rayford used to talk."

"Yeah, and you listened to him." Jackson smiled.

"I still do."

In the back room of Jackson's store the men argued over whether President Truman was good for the Negro, played games of checkers that sounded like the Battle of Bull Run and told stories they had known since before they were born. Their jokes testified to their expertise in surviving, their complaints to the stubbornness of yearning. The men carried first names like Jackson, Grant and Sherman. They had been given white men's names by parents who could imagine no other heroes. And despite designations that both sabotaged and saved them, carrying names of white warriors, they battled on their own turf to widen the boundaries that held them, their lives endowed them with names they knew but did not share, names that sprang from their truths and no one else's lie.

One evening, when Jackson's friends had gone and Esther was ready to close the store, she told her uncle what she had told no one else. "Sometimes I still talk to my daddy." Esther had dusted the counter, swept the floor, straightened the record displays and she stood beside Jackson as he counted the day's receipts. Jackson had returned from the war so bitter that he was unable to tell anyone what he had seen, yet Esther had coaxed tales of bravery and humiliation from her uncle, spotting his vulnerable moments and mining them with a precise innocence he could not resist.

"When do you do that?" Jackson asked, licking his thumb to count the dingy, crinkled pile of fives and ones that made Esther think of tobacco, so soft with handling were the bills.

"At night. He comes to me. Sometimes when I'm awake. Sometimes when I'm dreaming."

"What do y'all talk about?" Jackson placed a rubber band around the wad of money and folded it and placed it in his back pocket.

"Everything."

"I bet he's proud of you." He looked at Esther to say this. Jackson had saved his glance, thus far in Esther's extraordinary revelation, for those words.

"You told your mama?"

"No."

"How come?"

"She'd wonder why he didn't come to her."

"Maybe he does and she just didn't tell you yet."

"The last time we talked he told me to be careful."

"That's what a daddy's supposed to tell his daughter."

"I told him I was in love."

"With who?" Jackson asked her, alarm crinkling his face.

"You don't know him." Esther shrugged, her feet moving her suddenly away from her uncle to the end of the counter, where she slid the door of the case open and straightened the piles of sheet music that she had lined up in perfect order only moments before.

"I know everybody around here," Jackson blustered.

"He just told me I've got to be careful now," Esther said offhandedly, her eyes glued to the sheet music, avoiding her uncle's eyes.

"Well, he was right. And I'll tell you something else. Listen to your uncle for a minute. There's two kinds of men out there." Suddenly rapt and studious, Esther looked at her uncle, regretting her clumsy display of coyness. Jackson pointed through the glass windows of the store to the street. "There's trees and there's stumps. Your daddy was a tree. That's why he's still talking to you. I'm a tree. That's why I got this store. You can hold onto a tree, hide from the sun underneath it, climb all up in it and see what looks like the whole world from the top of its limbs. But a stump. A stump, all you can do with a stump is sit on it, rest on it till you catch your breath and are ready to move on or chop a little bit off and use it for kindling. A stump gives you them *easy* things, but they's things that you can't really do too much with. I don't want to see you with no stumps, you hear?"

"Yes, sir," Esther said meekly.

"Your daddy and all the men on his side and your mama's side was trees. You go out there and try to find the tallest tree in the forest."

Esther's father returned to her the first time when she was thirteen. He didn't come often, only when he was needed. Never once had Rayford's return frightened her. Neither phantom nor ghost, her father returned, Esther felt, because he had never really wanted to leave.

In life, Rayford Johnson had worn three-piece suits with vests that Naomi had custom made for him at Raleigh's and Esther would ask him the time over and over again just to see Rayford flip open the closed face of the gold watch that rested in his vest pocket. And he would always tell her the exact time, not ten minutes after three, but ten minutes and fifteen seconds after three. And every Friday evening he brought Naomi half a dozen roses. Naomi told Esther once, "Before I met your father, I used to dream about a man bringing me flowers. But I was sure the woman had to be Mae West or Claudette Colbert and the man Cary Grant or

Clark Gable. You know, I miss those flowers almost more than anything else." Rayford Johnson was a man—unequivocal and self-satisfied. A man whose wife owned the house they lived in, a man who still bought the groceries and named his child and brought flowers for his wife and didn't care whose name was on the deed.

And so, when Rayford returned to visit his daughter in her dreams, it was when he was needed. He came back when Naomi was being courted by a man who smoked Pall Mall cigarettes, called Esther *Sweetie* and who took off his shoes in the living room when he came to visit, just like he was at home.

Rayford came back when Naomi had to go to Freedmen's Hospital for a week because of some "female trouble" and Esther stayed with Cora and cried at night because they all said she was too young to understand why her mother had to have an operation. And he came back the night a boy in Esther's senior class took her to the Booker-T to see the movie *Porgy and Bess*, and slipped his hand beneath Esther's sweater and felt her breasts.

To Esther, her father's love had seemed a gift. Rayford had lived with them and for that, even in her seven- and eight-year-old prayers, Esther had thanked God. The other fathers Esther knew seemed to always be hunting hungrily for work, ashamed to live face-to-face with families they could not feed and so were afraid to love. Some of their neighbors on the street were on relief and she'd heard the men talk about how food bought with government money wouldn't go down in your stomach right and how they'd rather starve.

And now this was the summer Esther had decided to become a woman. The danger that lurked inside the love Esther felt would inspire Naomi to censor Esther's desire. For Naomi knew, as Esther was yet to learn, just how a woman's heart breaks. Her father could only inform Esther of the ways in which a man loves. Esther confided in her father and not her mother because Rayford Johnson told her that it was women and love that men could not live without.

Naomi had once told Esther she had a face nobody would ever think of not trusting and eyes that looked like they had seen more than they could bear.

During her secret walks to the Eden Bar and Grill twice a week, Esther could hear Naomi's judgment play like some haunted music that dogged each step. And sometimes the words would make her stop to cast a worried glimpse at her reflection in the store windows she passed. Esther was small but buxom and the lavender-print dress she wore had been wrinkled by a day of sitting on a stool behind a counter, ringing up sales. Esther had a generous pug nose and her cheeks seemed to bloom when she smiled. Esther clutched her mother's words like a charm on the days—without her knowledge—that she went to the Eden Bar and Grill.

The moment Esther crossed the threshold into the restaurant, she saw Forty Carats at the bar, loudly lecturing one of the waitresses, Geraldine, about Paul Robeson. Even standing at the entrance, Forty Carats's breath, sickly sweet, faintly sour with the odor of cheap wine, enveloped her. Once he had been somebody's husband, some child's father. Esther had heard the story of how he had left his five-year-old son alone in their Detroit apartment one afternoon while he went to the store and the child accidentally set a fire that killed him and two other people in the building. Some said that's why Forty Carats had crawled inside a bottle and couldn't find his way out. Some said he'd gotten fired from his job at a Negro school in the South after he "got involved" with one of his male students. Nobody knew the truth or cared to discover it, for the rumors fed speculation and stoked the eternal appetite for dismay, pity and surprise. And everyone called him Forty Carats (his real name was Walter Greene) because of the fake diamond ring he wore on his baby finger.

Forty Carats ran errands and numbers for people in the neighborhood and could be seen sleeping in an alley on Monday and riding beside somebody in a brand-new car on Wednesday, clean-shaven and dressed in a new suit of clothes. Over the objections of his waitresses, Randolph Spenser, the owner of the Eden Bar and Grill, gave Forty Carats a free meal when he needed it. And Naomi had said of him, "He just talks like a fool 'cause life's treated him so bad he don't know what to say. But that man's got sense and more than lots of people I know."

Two dozen tables covered with red-and-white-checked oil-cloths filled the dining area of the restaurant. A tiny vase with a plastic flower sat in the center of each table. Black-and-white photos of Nat King Cole, the Mills Brothers, Slappy White, Moms Mabley lined the walls around the bar, which at that moment was closed. Ceiling fans whirred overhead.

Esther nodded to the one or two other patrons and she felt the men's eyes probing her body with unapologetic interest. The waitresses—white uniforms tight, creasing their hips, the kind of women who, over ocher or brown faces, had dyed their hair red or blond—eyed Esther, as they did each time she entered, cautiously, quietly plotting her elimination. At times like this, before the place got busy, the waitresses stood, listless and impatient, behind the counter, snapping Juicy Fruit gum, polishing the countertop until it gleamed, the better to admire themselves.

Esther found Randolph Spenser in one of the booths that afforded more privacy near the rear. He was why she stopped in, trying to make her arrival two or three evenings a week after work appear casual, unplanned. He sat, as he often did, in the back booth, reading the *Washington Afro-American*. Esther knew that when he saw her, his silent yet pleased acknowledgment would calm the fierce gyrations of her stomach muscles and the manic pulsing of her heart. He would smile and stand up in greeting, just like she was a lady, and thereby distinguish Esther from everyone else in the room.

Randolph Spenser looked up from the sports page and saw Esther walking toward him and, as she expected, he stood up. He didn't know why he did this. No other woman evoked such a response. But there was something in the way Esther walked—her small frame erect, her shoulders thrust back, her ample breasts poised proudly before her—that made Randolph stand to honor her.

He was a patient man. He had not always been, but he'd

had to wait for anything that was really worth having, earning it through forbearance and a graceful acceptance of the limits of desire. He was patient. Yet every piece of luck he'd ever had had been of his own making. If he hadn't wanted it, coveted it, dreamed of it first, all the patience in the world would have gained him nothing. He was a married man and still he wanted this young girl. And he had learned to live with the sinfulness, the selfishness of his need, the way someone who is ugly or hopelessly deformed learns to bear the pitying gaze, the repugnant stare.

He had wanted Esther ever since she was a high school graduate who thought she was better than most of the people she knew.

Standing at the window of his restaurant in the afternoons, Randolph had watched Esther on her way home from Dunbar High School with two of her friends. Walking between the two other girls, who were obviously more innocent and less assured than she, Esther wore a secretive smile as she talked, as if she already knew something her two friends never would. Sometimes when they neared the restaurant, out of the corner of her eyes, Esther spotted Randolph watching her. And in response, she turned to look at one of her friends or gazed studiously at her penny loafers. And yet, before they had passed out of his sight, Esther would effortlessly grant Randolph a full view of her face. And on her face Randolph witnessed more confidence and hunger than he'd ever seen up close before. And watching the three girls walk down the street, their pleated skirts swinging above their knees, Randolph wondered how he could satisfy what he saw in Esther's eyes.

It was when she graduated from high school and entered Howard that Esther started coming into the restaurant regularly. Randolph and Esther had come to understand one another through what they exchanged in the brief, momentous seconds of communion several times a week. Randolph knew all he had to do was wait. One day Esther would walk through the door to claim him.

It started with them just talking. He knew of her mother, everybody in the neighborhood did, and the fact that Esther had entered Howard had set tongues to wagging with pride, envy and curiosity. In the beginning Esther would come in and order a Pepsi at the bar and just start talking to him, just like that. She'd tell Randolph about her classes and she talked to him like there was no need for them to get to know each other, like they already knew more than enough. Sometimes on Saturday nights she'd come in with some young boy, some kid too careful, too proper to know how to keep her. Randolph watched as Esther's eyes darted around the room right in front of the boy's. And when she saw him, she'd introduce the young man to Randolph, like he was the young man's rival, other times, like she sought Randolph's approval of her choice. And she'd come in the next week and pick right up where they'd left off.

Esther was drawn to Randolph because he didn't condescend to her, his voice didn't take on a lighter, less serious tone when he greeted her as she came through the door of the Eden Bar and Grill. He always seemed to have all the time in the world just to sit and listen. At first she had thought she was flirting, testing her womanly prowess, of which she became more aware each day. Esther had enjoyed the way their banter had seesawed back and forth between brotherly mockery and the vested interst of a man who had imagined what it would be like to call her his own. She had just wanted someone to talk to, Esther told herself. Somebody who'd done something. Randolph had made so much money from the restaurant that he'd bought a liquor store and had set his sister-in-law up in a beaurty shop in Northeast. He was tall and lanky, with an uncomplicated smile and a flat high-cheekboned face. Randolph's stunning granite eyes brimmed with evidence of a greed for life women could not resist. He had a .45 revolver hidden in the restaurant, bought after two patons nearly wrecked the place in a fight over Geraldine, his head waitress, and used to fend off a would-be robber. He lived in upper Northwest and nobody had ever seen his wife and kids.

Randolph Spenser was unlike many of the other men Esther had known, small men with small dreams, whose sheer ordinariness drove her from them.

One afternoon when the restaurant was nearly empty Randolph had told Esther who he was. And it was that day, Esther knew, that she fell in love with him because loving Randolph Spenser would require more courage than she thought she could muster.

"It took me a long time to settle down," he told her. "A long time. I left home when I was seventeen. Back in those days, seemed like colored folks stayed on the road—leaving the South to come North, then some even turned around and went back where they came from. Everybody was moving any way they could. Hell, if you couldn't catch a train, you'd walk. Sometimes that's how I traveled too."

"Where's home, where you from?" Esther asked, leaning back in the booth, already wishing his story would never end.

"Washington. Right here in this city, over in Southeast. But I got the itch and hit the road. I saw Baltimore, New York, Chicago and thought I was gonna see something like the Eighth Wonder of the World in each place. But everywhere I went I saw people struggling, hustling, hurting, just like me. In New York, I got into bootlegging, gambling, in Baltimore, I worked on the docks, in Chicago, cleaned up the stockyards and was a busboy, shoeshine, in every town in between."

"Is New York as pretty as they say?"

"In the daytime you don't see it so much. You just feel the buildings and the people. But Lord, at night, when that city gets dressed up, lights all on the Chrysler Building and strung along the Brooklyn Bridge! And Broadway lit up like a mile-long smile, I tell you the city looks like something God made just to show off."

"What were you looking for in all those places?" Esther felt the questions clogging her mind, backlogged and restless. Randolph sat telling her everything and still that wasn't enough.

"Only thing I can think of is I was searching for somewhere I could be me. And you know, I didn't do that till I came back home."

And of all the things he did, he told Esther, back then before settling down, he'd liked gambling best of all. "Shooting craps especially. Give me a thrill to know a coupla black dots on two little white cubes could make or break me. But I had to use everything—my mind, luck, will. I had to strategize. Hell, I even prayed sometimes while shaking the dice in my hand. If I lost, I had to start from scratch, if I won, I might not leave alive. You never came to a crap game unprepared to defend your winnings. And if things got tight, you let your razor or switchblade do all the talking for you."

He was stabbed once in an alley in Harlem, stabbed over fifteen dollars. And then left for dead when the other men scattered at the sight of his slashed chest and the blood gushing out onto the mean, gritty surface of the alley. Randolph lay there, the odor of his blood mingling with the smell of defeat around him. He was unconscious and suddenly wrapped in a splendid white light as piercing as a spotlight, as soft as the moon's glow. Randolph felt himself healing, his spirit elevated and thrust outside himself. The light expanded and smiled upon him, the light blinded and blessed him, assuring him he would never die.

A day later Randolph woke up in a bed in Harlem Hospital, knowing he had been saved not just to go on living but to find out why he was living. The day he was released from the hospital Randolph returned to the same alley. Among a different set of men, he won big. And this time he pulled out his knife before anyone else.

"That light, that taste of death, that's what brought me back home," he told Esther. "I thought I was on the road all that time looking for a place to live. But I was really trying to find a place to die."

With the money he won in the alley Randolph returned home. One evening he visited his widowed father, whom he had not seen in a year. His father was a truck farmer who sold produce and supplied small stores and vegetable markets.

During Randolph's visit the niece of one of his father's regular customers came to the house. Mary Littlejohn had long-fingered elegant hands that made Randolph think of a swan. And when he stood behind her to introduce himself, the scent of Ivory soap rose from the skin on her neck. Randolph cleared his throat and said hello. Mary Littlejohn turned around and inside her smile he saw a fireplace, stacks of clean sheets and felt the warmth of a naked thigh resting against his stomach. A year later they were married. And when America entered the war Randolph was rejected by the army because he had a bad heart.

"But I thought you wanted to be free?" Esther asked, irritated by the end of the story.

"Life's not always wanting the same thing all the time," he told her almost sadly. "Freedom's a good thing. It's just that it's not the only thing that matters."

Folding the sports page of the *Afro* hurriedly and slowly reseating himself, Randolph asked Esther, "How you doing today, Miss Lady?"

"I'm fine."

"So I see."

Randolph threw the paper on the seat beside him and watched Esther sit down.

"You want something to drink?"

"I'll have a Pepsi."

"Geraldine, a Pepsi," he called out.

"How'd work go today?"

"OK."

Geraldine roughly set the soda down before Esther and turned on her heels, aggressively switching her hips as she walked away.

"She doesn't like me," Esther said, reaching for the glass.

"She's jealous."

"Why? What've I got that she hasn't?"

"She knows I like you." The admission came easy, natural, and yet Randolph hurriedly moved to sabotage the words by observing, "In another few weeks you'll be going back to school. You ready?"

"I'm not going back."

"Why not?" he asked, lazily lighting up a Lucky Strike.

"I've learned as much as they can teach me."

"Now, how do you know that?"

"I've talked to some of the seniors and they're less interesting than the freshmen. That scares me."

"Your mama won't like that."

"That's all I been thinking about."

In her complaint Randolph heard Esther's longing and he knew she was ready to be his. Still, he trembled at the thought of what he was about to do. After seven years and two sons, Randolph knew that with the woman he had married his happiness would be sporadic but his loyalty to her complete. Mary would forgive him anything as long as their life together remained unchanged. His wife was bedrock rather than inspiration, their marriage a healthy silent pulse. But Randolph was so wearied by a mere glance at the curves of Mary's body now, changed to bulk by childbirth, the touch of her hands, that night after night he sat up listening to the radio hoping Mary was asleep when he pulled back the covers to lay beside her.

Randolph wanted to ask Esther to go out with him, yet he sat gripped by exhilaration and shame. Esther saw his uneasiness and asked, "What's wrong?"

"Nothing, nothing." he assured her. "I was just wondering if you'd like to go to the Howard with me to see Sarah Vaughan Friday night?"

"I think I'd like that." Esther smiled, allowing herself to touch him for the first time ever, her fingers gently massaging his wrist as she said, "I think I'd like that a lot."

Naomi tended her houses like a garden. And of the houses she owned, none had bloomed beneath her hand with more grace than the house on Harvard Street that she now called home. The pale yellow-brick Victorian structure exuded a stern elegance and guarded the lives it sheltered like a sentry. The dwellings that lined the block achieved an almost royal distance from the street, separated from it by three, sometimes four levels of steps. These were homes approached carefully, wondering, as one neared the portal, if it was possible to live up to the expectations the inanimate yet forceful exterior imposed.

Single families resided in only a few of the residences, most gave shelter to two or three families living on each of the three floors, sometimes even the basements as well. The entire first floor was Naomi's private domain. Naomi had gleaned a sense of decorating style from the white homes she had worked in years before, from magazines and the movies. An upright piano that only Esther could play claimed one corner of the living room, standing on an oriental carpet of deep tones of green, yellow and red. Lace doilies lay on the arms of the broad, solid sitting chairs. Large gilt-framed mirrors were poised behind the sofa and over the mantelpiece. From her childhood, Naomi still harbored memories of harsh winters dressed in flimsy dresses and jackets that offered little resistance to wind or cold. And so, more than any other feature of her house, Naomi cherished the fireplace that was the centerpiece of the dining room. In winter she preferred to eat her meals from a tray sitting before the fire, watching the blue propane-gas-produced flame thunder with quiet glory against the asbestos lining. It didn't even matter that it wasn't a *real* fireplace, the kind that required wood and kindling. It had taken Naomi forty years to finally get warm and the glorious heat almost erased memories of sleeping beneath a too thin blanket, fully dressed, dreaming of the kind of fire she could turn on anytime she pleased. And when friends came to call, no matter what time of year, Naomi led them to the fireplace and urged them to pull up a chair.

When Esther arrived home, exultant yet troubled by the plans she had made, she found her mother sitting in the bedroom before the lace-curtained front window, fanning herself with the graceful fatigue of a slightly bored monarch. Naomi had opened the front of her dress and baby powder covered her chest and creased the valley between her ample breasts. The nearly ninety-three-degree heat had gripped the city by the throat and the small electric fan on Naomi's dresser merely circulated a steady steam of humid air. Esther stood at the entrance to her mother's bedroom, fearful for the first time in her life of crossing the portal of the french doors.

Esther was the child of Naomi's dreams and she had created for her daughter a world that was wondrous and expectant. Esther's bedroom, even now, was decorated in a soft white virginal color scheme of eyelet lace. The boarders, sensing the special requirements Naomi had erected around the life of her only child, had doted on Esther as insistently as her mother. And so Esther had grown up supposing that the world would always be kind.

"That you, Esther?" Naomi asked without even turning to see who was behind her.

"Yes, ma'am." Esther said, freed by her mother's words to enter the room.

"What you just standing there in the doorway for?"

"Nothing."

Esther forced herself to enter the bedroom and cautiously sat on Naomi's massive four-poster and quietly listened to Naomi's account of her day. "After you left this morning, I got up and started to make breakfast, but it was just so hot I couldn't eat a thing. Then Forty Carats knocked on the door—just in time too, hadn't had his morning taste yet, was sober as a judge and him and Mr. Franklin set that old furniture in the basement out in the alley for the trashman. Then I got up my nerve to go out in the heat and drove over to Monroe Street to collect some rents from the management company and by the time I got back home I felt like I'd been out working in that heat all day long. I laid down, then got up a hour later, took a bath and got dressed all over again.

I've been sitting here near about two hours. This is the happiest I've been all day."

Naomi's hair was swept back from her forehead into a bun, revealing a face that, powdered and streaked with rouge, resisted the arrival of each new year, viewing it as an unexpected interloper. Naomi had told Esther, "I know I have to die, I can handle that, it's the getting old part that burns me up."

"Some boy named Bruce called for you." Naomi tossed the information at Esther with disdain. Her daughter was almost a woman and yet the young men who courted Esther still qualified, in Naomi's eyes, despite their jobs, their deep voices and their persistence, as mere boys. Esther stretched out on Naomi's bed and lay against the thick, fluffed pillows.

"Girl, you better get your shoes off my spread," Naomi snapped. Kicking her sandals onto the floor, Esther felt a sudden sensual tingling that ran like hot lead through her muscles and gathered her breath in her throat. She stretched her small body, lithe as a cat. The thought of Randolph perched gleefully in the corner of her mind.

"Girl, what's wrong with you today?" Naomi asked.

"Nothing, Mama. Nothing's wrong." Esther whined, offering, as assurance, a large clownlike smile.

"You want some aspirin? This heat can affect young folks too, you know."

Rolling on her back and staring at the ceiling, Esther asked, "Mama, how much did you love Daddy?"

"What kind of question is that?"

"Mama, please. You hardly ever talk to me about him."

"I still don't understand what . . ." Naomi said, fidgeting and fanning with irritable urgency.

"It's something I need to know."

Naomi gazed through the sheer lace curtains at the street. Lying on her side, Esther could see the sun's rays filtered through the curtains, translucent, dancing in the air around her mother's face as if they too awaited her response.

"You see, I never loved nobody else," Naomi blurted. "There's been men that would've gave anything to marry a widow with property. One or two even felt something and made me feel something too. But your daddy filled me up, gave me enough to last all the years without him and not be lonely. I never had much education, you know that. Even now, my reading's not all that good. But your daddy had a mind! Ummph ummmph! Seemed like he'd read everything and knew the rest. And he didn't make me feel small 'cause I didn't know as much as him. Made me feel like what he knew and I didn't was just a way for us to get closer. You know, when we'd be in bed at night, sometimes he'd read me stories, not like for a child, but for grown-ups. Stories by Charles Chestnut, some of the poetry of that man Hughes and some of Dunbar, and he'd even read white folks too, read *Oliver Twist* one time, though I didn't like that so much, I already knew what it was like to be poor. And when he read the story of David to me from the Bible, I thought that was the most beautiful story I'd ever heard. I had the money and he had the brains and nobody thought we'd last—nobody. The women swore he'd spend every dime I had, the men hoped he would, so they could take his place. But we were a team, that's what nobody saw. And I never tried to figure out how much I loved him—I wouldn't have even known how to do that. Even with all the education you've got, you couldn't pull that off. But I guess I loved him enough to let him make me a better woman for knowing him. I didn't resist him. I had sense enough not to do that. Why do you ask me something like that?"

"It's important for me to know."

Naomi let the cardboard fan from Gilchrist's Funeral Home fall into her lap and assessed her daughter, stretched out on the bed, wrapped in the too-neat tranquil repose that precedes upheaval. She wanted to ask simply and boldly, "Who is he?" but she could not bear the thought of hearing a lie and the sensation that had come upon her informed Naomi that Esther would interpret curiosity as trespass. Naomi picked up the fan and felt the warm air against her cheek as forlorn as a goodbye kiss.

The phone rang and Esther said, "If it's Bruce, tell him I'm not here."

"I'm not gonna lie for you, young lady. You're big enough to do that for yourself."

The phone rang several times with a persistence that Esther associated with Bruce. She had met him at Howard. He was a mannerly young junior from Newark, New Jersey, who wanted to be a lawyer and who bored Esther more than she'd imagined possible. The phone was finally silent after the twelfth ring.

"What's wrong with this Bruce anyway?" Naomi asked.

"He's so young."

"Young, well, *you're* young. What do you want? A man? You're not ready for that. A man right now wouldn't do you nothing but harm."

"You married at seventeen."

"Yeah and I wish I hadn't. And that don't mean I was ready for it. That was the only thing a girl could do, where I come from, to prove herself."

"I just can't stand Bruce. He's got no imagination."

"Sometimes I'm sorry you're in college. You come home throwing around all those words like they've got something to do with life. Man don't need imagination to love a woman. He needs to look her in the eye and see her for everything she is when he finds her, forget about fantasies and dreams and what he thinks he got to have, man has to look at a woman like she is and love her anyway."

"Imagination got you everything you have."

"Being hungry got me what I own. When you're hungry

you'll do almost anything, when it's imagination that's driving you, you get picky."

Naomi stared out the window for a while in silence and then she said, turning to Esther, "I wanted you to go to Howard, not just so you'd be smarter than me, but so you'd have peace of mind. I listen to you and look at you sometimes and I know you're on fire with something that school started but can't put out."

"I'm not happy there," Esther said, turning on her stomach and clutching a pillow.

"There's not too many places in this world you're gonna be happy—not like you mean anyway."

Esther closed her eyes as Naomi's complaint droned on and saw the girls of Howard University—a rainbow of light tan saffron-colored faces. And then the young men came into view, the campus big shots, the ones Esther longed for and who looked at her, their eyes indifferently rolling across her face, as though there was nothing there to see because of her dark skin. The two years Esther had endured at the school had nearly defeated her. And the fact that it was necessary to defend, in the way she walked across campus, entered a room, spoke English, her claim to serious consideration quickly extinguished the joy Esther felt when she first enrolled.

What terrified Esther most, however, was the air of smug self-satisfaction, the complacency that hung like a fog over much of the school. The young women, demure and proper in pearls and saddle oxfords, were ladies-in-waiting for just the right young man to escort them into the future. The sororities determined what the young women would think, who they would befriend and whom they would deem it possible to love. In the thrice-weekly required chapel, Esther learned there was a difference between faith and religion and that the God of Howard University did not speak in the passionate tongues unleashed in Greater Faith Baptist Church but in modulated patient tones that roused no one from sleep or sin.

Her teachers were prim patrician males. Their serious, staunch bearings, tight lips and three-piece suits informed the word they were reasonable men.

Yet there were discordant and to Esther's ears, joyful noises of dissent—the Law School worked diligently with the NAACP, developing cases to challenge the legality of segregation. Students from Africa and the Caribbean sat in Esther's classes, the kind of men who confidently told her that when they graduated, they planned to "go back home and lead my country to freedom."

Esther did not know what she wanted to do, but she knew she did not want to be a schoolteacher, social worker or get married exactly one year after she graduated and move to LeDroit Park in Washington or Sugar Hill in Harlem.

Naomi sat clicking her tongue, murmuring disapproval of her daughter's discontent.

The fatigue in Naomi's voice, the sadness, the resolution told Esther that she was free to make a choice. And so she said, "I'm not going back." At her words, Naomi dropped the fan on the floor, rose from her chair and walked out of the room. As Esther watched Naomi walk past her, her carriage stooped by the knowledge of her fast-shrinking influence, Esther realized for the second time that day that she had been granted the freedom she had prayed for. The thought charged her with such a rich fusion of emotions that Esther lay on her mother's bed and wept, completely and quietly, until dusk filled the bedroom with a willful calm. When Naomi entered the room again, she saw her daughter's sleeping tear-stained face, covered her with a summer blanket and stroked Esther's hair and wondered how she would love her daughter as a woman instead of as a child.

N A O M I

sther dropping out of Howard like that near about broke my heart. I hadn't had a whole lot of education, as I told you. But education is the one thing that nobody can take away from you. There'll be times when you've got money and when you're broke, when you've got somebody to love and when you're so lonesome you feel *worse* than a motherless child. But get you some education and you've always got it. I think if my folks had had an education, their lives wouldn't have been so hard, they could've done more than just work like mules. And even me, getting my houses and the little money that's mine, well, that made me feel pretty good. But knowing how to talk and understand books, that must be something. Oh, I've always preached about "motherwit" and common sense and even the smartest person won't last long without them. But I used to get jealous of Rayford sometimes, how he could read a book and act like it was almost better than having sex with me or talk about things because he knew so many different words, so many different ways to think about a thing, to find out what it meant. And I wanted that for Esther, since I'd never known it, that real love for learning.

I remember Rayford read a poem to me one time by this man who put words together like he was spinning gold. And in the poem he said that God had just loaned us our children, we were just caretakers and that in the end our children belonged to Him, but mostly they belonged to themselves. The day Esther told me she wasn't going back to Howard, I knew I had to let her go, to find some way to love her but not hold on so tight. It's like when she was little, I'd pick her up and carry her in my arms. Now I had to be satisfied with holding her hand and that only if she wanted me to.

I'd imagined Esther being a teacher like Rayford or maybe something even more. But I can't tell her what to dream. What to want. Still, I wish I could. I talked to Cora about it one night and she told me Esther was just doing what I had done—the unexpected thing. She reminded me how my leaving Isaiah and even coming North wasn't the kind of thing a woman was supposed to do. And she reminded me that I didn't turn out too bad. "How you know?" Cora said. "Esther's gonna surprise you yet. One dumb decision don't have to wreck a life. They thought you were crazy for leaving Isaiah when he had all that land. Didn't matter that he was too small a man for a woman who thought as big as you. And even when you left Spring Hope, you and I both know, there were folks just counting the days till the North drove you back home, raggedy and broke. You don't know who your daugher's gonna be. She don't neither. Just give her time, Naomi. Give her time."

I thank the Lord for friends. They can see you and your life so clear 'cause it's not their hearts all tangled up in it. And I prayed on Cora's words a long time and made my peace. But Esther had still took a piece of my heart I knew I'd never get back.

S taring at his face in the mirror as he buttoned his white shirt, Randolph Spenser was an almost happy man. He savored the illicit expectation that had, in the past few days, when he least expected it, set his hands to trembling and stoked his mind like a fire. He was an almost happy man because in a few hours he would once again receive more than he deserved. He was a man who regularly and methodically risked everything, in order to test the endurance of the people and things that claimed him. To Randolph Spenser, existence was merely a fate to be outsmarted.

He gazed at his face closely in the mirror and saw that several unruly hairs poked from his mustache. He took a tiny pair of scissors from a manicure set his wife had given him for Christmas and began to even the sides.

Randolph Spenser had always had more than one woman at a time in his life. And because women occupied a place in his imagination and were a need, more intense than for many other men, he always called what he felt for a woman "love."

He was born and grew up in Anacostia, named for an Indian tribe that once lived on the banks of the river that separated the Washington of myth, pageants and history books from the grubby, more mundane city across the river.

Randolph's grandfather Ellis Spenser was a slave and declared contraband when the Union Army evacuated thousands of slaves to Washington from their native plantations during the last stages of the Civil War. Along with the other "human spoils of war," Ellis Spenser, when he arrived in Washington from the Virginia plantation where he had spent his entire life, was housed in a barracks, one of hundreds erected as temporary shelters in the swampy wasteland east of the Capitol.

The government purchased large tracts of hilly, rugged woodland, which was cleared by the freedmen who built homes on one-acre plots purchased with a subsidy from the government. Ellis Spenser built a one-room cabin in 1865 in what became known as Barry's Farm, a settlement of Negro freedmen. With unmatched civic pride and fervor, the inhabitants of Barry's Farm quickly organized a Baptist church and built a one-room schoolhouse.

Ellis Spenser became a successful and busy carpenter who married a former slave, Anna Stiles, in 1875. Anna Stiles was a widow whose husband had been killed in one of the last battles of the Civil War and she was the mother of three children.

The newly freed slaves lived lives that were rural, often rustic, yet endowed with a pride that knew no bounds, simply because, for the first time in their lives, their lives belonged to them.

Emancipation Day, April 16, was in those days celebrated with a parade of floats from Anacostia to the White House and down Pennsylvania Avenue, to the Capitol and then to Lincoln Park, where Frederick Douglass might deliver a speech to mark the historic proclamation. And every year, in honor of John Brown, there was an excursion to Harpers Ferry.

In 1880 Anna Stiles Spenser delivered to Ellis Spenser his only child, a son whom he named Ezrah. After his father's death, Ezrah Spenser, then twenty-one, cleared away the log cabin his father had built and erected a five-room house that eventually became home for his mother, his wife Ida, and their son Randolph.

Randolph was raised by his father after his mother died of a stroke when he was six. His father, Ezrah Spenser, was as frugal with affection as with his money. And the rambling house in which Ezrah Spenser raised his son alone after the death of both his mother and wife in the same year was bereft of all but the most essential furniture, a house haunted by the silence that, after a while, Randolph preferred to the gruff sound of his father's voice, ordering him to chop wood for the stove or to feed the horses that pulled the wagon loaded with his father's farm produce. Randolph hated most of all the sound of the coins dropped into a tin box his father hid beneath his bed and opened each night to deposit money from the day's sales. No one else knew it, but Ezrah Spenser was a rich man. He lived like a pauper, perfecting denial, yet able to sleep at night only after the sight of the coins in his box filled his parched, withering spirit with the one pinprick of excitement he allowed himself. When he left home at eighteen, it was the drumbeat sound of those coins over the years that pushed Randolph into the night with only the clothes on his back.

There had been no mother's kiss planted on his forehead in the middle of a night's sleep, imprinting and shaping the quality of his days. And Randolph greedily watched the unabashed favoritism his friends' mothers showered upon them, defending them against stern, unjust fathers, saving the last piece of cake for the son whose manhood was enigma and wealth, gazing at the boys sometimes and seeing in the pubescent face the best thing she had ever done.

For Randolph, women existed on the periphery, an occasional visit from an aunt, his schoolteachers, the storekeeper's wife, the "fancy lady" who sent him to the store to buy cigarettes and stockings and who took him to bed with her when he was fifteen. Yet none of the women of his youth penetrated the hermetically sealed world his father created for him. And so, in the years since he had left his father's house, Randolph had sought in the love of women what he had been denied in all the years before.

He had loved many women and still the loneliness of his father's house gripped him, as he lay in the embrace of a woman who was not his wife. The silence, the mute hunger of his childhood, overtook the words he vainly chiseled as he cradled his wife Mary in his arms. Randolph knew that he would always be alone beside any woman he touched because of the chasm carved in place of his heart.

Still, he was a good man. He heared Mary tell her friends that all the time. Randolph paid their bills promptly, spent time with his wife and two sons, remembered everyone's birthday, had never offended his in-laws, worked hard and had money in the bank. There were moments when he was filled with a numbing anger at the thought of how little was

required to be considered "good." Still, his wife's designa-
tion, over the years, freed Randolph to be both the man his
wife thought him to be and the man his childhood had made
him.

"You going out?" Mary asked, as she entered the bedroom
and placed a stack of just-pressed slacks and shirts on the
bed.

"Yep, I'm going out."

Gazing at Mary in the mirror, Randolph wished she would
ask him where he was headed, but he knew that she would
not. She was a good woman. He had almost thought about
not going to meet Esther and that possibility struck him as
much of a betrayal as his promise to see her.

Finally Randolph was satisfied with what he saw in the
mirror and turned to face his wife. She was the mother he
had never had, the wife who knew him better than he could
accept. And they lived together aware of their neighbors'
envy, each aware of how undeserved the envy was. Randolph
cherished most Mary's righteous and turbulent anger when
revealed in full dress and her short-lived rebellions against
his patriarchy. Three times so far she had gotten out of bed
in the morning, dressed their sons and annouced to Randolph
from the bedroom door, "I need to get away," and driven
to Richmond to spend a week with a cousin.

Randolph pulled Mary up from the bed, where she sat
counting socks, and hugged her.

"What time will you be back?" she asked, her light brown
eyes reflecting knowledge.

"I won't be late," he assured her.

"Should I wait up?" she asked hopefully.

"There's no need."

"I never sleep until you're beside me. After all this time, I
still can't do it."

"What, are you scared I won't come back?"

"I know you'll come back," Mary told him, then, firmly

removing his hands from her hips, she added, "I just don't know when and my life is on hold until you walk back through that door."

As Esther stood in front of the Howard Theater, waiting for Randolph, beneath a neon marquee advertising Sarah Vaughan and Slappy White, she mulled over the etiquette of deceit. Recalling the words and actions that had brought her out of the house alone to stand waiting on the corner of Seventh and T for Randolph, Esther concluded that deceit depended for its power, on at least a partial union with the truth. And so Esther told Naomi that she was meeting a friend.

It was Friday night and across the street Scott's Billiard Hall was filled. Through the glass windows Esther could see men hovering around the green felt tables as intent as surgeons trying to save a life. Women in high heels and fox fur throws and men in zoot suits passed her on the way to the Stagedoor Bar and Grill, their walk, their smiles testimony to genteel lust. Howard University stood atop the hill, looking down at Seventh and T in fascination and disdain at the pool sharks, prostitutes, lovers, hustlers, good-time chasers, 'bamas, tan and high yellow mamas that gave the street its particular and peculiar kind of life. Seventh Street, dressed in neon, scented with the hungry perfume of passion, hummed and whistled and scatted its way into the night.

The minute technicalities, the subtle shades that could color a lie, suddenly fascinated Esther, who before tonight had hardly ever been less than honest with her mother.

This first major deceit had the feel of a game whose dangerous potential merely heightened the longing to master it. Esther had made herself an easy target for the sting of regret and dismay as well as the depths of the kind of passion she had encountered so far only in the pages of *True Confessions* magazine and in the fantasies that bloomed in the darkness and starred Randolph, his face darkened by shadows but his hands firmly reaching for her. And because Esther was determined to discover with Randolph more ardor than despair, she had stopped by a florist shop in the afternoon and bought a gardenia. In the taxi on the way to the Howard Theater, she had pinned the flower in her hair.

After the show Randolph took Esther to a nearby Chinese restaurant. They had settled in a booth and quietly sipped their drinks—Esther's colorful and fruity, Randolph's a shot of bourbon. They nervously assessed on another, neither quite believing what they were about to do. Finally Esther said, "You know, every Sunday I go to church with my mama and now I'm sitting here with you, but I don't feel like a sinner."

"No need to." Randolph smiled. "We ain't started sinning yet."

"According to the Bible, we've been sinning all along," Esther informed him primly, as though correcting some grave basic error in his reasoning.

"I didn't know you were religious."

"I never felt the need to be until now."

"You scared?" Randolph whispered, leaning forward, as if to share a secret.

"Aren't you?"

"Uh-uh." He smiled again. "You the one read all those books. I ain't got sense enough to be scared."

His words had not relaxed her and Esther sat across from Randolph, twisting a small white handkerchief into knots, pulling on each small knot like a noose.

"I ain't even asked you to be mine yet, but we both know my intentions. But I'll let you go right now, if that's what you want. Let you go and won't be no harm done."

Esther looked at Randolph, startled, afraid, until she saw, flickering in his eyes, a staunch denial of his words.

"I'm not gonna lie," he rushed on. "Say I hate my wife. Tell you a bunch of bullshit about how I'm miserable. Dishonest as what I'm doing is, somehow there's got to be room in it for the truth. I want you. And nothing and nobody else matters. I want you. But don't ask me to be or do what I can't."

"Mama told me that I'm still too young for a man, said a man wouldn't do me any good," Esther said weakly.

"And she was right. *Any* old man, *a* man, *some* man would do all the things she warned you about. But your mama wasn't talking about me. I'm not *any* old man. I'm yours."

"I'm ashamed, no matter what I said," Esther finally confessed, her voice riddled with the urgent sound of retreat.

"Your mama don't want you to grow up. Don't want nobody to break your heart. I ain't gonna break your heart, baby. I'm gonna make it mine, take it around with me wherever I go."

"What happens if . . ."

"And you want that, you know you do." Randolph enfolded Esther's hands in his, calmed their tense, aimless wandering. "Your mama only told you half the story. She didn't tell you how good a man feels next to you. How come mamas don't tell their daughters that?" He eased the handkerchief, smudged with perspiration from Esther's hand, and she released it, asking, "And what about . . ."

"You think I'm gonna take what you got and then don't want to see you again. You want me to respect you. And I do. I couldn't want you if I didn't respect you. And what's underneath your dress, baby, that's no big deal. And it ain't why I'm sitting here with you tonight."

Randolph reached across the table and removed the gardenia from Esther's hair and placed it in the center of the table. The flower lay between them, slightly wilted and damp, its veins brown and bulbous against its white skin.

"You didn't like it?" Esther asked.

"Reminds me too much of Billie Holiday. You don't need to be looking nothing like her because I don't plan to give you no reason to sing the blues."

When Randolph took Esther home, he asked her, "You still scared?" And she answered him with the kiss of a woman who had never been less afraid at any moment in her life.

Still, he did not touch Esther for several weeks, preferring to savor her burgeoning assurance and to lock in his mind memories of the naïveté Esther would have to shed in order to become his lover. Everything would change once he made love to her. And Randolph eagerly awaited the tension, pulsing and alive, that would engulf them in the aftermath, dictating and determining what they felt. Yet he dreaded the loss of the virtue that marked them now.

Because Esther had been inevitable and necessary for him since the first day she entered the Eden Bar and Grill, making love to her would matter to him in ways that seared his imagination. The thought of it plunged him into mournful silences at the dinner table with his wife and sons and made Esther's laughter startle him as boldly as a siren when they were together.

Finally, one night they went to a tourist home in Northeast and as Esther lay against his chest, silent and warm, Randolph kissed her forehead and told her, "Now, baby, now I'm scared."

One afternoon a few weeks later Esther and Randolph went to Carrs Beach. It was the middle of the week and the beach was nearly deserted. Esther had packed a picnic lunch and strolled into the Eden Bar and Grill at twelve-thirty to claim Randolph with a shy yet provocative gaze that made him hastily untie his apron and shout over his shoulder to Geraldine that he'd be back before six o'clock. They jumped into his sky-blue 1948 Cadillac, which was as forbidding as a Sherman tank, as beautiful as the most thoughtful work of art, and headed for the beach.

LONG ■ DISTANCE ■ LIFE

"What you gonna do, now that you're not going back to Howard?" Randolph asked, his shoulders flecked with sand and sweat as he lay on one of Naomi's old blankets, gazing at the sun overhead.

"Take the civil service test, I guess. I took a typing course one summer."

"Civil service?" he asked, turning to look at her. "I figured you for something more exciting than that."

"Like what?"

"Oh, I don't know. But anything besides sitting at a desk all day long, working for Uncle Sam."

"It's a living," Esther said, putting on her sunglasses and staring at the sky.

"You could say that about almost anything."

"There's not but so many things for a Negro woman to be," Esther said defensively. "I'm not as smart as Mrs. Bethune, I don't look like Lena Horne, I can't play the piano like Hazel Scott."

"You grew up in your mama's house and you believe that?"

"My mama had to find her own way. She made mine for me. All those ballet, piano lessons, even sent me to a colored charm school one time—only thing I learned from all that was how boring it must be to be a lady."

"You got your mama's grit?"

"All the lessons took it out of me," Esther sighed, hugging her knees.

"You got her guts or you wouldn't be here with me," Randolph assured her, his voice brimming with a satisfaction so manifest that it inspired a sudden defiance in Esther.

"Who knows, I might just hit the road one day like you," she said, leaning back on her elbows.

"I'll take you anywhere you want to go," Randolph promised.

"One day when I'm ready, I'm gonna just take off," Esther

said coyly, then added, pushing her sunglasses onto the top of her head and gazing at Randolph for effect, "and I won't look back."

"You better look back and you better come back too. By the time you have your children, things won't be segregated, not like now. Who knows what'll be waiting for them?"

"You think things'll change?"

"Honey, that's all they do."

"You know, I never felt Washington belonged to me."

"That's 'cause it don't. It belongs to those congressmen and senators and all the tourists."

"You know what I mean."

"Yeah, I know." They watched a group of boys, wet and glistening beneath the afternoon sun, playing in the surf, then Randolph said, "So you thinking about going someplace else."

"No, I was just talking."

"Don't *ever* talk like that," he said, turning to Esther, his voice filled with the muscularity of a threat. The fear on Esther's face made Randolph gently rub her ankle as he said, "*Please* don't talk like that."

"What is it you want me to say?"

"I sure don't want to hear that."

"You act like we have a future."

"As long as you want me." Randolph stretched his body on the blanket like an offering. He wore a pair of red skin-tight trunks and his lean body was radiant and hard.

"Is that the best you can do?"

"There's more to what I said than you can hear right now," he told her solemnly. Then he asked, "Does your mama know about me?"

"No."

"You think she doesn't. I'll bet she does. If she's the kind of mama I think she is. She's got it all figured out."

"I can't lie forever."

"Nobody asked you to lie at all."

"Everybody's not *free* like you," Esther said angrily.

"Ain't none of us free."

"*You* act like it."

"You still ashamed, ain't you?" Randolph asked, rubbing her calf gently.

"This is adultery."

"No it ain't, Esther. This is life."

"How do I tell my mother?"

"You don't. She'll come up to you one day and tell you everything you've already done. You won't have to tell her a thing. You just got to figure out how to stand up for what you doing and what you feel when that day comes."

"Does your wife know about me?" Esther countered, brazen and bitter.

"No and if she did it wouldn't matter."

"To who? You or her?"

"To neither one."

"How can you be so sure?"

"You never been there, honey. You think marriage is about love and kisses and babies. It's about making a tiny little world—imperfect as it is—where you can be who you are and now and then be content. And you know when I'm happiest? When I see that my son's grown another inch or look at the other one and tell what part of him is me, just by what he says or how he says it, or laughing with my wife over some dumb thing in the newspaper. Ain't nothing earth-shattering about what I got. Nothing monumental. But it's the best I can do. And I ain't giving it up and neither is my old lady."

"Marriage must be awful," Esther said, wrapping her arms around her body as if brushed by a chill wind, so chastened by Randolph's words she felt near tears.

"Baby, it's all awful," Randolph told her, pulling Esther by the leg down beside him. He tried to kiss her, but she fought him, forming her arms into a barricade which he easily broke through. When he calmed her, he said again, "It's all awful, honey, being with somebody and being without, it'll kill you fast as it'll save you. That ain't too romantic, but it's the truth. But every minute we're together, at least, we're fighting back."

Now Esther had a lover and so she was afire with emotions that set her skin tingling and her eyes sparking with a wisdom whose price she could not calculate. This same unspeakable feeling, on other days confined Esther to bed with headaches and a sadness that was taut and burning inside her bones. She became obsessed with mirrors, gazing in them constantly to monitor the physical manifestations of the turbulence locked inside. And yet her reflection revealed no clues to the burgeoning ripeness Randolph had unleashed. This disappointed Esther greatly, for a secret, she felt, depended for its value on the everpresent possibility of discovery.

When they were together, Esther affected the mannerisms of the woman she was convinced he wanted—confident but uncertain enough to make her need for him apparent; childlike but willing to master the kind of feminine prowess that he liked periodically to succumb to; and compliant but able to harbor the potential for rebellion. Randolph remained attentive, yet Esther found that now she had little to say. And her silences provoked in Randolph a frenzied guilt, the very thing that he denied could ever claim him.

He gave Esther an emerald friendship ring so expensive she was afraid to wear it in Naomi's presence, for the questions it would provoke. On her birthday Randolph handed her an envelope containing a five-hundred-dollar U.S. Savings Bond and told Esther that she was to come to him for anything she needed, anything at all.

Esther rarely went to the Eden Bar and Grill anymore. She

could not bear the glances of Geraldine and the other wait-resses, stripping her as she entered, assessing her as she passed. Their gazes promised Esther that Randolph would hurt her one day, simply because he was a man.

And so, to make him break her heart, Esther found herself testing Randolph, and the resilience of their bond. She told him she'd meet him and didn't show up, demanded money she didn't need, lay unmoving and unmoved beneath him when they had sex, picked a fight when he could not see her when she wanted. Randolph knew what she was doing. One night when he took her home after a dinner over which she had not spoken a single word, Randolph told Esther, "I know what you're trying to do. But it won't work. If you want this thing to end, it's on you. You'll have to break my heart 'cause, like I told you at the start, I got no plans to break yours."

What Esther hated most was the claustrophobic atmo-sphere in which they played out their union. The neat but drab decor of the tourist home they frequented threatened to drive her mad. The pale floral wallpaper seemed to promise life without hope and the clean but shabby carpet and the cheap curtains made Esther want to turn around and go home. The small twin beds felt more joyless and accusing each time her back touched the overstarched white sheets.

And because they could not share one another with friends they had no other vision, besides their own, to compare each other to. Esther feared that what would destroy them would not be some act of betrayal, but that they would simply implode, the sheer weight of their sealed universe causing the fatal collapse. Vainly she tried to tell Randolph this, but could only say, one night as she sat, her nakedness covered by his shirt, sitting in the chair facing the bed, with Chinese food cartons littering the bedstand and bureau, "This room is driving me crazy."

"We can start going someplace else," he offered gener-ously.

"I don't *want* to go someplace else."

"What *do* you want?"

"I want to be normal," she cried. "I want to stop hiding my life. I want to let people know I'm in love."

"It won't always be like this," Randolph assured her.

"Why?"

"It just won't. I guarantee." He got out of the bed—tall, nude, his member now as harmless as a toy—and picked up his wallet from the bedstand and approached Esther, saying, "I've been meaning to give you this." He handed her a business card with his home phone number written in. Esther gazed up at him, her eyes grateful, wide with surprise.

"I trust you," he said, kneeling down before her, cupping her face in his hands and kissing her gently all over her face. When he finished kissing Esther, Randolph told her seriously, "It's only for emergencies, that's the only time you're to call, promise?"

"I promise," Esther said, submitting to his embrace, not sure why the card had extinguished her anger, clutching it as she held him tightly and felt his large hands rub her hips beneath the long tail of his white shirt. He lifted her from the chair and held her straddling his waist. She felt his sex, groping, fervent, as he whirled her around the room, laughing, she holding on to his shoulders, the card a white blur as they twirled in the room's dim half-light. Finally they fell on the bed, Esther astride him, her breasts spilling out of the shirt onto his face, he greedily sucking her as her body was startled by a nearly painful arc of desire; and she, sweating, hungry, worked her way out of the shirt and rolled onto her back, pulling him atop her and parted her legs in order to bring him home.

Only once had she used the phone number. She told herself she was testing to see if it was really his. A woman answered. And it was then that Esther realized she didn't even know his wife's name. The voice was friendly, the hello was almost sung, rendered with an expectant lilt, a rise at the end, that implied that happiness or good fortune must await such a greeting. Esther hung up the phone quickly, nearly dropping the receiver, so drenched in sweat were her palms.

Just before Thanksgiving Esther was hired as a file clerk by the Patent Office. Now she worked "for the government." Just like everybody else in town. Naomi was pleased for Esther, watching her leave for work each day as proudly as she had watched her leave for school. Everyone congratulated Esther now, for she was "set." All she had to do was go to work every day, not make too many mistakes and by the time she was sixty-five she'd have a pension.

But the deadening repetitiveness of the job soon dulled Esther's spirits so much that she had to drag herself to work. The other young colored girls on the job, over lunch in the cafeteria, talked about boyfriends, clothes and money. Esther sat in their midst, horrified into muteness by the thought that she had reached both the beginning and the end of her life.

N   A   O   M   I

t took me some time, but I finally figured out
what was going on. I watched Esther, all moody
and strange, acting like a crazy person. And for
the first time in my life, I heard my daughter lie
to me and I let it go. I was scared for her to tell
me the truth 'cause deep down I knew what it
was. I knew there was something just plain
wrong with whoever she was seeing. Esther
didn't come to me this time, complaining about
a broken heart or sharing a happy one. And

she'd changed, but it wasn't something you could see. It was in her voice, like she was tired all the time or sometimes so excited she couldn't stand it. And she never brought the fella to the house, that told me everything. Whispering on the phone, running out of the house to meet him like she'd been spirited out the door. I kept my eye on her real close. Thank God, she didn't miss her period. I made sure of that.

I had always been pretty strict with Esther about boys. Watched her pretty close. And I always tried to teach her that a man wasn't some savior who would make everything right. I told her to always love herself more than any man. That way every man would have to respect her and treat her right. But love is a powerful thing. A terrible thing. There's some kinds of love I wouldn't wish on nobody. And that's the kind young girls seem to fall into first. I had always watched Esther real close. Maybe too close. Maybe I drove her, in the end, to discover what I was afraid for her to find out. And when I found out who the man was, well, I was surprised, but then it all made sense. It was Forty Carats who let the cat out the bag. I caught him leaning on my car one day in front of the house, he was just coming off a three-day drunk and I got so mad at him, how he was just killing himself and wasting his life. I told him to get offa my car and even hit him with my pocketbook. He starts ducking while I'm hitting him and says, "Don't worry 'bout me. You need to be looking after that daughter of yours. Out here messin' with a married man." I grabbed him by the collar of his shirt and says, "What you talking about?" Then it all comes out, just like a dam bustin'.

"Miss Naomi, I ain't trying to get in your family business, but everybody knows it. Everybody. Esther and Randolph Spenser. I saw them parked out front of the Tivoli two nights ago, hugging and kissing for their lives."

Then I damn near tried to kill him. And when he started

running, I was so mad I picked a rock off the ground and threw it at him. "You keep my daughter's name outta your mouth. You hear me?" I shouted after him. I didn't know who made me more mad—Forty Carats 'cause he threw it in my face or Esther 'cause I knew it was true.

Well, the next night he called. I knew it was him by the whispering secretive tone Esther used on the phone in the hall, the way her voice got all excited, like mine used to when I was young and had no sense and thought I was in love. They talked for about half an hour. I had taken to timing Esther's calls. I was listening to "Amos 'n' Andy" on the radio and he'd called when the show came on and Esther hung up about the time the show went off.

"I'm going out," Esther called into the living room and nearly ran to the back of the house to her room to get her things. I turned the radio off and stood up. I figured I might not be able to stop her, but I'd at least try. I was determined, but I'll tell you, I had no idea what was gonna happen. I walked to the front door and stood in front of it like a guard. Then I heard Esther humming as she got close to the hallway.

"I'll be back in a few hours," she said, not even looking at me, like I wasn't standing in front of the door and like she was too ashamed to look me in the face. I had practiced what I was gonna say, put my foot down and not let her out the house. But Esther looked so scared seeing me blocking her way I just broke down and begged her, "Don't go out tonight, Esther, I'm not feeling too well and . . ."

"Mama, I'm not going to be long," she said.

"Why you got to go out now?" I pleaded. "It's almost ten o'clock."

"Mama!" she whined, like I was a child, getting on her nerves, and then she reached behind me for the doorknob. I grabbed her wrist and squeezed it, saying, "You're not going nowhere tonight."

Then Esther struggled with me and got her wrist free.

"What're you talking about?"

"Oh, baby, Esther," I said, reaching out my arms to her, watching her back away like I was gonna hurt her. I was hurt and mad so I shouted, "You're no whore, can't no man just call up here and you come running. Not my daughter. Not in my house."

"You don't know what you're saying."

"What kinda man is this anyway? Why can't he show himself? Show his face? Come meet your mama? Respect you and himself enough for that?"

"Mama, leave me alone," she said, closing her ears with her hands.

"I can't, Esther. I'm your mama. I got to say something. You won't."

"It's none of your business," she said, moving again toward the door.

Then I slapped Esther and I watched her eyes begin to tear and her hand touch her cheek that I had hit. "You are my business. You are my child. Don't ever tell me you not my business."

I reached out to hold her, but she bolted and I ran after her and caught her in the living room, caught and held her, her back to me, her face hidden in her hands. "Don't hide your face, Esther. Why won't you let me look at you, baby? I'll always love what I see." But she wouldn't let me look at her face and she bolted again and ran to her room, where she stayed locked up for the next two days.

The next week I went to the Eden Bar and Grill. I got there an hour before closing time and ordered a fried chicken dinner. While I waited for my order, I watched Randolph Spenser joking with the waitresses, talking with the customers, and I saw why Esther wanted him. When I finished eating, I called over one of the waitresses and asked to speak to the owner. Wiping his hands on his apron, he came over and said, "Can I help you, ma'am?"

"I'm Esther's mother," I told him. He didn't act surprised. Just sat down across from me in the booth.

"I know. We've never met. But I've seen you, people have told me who you were."

I pushed my plate out of the way and wiped the corners of my mouth with my napkin. I folded the napkin real neat and placed it in front of me on the table. I was doing all this, just stalling for time, while I got the nerve to tell him, "I want you to let my daughter go."

"I can't do that."

"Why? You've got a wife and a family from what I hear."

"And Esther's got nothing to do with them. They got nothing to do with her."

"You didn't look like a liar," I told him, sitting back in the booth, so disgusted I didn't think I could look at him one more minute.

"With all due respect to you, Mrs. Johnson, I can't let your daughter go because I don't want to. And even if I did, wouldn't be too long before we went right back together. If she didn't make that move, then I would."

"What do you want with her?"

"The same thing any man wants with a woman he feels something for."

"And what is that?"

"That's between me and Esther."

"She knows you have a wife?"

"Yes, she does. You see, I'm *not* a liar."

"She knows and she still . . ."

"Yes, ma'am."

"What do you think you can possibly give her?"

"Everything but a ring."

"You're making light of marriage."

"I wasn't talking about marriage."

"If you hurt my daughter, Mr. Spenser . . ."

"I hurt her already. I hurt her every time I leave her and go home to sleep beside my wife."

"God, but my little girl is strong," I sighed, rubbing my temples. The man's stubbornness took my breath away.

"How come you think she can't hurt me? You know how many times she's said she didn't want to see me no more and how many times I was scared she meant it? Esther ain't a little girl, Mrs. Johnson. I can vouch for that. And that's what's got you so upset."

"She's my child."

"But she's also her own woman. And she ain't never been that before."

"And so I've got to share her with you?"

"I'm not a bad man. Ask anybody around here. Esther's your child. And so she's not stupid. She didn't choose nobody who'd hurt her on purpose. My sins'll be just like yours— the kind I fight against but can't help. What you worrying about all those rules wasn't made with colored folks in mind for? Esther told me how you hustled and pushed and pulled to get what you got. You a self-made woman. I'm a self-made man."

"Some rules are made for *everybody*. I don't want her hurt," I told him.

"Then you must want her dead. That's the only way she can keep from being hurt by something or somebody."

"You're pretty smart, Mr. Spenser."

"Bet you thought 'cause I owned a restaurant instead of carrying a briefcase you could march right on in here and leave having heard everything you wanted to hear. Go home and ask Esther if she wants to be free."

The man had beat me at my own game—talking. And I felt like a old woman.

"You gonna have to excuse me," he said, real curt, looking at his watch. "We're about ready to close."

"I'm sorry I came."

"No, you're not. You're sorry you didn't get what you came for."

I put on my glasses and picked up the bill beside my glass of water. Randolph Spenser pulled it outta my hand and said, like he'd just conquered the world, "Don't worry, it's on the house."

You can bet I didn't go home and ask Esther if she wanted to be free. I knew what she would've said. But Randolph Spenser, with his conceit and self-righteousness, set me on edge for days after I saw him. Claiming my daughter just like he had a God-given right to her! I had a pain in my neck and my eyes ever since I walked out of the Eden Bar and Grill. Men like Randolph Spenser are the kind of men I'd warned Esther about—men who made their own rules, who thought they could do anything they wanted when it came to people and especially women. He was right. Sure, I had roughed and smiled, sometimes lied and conned my way into what little I'd got. And him knowing all that made me madder almost than him calling Esther his. But no matter what I did to get what I got, when it come to people, I always tried to live in a way so I wouldn't have to lie to nobody about nothing. I married Rayford Johnson and never once thought of doing anything else with another man. And after Rayford's death, I went and got a high school diploma through the mails, one of those correspondence schools, 'cause I knew Rayford was still watching me and I wanted him to be proud. No, I wasn't always no angel, but I come too far depending on people who trusted or loved me to twist the rules now. And besides, I wasn't the issue. My life wasn't the one that was blasphemous and sinful.

And now that it was all out in the open, Esther and me kinda got close like we used to be. But I was so angry I couldn't bring myself to say a word about Randolph Spenser. And Esther, well, she never mentioned his name. Every night

I fell asleep in my bed I'd be clutching the Bible in one hand and have a prayer on my lips to protect my daughter. All my life, when I didn't know what to do, I just turned the problem over to the Lord. His hands got more experience than mine. And never once, yet, did He let me down.

t started innocently enough or at least that's
what he told himself to explain his suspicion
that he was losing her. More and more he felt
it in the pit of his stomach, a hunch, nagging
and complete, the kind that's like a crazy vision
of the future coming at you with the swiftness
of a fastball. He thought he was losing her and
he was afraid. One day he surprised Esther and
showed up at her office to take her to lunch.

Esther worked in one of seventy divisions in

the huge Commerce Department Building on Fourteenth and Constitution Avenue that housed the Patent Office. Her small office was connected to a series of four much larger rooms, where the professional staff—mostly white men—sat with a typing pool and a supervisor. Each time Randolph had entered Esther's office in the past, he'd nearly broken out in a sweat at the sight of so much enforced conformity, the typists lined up in rows like female robots, the white men who supervised them, bland and anonymous in white shirts and ties, the pale green walls that reminded him of a hospital.

There were only a few Negroes in this office—but more than he had expected to see—and Randolph marveled at how easy and comfortable Esther was with the business-suited white men who worked at desks around her or passed by with a nod of the head. She had seemed surprised, even a bit embarrassed, he thought, to see him standing before her desk when she looked up from her typewriter. Was it he that made her look at the coworkers on either side right after she mumbled a hushed, surprised hello? Or was it the sight of his jacket and casual slacks that made her hurriedly bring order to her desk, the stacks of official-looking papers, as if she had something to hide.

"I thought we could have lunch," Randolph explained, suddenly weak-kneed with regret. Esther looked at the round-faced clock on the wall that loomed over the office like an omen and marveled, "I had no idea the morning was almost over." It was twelve-thirty, her assigned lunch hour. Esther reached for her purse in the bottom drawer so quickly that she put a run in her stocking when her leg snagged the edge of the chair.

The irritation in Esther's voice when she asked, "Why didn't you call?" offered Randolph an intriguing potential source of anger as they headed out of the office. Walking down the wide marble hallway, their heels echoing with each step, Randolph asked, "Why? Did you have other plans?"

"No. But I might have," she told him and he felt like he'd been slapped.

In the cafeteria Randolph had no appetite and picked at his hamburger and fries. But he couldn't seem to look at Esther long or hard enough, searching for the young woman he had asked out barely eight months ago. She had a new hairstyle, the same one his wife was wearing now, the same one all the women were wearing. She looked like a young girl trying to look older. She didn't look anything like the girl he took to see Sarah Vaughan.

And Esther had nothing to say, she gazed steadfastly at her food and ate two slices of apple pie. He walked her back to her office and hung around her desk for a few minutes, mostly because he could feel how edgy and nervous it made her. People were returning from lunch and the desks were being reclaimed. Randolph watched Esther open a compact and look at herself in the small mirror as she applied a fresh coat of lipstick. Randolph suddenly felt like a stranger annoying her on a street corner. When she closed the compact, its click sounding like a clue to leave, she looked at him and said apologetically, "There aren't too many of us working in this agency. And you know how they are, if they see two of us together, they think we're planning something."

"Sure," he said and this time he wanted to slap her. "I'll talk to you tonight."

"OK. 'Bye," she said, already facing the typewriter.

And so Randolph found himself driving around downtown at just the time Esther got off from work, stalking Constitution Avenue with a determination all the stronger because he wasn't certain what he hoped to find. Once or twice he'd waited across the street, honked his horn and called her when he spotted her dark face among the crowd of whites streaming out of the Patent Office at five o'clock. The first two times he did this she was surprised and grateful, chatting about the day at work, sharing anecdotes and complaints. They had stopped for something to eat and a drink. But the third time Randolph showed up unexpectedly Esther told him that she'd let him know if she needed a ride home.

"You hiding something?" he'd asked, moved by Esther's increasing self-sufficiency to offer her a long gaze of nearly clinical assessment.

"What are you looking for?"

And that was all they had said during the long ride home.

Randolph woke up one morning and decided that he would park his car a few blocks away, hide behind one of the huge oaks in the park across the street. Sometimes she came out with two or three other colored girls and they stood, laughing and talking, and then walked together to the bus stop. One day they all got into a car and he followed them to the home of one of the girls, where Esther stayed until nine o'clock, Randolph knew, because he sat in his car, feeling foolish, hungry and justified, until they came out of the house.

Soon he found himself parked in his wife's car a few doors down from Naomi's house three times a week, watching and waiting for Esther to enter or go out. He didn't know what he was looking for but was sure he would find it. When after several months of surveillance, no evidence presented itself, Randolph was merely convinced of his own ineptitude rather than Esther's loyalty to him.

Although Esther was seeing no one else (he knew this, but he did not believe it), she had become more elusive and therefore more irresistible. Asking less of Randolph, he ached to give her more. Once he stayed out all night with her, something he had never done before, so afraid was he that she would leave him only to seek, even for a moment, someone else's arms at six in the morning. He helped her to buy a fire engine red Ford, although the mobility she would now have caused the loss of many of his nights' sleep. He didn't know how long he could go on like this. He only knew he had no choice.

When Esther knew that she was pregnant, what she dreaded most was telling Naomi. She and Randolph had been lovers for a year. All along, some part of her had waited for this, expected it. And yet she felt no fear, only curiosity, more medical than maternal, more about who she was than who she would soon become. Randolph had told her that change was the only thing life did and he was right. She almost looked forward to this change. And in these days and hours that still belonged only to her, shared with no one, uncensored by responsibility, unchecked by obligation, Esther did not think so much of the child but rather how the child would change her. She thought of how Naomi had loved her—strongly, possessively—and how that love had stoked and quenched her spirit. And Esther promised to love her child as though he belonged to himself, to love him as her echo, not her shadow.

"You don't have to have it," Naomi said simply when Esther told her. Naomi lay in bed, comfortable against several fluffed pillows, and Esther sat at the foot of the bed, sprawled across the pink chenille spread. "And I'll be honest with you, Esther, I wish you wouldn't. I know a doctor who can . . ."

"Mama, please, don't talk like that. I *want* to have the baby."

"Have you told *him* yet?"

"No, I wanted to tell you first." A long silence erupted in the wake of Esther's words. Mother and daughter sat, joined and autonomous, expectant and afraid.

"I'll help you all I can," Naomi finally said.

"Does it hurt like they say? When it's time?" Naomi heard Esther ask the questions eagerly, only slightly worried. The question sounded very far away.

"Not always, you were an easy baby. My water broke at midnight and you came out two hours later. You just couldn't wait."

"But what about the pain?"

"I just closed my eyes and tried to wish it away or I'd start humming to keep from crying and sometimes I'd just let out a big old fat scream and doing that seemed to work best of all."

"What did I look like?"

"Like a little brown ball, crying and raising Cain," Naomi laughed. "You were the prettiest little thing when you first come into the world."

"Mama, I'm sorry. I know you wanted something different for me. Something better than this."

"Don't matter what I wanted. It matters what you think you got to have." Naomi pursed her lips at the lie so hard she produced a warm sliver of blood on her bottom lip.

"Right now, I've got to have him," Esther said. "And I've got to have his baby."

In the fourth month of her pregnancy, Esther quit her job. As she grew larger, Esther noticed that people saw only her stomach or looked at it openly, staring rudely. She felt like an elephant and yet remembered that in their massiveness elephants had acquired more than a little grace.

The first time Randolph Spenser entered Naomi's home it was nine o'clock in the evening and it was ninety-two degrees. All along Harvard Street the front stoops were lined with people trying to cool off. The yards were full of children, armed with glass jars, chasing fireflies. Young seventeen- and eighteen-year-old boys "bopped" down the streets in pairs beneath the lamplight, crooning words melodic with a plea for love or forgiveness. Esther had walked up to the corner deli to buy a magazine. When he drove up to the house, Randolph saw Naomi sitting in a chair on the front porch, among several of her boarders, who sat smoking, talking, laughing in boisterous celebration it seemed of nothing more momentous than life itself. Naomi looked, even in the dark, like the Queen of Sheba holding court. Randolph approached the house on slow, dreading feet. As he walked up the steep steps, the conversation slowly halted and he watched the boarders cast furtive glances at Naomi. When he was finally face-to-face with Naomi, Randolph said, "Good evening, Mrs. Johnson, I've come to see Esther. She's expecting me."

Wordlessly, Naomi stood up and dropped her fan in her chair and led Randolph into the house. She motioned for him to have a seat in the living room on a gold-colored plastic-covered sofa.

"Would you like something to drink?" she asked graciously.

"I'd like that, ma'am. Yes, I would."

Naomi brought Randolph a glass of RC Cola and as he took it he said, "I'd like to apologize for the last time we talked. I said some things I had no right to say."

"I'm glad to know you can tell when you've spoken out of turn."

"I don't think she knows yet what's hit her," Randolph said after drinking the glass of soda empty and placing it on a napkin Naomi had put on the coffee table.

"And do you?"

"No, ma'am. I can't say as I do."

"I tried to convince her not to have it. I want you to know that," Naomi said, pleased to offer this information in the name of honest principle.

"Well, *I* didn't."

"We both did what was expected then."

"I wouldn't have expected you to tell Esther to get rid of her own baby."

"Then you don't know me as well as you thought you did."

"The child's gonna have my name."

"I wouldn't have expected you to say anything else. The child will be your responsibility."

"I *know* that. And you're just waiting for me to deny it. But you won't live long enough to see that."

"I'm going to live a long time, Mr. Spenser. Who knows? Maybe even longer than you. It wouldn't bother me a bit to see you deny my daughter. But I hope you keep your word and if you're the man I think you are I think you're right— you'll never deny your child."

As Naomi offered this judgment to Randolph, which sounded to him like a completely intended form of damnation, Esther entered the living room. She gazed in curiosity at her mother and Randolph, facing one another, locked in a brutal quiescence. Finally Randolph explained, "Your mama and me was just having a little chat while I was waiting for you."

And when he told his wife, of course it mattered. And, watching Mary's face, it made no sense. "She's a girl I've been seeing a coupla months now," he explained, despising the words that denied Esther's importance and at the same time wounded his wife.

"I wanted you to hear it from me and nobody else."

"I suppose that makes you a hero," Mary said. Then she asked almost disinterestedly, "How much does she mean to you?"

"I won't deny my child."

"I said, how much does she mean to you?" she shouted.

"I love you, Mary."

"But you still have to have her?"

His silence shocked them both.

"You never thought you might be risking your home?" she wailed.

"I've been a good father, a husband, all this time. Nothing changed between me and you."

"Nothing changed? Are you blind? Or is it only what you want to see that's clear before your eyes?"

"She's got nothing to do with you or anybody else in this house except me." Randolph had repeated this lie so often to himself, to Esther, in his dreams that now it stunned his own ears with the force of an obscenity. He stood with his back to Mary as he said this and he suddenly felt her punch him in the back—once, twice, then her fists, balled and furious, pummeled him in time with a string of curses that injured him more than the blows. Randolph allowed Mary to hit him again and again until she was exhausted and the hoarse bitter sound of "Bastard, you bastard" caught in her chest and died in her throat as she sank into the carpeted bedroom floor at his feet, sobbing, flailing against him with arms and legs when he tried to lift her from the floor to the bed.

The next day Randolph moved out of his house and into a room around the corner from his restaurant. He went to see his father one evening and the old man told him, "If you'd loved money the way I do, more than any woman, none of this would've happened."

He stayed at the restaurant long hours, making overdue repairs, painted and remodeled the dining room and kitchen, sat at one of the tables behind the locked doors of the Eden Bar and Grill some nights, smoking cigarettes and watching the sun come up rather than sleep in his rented room.

Even now, as he clung to Esther and their child with a tenacity that astonished him as certainly as it distressed his wife, Randolph was not sure why Esther had become so essential. He knew that men married or sought women who possessed qualities they feared they would never have. And Randolph suspected that Esther was capable of both the surprising and the wondrous. She had opted for the mundane, embraced heartache with her eyes wide open in their affair. But Randolph was thirteen years older than Esther and so he knew what she did not—that her life still lay before her unchartered and virgin and no resistance would quell the pull of whatever belonged to her.

She had come from amazing stock—a father whom, when Esther told Randolph about him, he wished he had met and a mother who had defied every expectation of what a colored woman was supposed to be and do. Randolph remained with Esther partly to witness her own unfolding, given the heritage she would find herself unable to deny. She was, even now, heavy with his child, an ember. Randolph awaited the moment when she grew into a blaze. He was not convinced they would survive the flames intact, but it was a sight he would forsake anything to see.

In her seventh month Esther blossomed, her belly hard and ripe. Weekends she spent with Randolph in his room and they lay in bed beneath the sheets, naked, sweating, eating fruit, potato chips, drinking sodas and reading the Sunday papers. They argued about boys' names, debated names for a girl. He did not make love to her, but instead gave Esther cool sponge showers, poured Pepsi-Cola on the mound of her stomach, watched it drip, slide between her legs and he licked the skin, rejoicing in the bubbly sweaty taste of her. And she—bulky, beautiful, her body some splendid ominous sculpture—took him anyway she could, held him, his unhappiness and joy warm, so drenched in pain that the sound brought tears to her eyes.

"Will you go back?" Esther asked on Sunday afternoon as they listened to a ball game on the radio, Randolph's head resting beneath her breasts.

"If she'll have me."

"What happens to me?"

"I've got to have you both." he told her. "You and her. *My* kids and *our* baby too."

"One day I'll leave you."

"Until then I want you," he said, touching Esther's face softly. He dropped his hand and turned his gaze to the ceiling as he said, "You think having you both makes me king? Uh-uh. I'm y'alls' slave."

Chapter Eleven

N A O M I

Wouldn't you know it, that baby looked just like his daddy. Two days after they started fighting over in Korea, Esther went to Columbia Hospital for Women and had her first child. I'd always figured on the day I become a grandmother to be one of the happiest days of my life. But I looked at Esther holding her baby for the first time, twelve hours after she delivered, and I just started trembling inside and felt afraid for her and the child. Maybe it was what I saw in Esther— how much like a child she still was herself, how she held the baby like it was a doll and how often she looked at me when she touched the child, her eyes begging for help.

I never counted myself no prude, but I sure hadn't raised my daughter to go having a baby with a married man. And while I thought I'd made a kind of peace with Randolph Spenser, the sight of his child in Esther's arms made me so mad I could feel my pressure going up. All I could think of was what Rayford was thinking, looking down at us. Near about every month since he'd died, I'd gone to visit Rayford's grave. And when Esther had her baby, that meant I'd been visiting Rayford at the cemetery for ten years. Nothing had changed between us. Nothing at all. I talked and he listened and he told me what I should do. I told him everything— about Esther leaving school, Randolph Spenser, the baby, everything. I'd usually get my answer from Rayford about what he thought of things a few days after my visit. Maybe I'd be cooking or sewing or listening to the radio and his answer would just pop into my heart and set me to shivering. And just like when he was alive, Rayford had more patience than me and he just counseled me to remember that Esther was our daughter no matter what. I'd forgotten you couldn't put conditions on love.

So when Esther handed me her child for the first time, I just looked into his little face and his eyes that even at one day old were Esther's. I just looked at all that and wondered how I could do my part to help make him a man.

Chapter Twelve

They named the child Logan and he carried his father's name. With the birth of her child, Esther's world contracted into a domestic routine that made her feel as though she were imprisoned. For the first three months after Logan's birth, Esther lived with Naomi and within a few weeks depression set in. She had no appetite. Her milk dried up. Randolph visited regularly and Esther watched him swell with pride and affection that was absent from her heart. She had what she said she wanted—this child, Randolph's child—but found herself unwilling to claim it.

When Logan was six months old, Randolph moved Esther and the baby into an apartment. Esther and Logan lived a life dominated by schedules—when he was to be fed, dropped off at Naomi's so Esther could go to work, picked up from Naomi's, fed at night. Motherhood invoked in Esther feelings of ambivalence and confinement. No one had told her she could love *and* resent the child she had borne.

As the years passed Logan grew into a precise boy, whose eyes were dense with the same agelessness that appeared to give his mother's eyes a kind of second sight. He was not a child given to easy or frequent laughter, and yet when he did succumb to the impulse, his father's look and presence suddenly and completely claimed his face. From Naomi, Logan inherited a chin that, even as a baby, jutted out solid and daring, undermining the tranquillity of his manner with a host of disturbing possibilities.

Because he was an only child, the adults around him burdened Logan with more attention than he wanted. Logan's singleness—the sometimes threatening, often uneasy fact that he shared them with no one else—made adults choreograph their responses, as though their lives contained only one chance to please him. His favorite toy was his imagination—private and perfect, unencumbered by the self-doubt a sibling could inspire.

And in his imagination he was like everybody else, fulfilling his yearning to be ordinary, nondescript. Still, everything in his life informed Logan of his distinction. Randolph came to see Logan and Esther once or twice a week. And Logan associated his father's arrival with bags of groceries that Randolph brought with him and long white envelopes with money inside he left on the kitchen table. Sometimes Randolph spent the evenings with them and watched Milton Berle or Red Skelton on the television set he had bought Esther for her birthday. While Esther cooked dinner, Randolph carried Logan around the living room on his shoulders or wrestled with him on the floor.

Logan thought that his father was a magician for the swiftness of the transformation from father to friend. And their play possessed a noisy passion, a raucous intent, that sprang from Logan's fear that his father would, at the moment he would least expect or bear it, become a grown-up again or say simply that he had to go.

Still, in those moments, Logan merely cherished his father's love. Some nights Randolph was there to put him to bed and drop a dime in his piggy bank. And when Randolph kissed him goodnight, Logan smelled Crisco and sweet potatoes, the deep-fried fragrance clinging to his father from the kitchen of the Eden Bar and Grill.

On other nights, huddled beneath his Roy Rogers sheet and blanket, resisting sleep, Logan heard, in the next room, the muffled dark voices of his parents. They often went into his mother's room and closed the door and turned off the lights after Logan went to bed. Sometimes Logan climbed out of bed and padded softly into the kitchen for a drink of water. Whatever his parents did in his mother's bedroom seemed always to make her cry. But it was a strange cry, like she was catching her breath and trying to hold it back and not let it go. And he hardly ever heard his father's voice, but once, as Logan stood next to the refrigerator clutching a cup of water, he saw Randolph leave Esther's bedroom with no clothes on and walk to the bathroom.

Mornings came and Logan longed to stay in bed because he knew his father was no longer there. By the age of eight, Logan wondered where Randolph went when he left them, where he really slept and spent the night, but Logan feared those questions would shatter the delicate equilibrium that gave him his father like a gift found beneath his pillow. It was apparent that Randolph's presence represented a trespass of something Logan did not understand but that he respected with the staunch obedience of the well-trained child.

His father smoked Lucky Strike cigarettes and used Dixie Peach pomade on his hair and drove a Cadillac. Because he could not penetrate the essence of who his father really was, Logan settled for this specific, telling knowledge.

Weekends were spent with his grandmother. Naomi's house was so big that Logan cried whenever he was told to sleep in the room at the other end of the house, the room that had once been his mother's. The bedroom seemed, to him, miles and miles away in the dark from his grandmother. So some nights Naomi allowed Logan to sleep on a cot in her bedroom. In this darkness the odorous fragrance of Ben-Gay ointment hung, heavy and tangible as the colorful sturdy quilts Naomi made and under which they slept.

Before bed Logan watched Naomi rub the liniment on her thick knees, pulling up the bottom of her gown to expose her thighs—large and imposing with lives of their own. "Why you put that stuff on?" he'd ask, twirling his feet in the air, wondering if it hurt and how a woman's breasts could hang down like his gramma's did when she took off her clothes. Naomi rubbed the liniment into her knees and thighs with a sponge applicator, as though painting a masterpiece. And then, as she waited for the medicine to dry, she told Logan, "I got arthritis. Old arthur and me been friends for a long time now." Then Logan watched as she removed her teeth and put them in a glass of water on the night table. One day Naomi caught him standing before her bedroom mirror, struggling with his teeth, trying to remove them, and she told him, laughing and shaking her head, "You got to grow up and get old before you can do that."

On Sundays they went to church and Logan nearly always fell asleep against Naomi, the weight of the preacher's words, the rhythm of the choir, the warmth of the bodies rocking him into slumber. On the way back home they'd stop at an Italian bakery near the house and buy a dozen "pocketbook" rolls to eat with Sunday dinner.

One Sunday afternoon Logan was playing in the backyard of Naomi's house with a little boy who lived next door. Naomi sat on the screened-in back porch with Cora, an oilcloth covering the card table, their glasses filled with lemonade.

The two women sat talking about Little Rock, Arkansas, where federal troops had been reluctantly ordered by President Eisenhower to ensure the peaceful integration of that city's high schools. The city fathers in Little Rock would eventually close the schools for a year to avoid integration. And Logan had heard the adults around him say the words *Little Rock* so often that the words began to sound like a secret code, for they nearly always produced worried, agitated expressions or declarations filled with anger. The years after the end of World War II had unleashed a concentrated campaign on the part of Negroes for equal rights. Lawsuits, picketing and boycotts in cities across the country paved the way for two decades of wrenching, irreversible social change.

And there was now a candy named after the Sputnik satellite the Russians had launched into space. Logan bought fistfuls of the hard round marble-sized candies on his way home from school. Once a month all the students at Harrison elementary school practiced Air Raid drills, so they would know what to do when the Russians, who even Logan knew had made something called an Iron Curtain, bombed America.

But this Sunday, as Naomi and Cora sat on the back porch, their voices rising in a fluid cadence, sparked by the words *Little Rock*, Logan played with a friend.

The little boy's name was Rodney and Logan had begun to like him, for like Logan he had no sisters or brothers. Rodney understood, without saying, that his aloneness was not always lonely, the way grown-ups thought. They were shoveling dirt into their dump trucks and then emptying them, moving their G.I. Joe men up and down the steep dirt hills, when Rodney suddenly said, "You ain't got no daddy."

"What you mean? I sure do got a daddy," Logan cried in befuddled indignation.

"My mama said you don't. I heard her. She said you're a *bastard*." Logan saw the child's face tighten with misery, clench in contempt for Logan and, because of the meanness of his thoughts, for himself as well.

"A *bastard?*" Logan dropped his toy men.

"Yeah. That's somebody who ain't got no daddy. Your mama don't have no husband." Rodney spewed the words forth like a rote lesson he'd learned in school, recited now to reveal his brilliance. Logan furiously threw several handsful of dirt into the boy's face and ran up the stairs, past the two women, into the house.

Naomi watched Logan run past her and then before she could reach the banister, she saw Rodney scamper next door. She found Logan sitting in a corner of the kitchen, behind the stove. Looking up at Naomi with a tear-stained face, he asked, "Gramma, what's a *bastard?*"

"An ugly word that don't mean nothing."

"It must mean something," Logan said weakly.

"Sometimes people use it to hurt other people."

"Why would he want to hurt me?"

"He's got no home training, that's all."

"It's 'cause my daddy don't live with us. It's 'cause he never stays, that's why I'm a bastard, ain't it?" Logan asked, his voice rising.

"Logan, don't you mind," Naomi said, reaching for him.

But the child ran past her to the front door, jumped on his bike and rode down the street. Naomi called after him. But all she could see was Logan pedaling towards Sixteenth Street. Two hours later Logan returned. He had ridden his bike past All Souls' Church and then to Meridian Hill Park. He had ridden his bike around and around the park, simply to keep from crying. Logan watched the waterfalls on the lower level of the park and felt covered in shame as enduring as the water.

That night, while Naomi thought Logan was in bed, he crouched at the door leading to the dining room and heard Cora and Naomi talking.

"I don't know what all this sudden interest in legitimacy and illegitimacy among colored folks is anyway," Cora said in disgust.

"Negroes won't never be legitimate to white folks, don't care what we do." She laughed. "Down home, folks never worried about who your daddy was. They knew you had to have one to get here."

"Folks are changing," Naomi said.

"All this talk about integration, colored want to act like they white. What have they told the boy?" Cora asked.

"Nothing. Nothing that I know of."

"The poor thing."

"What can you tell him that he'd understand?" Naomi asked. "What can you tell him that wouldn't hurt him one way or the other?"

"They better tell him something," Cora warned.

"It won't be Esther, that's for sure," Naomi said. "She comes over here, talking about one day he's gonna leave his wife for her. Some days I think the child's got more sense than her. I tell her she should find somebody else and she says she don't want nobody else."

"Give her time," Cora said gently.

"Time? Ain't you heard? Time don't wait for nobody."

"But you know, sometimes a married man is better for you." Cora eyed Naomi cautiously as she said this.

"Oh, hush that."

"Naw, I mean it. Better than those old single fools out

here. A married man lives with a woman so he knows what she wants."

"Hell, Esther wants to get married."

"You know what I mean."

"And I don't think I like it."

"Don't worry, Naomi, at least Logan's daddy don't deny him."

"But others will."

"It'll make him strong, give him something to prove. Might as well be dead without something to prove," Cora insisted. "Never know what you made of if you ain't arguing with the world about something. Half the folks in the history books was outcasts, raising hell, discovering things, inventing, just 'cause folks told them they was ugly, dumb or nocount or didn't know who their daddy was." Naomi shook her head in disagreement. But Cora insisted. "Don't worry too much, that boy'll be OK."

That night after she took her teeth out and rubbed liniment on her legs, Naomi went into Logan's bedroom. He lay huddled beneath the spread, feigning sleep. But Naomi knew Logan was awake so she told him, "I want you to always love your daddy. I've had my differences with him, but he's the only daddy you got."

"But I'm a bastard, Gramma, and because of him," Logan said, bolting upright, throwing off the covers in a dramatic movement he had waited for all day. Naomi took hold of Logan's slender shoulders and shook him hard. "Don't *never* use that word. Don't never even think it."

"Yes, ma'am."

"You're what you *think* you are. White folks used to call colored folks *nigger* all the time, *nigger* this and *nigger* that, *Come here, nigger, Go on, nigger.* Even went to putting it in front of our names. But I never in my life answered to that. Let the word roll off me like water off a duck's back.

I wouldn't let them make me a nigger. You not gonna let people make you a bastard now, are you?"

"No."

"No what?"

"No, Gramma."

"He's the only daddy you got, Logan. He belongs to you. Love him, boy, need him. And thank your lucky stars he owned up and claimed you and never once thought about running from you and your mama."

Exhausted by anger, Naomi sank onto the pillow beside Logan, sweating, her breathing raspy and heavy. Fearing Naomi was sick, Logan shook her, "You OK, Gramma? You OK?"

"Just say your prayers, boy. Just say your prayers and go on to sleep," Naomi told him. Logan slumped back onto the bed. Before he drifted off to sleep Logan heard Naomi whisper, her back to him, her words burnishing the darkness with a thousand wonderful promises, "Lord, make him strong. And don't let him mind what nobody say."

sther felt as if her life was encircled by secrets. Randolph by now was an open secret, acknowledged by everyone who knew her, yet unchallenged out of politeness or awe at such stubborn obedience to romantic fantasy. And then there was the secret that no one else knew, how poorly motherhood suited her, how the affection she felt for Logan was tempered by disdain for the responsibilities he imposed. She had given her son life and wished, more than anything, to observe his life from afar. Esther had never been gripped by the maternal instincts that she had supposed lay inside the genes of every woman. Her affection for Logan was functional, pragmatic, devoid of the delicious sense of the irrational that could make a woman give her own life for her child or find meaning for her life in the essence of what her child did with his. She had left her mother's house to live in a liaison with a man who could promise her neither contentment nor a glimpse of happiness—only that he would be there.

Logan was, as Naomi had called him once, "an old spirit." He had skipped a grade in school, never brought home grades lower than A's and B's on his report card and his teachers complimented Esther during conferences on his manners and seriousness. Each year his face was etched with deeper, more prominent lines of determination, as his chin seemed to jut out a little more. He tried hard to please adults, as if proficiency in their world assured his worth. Randolph taught him how to play chess and Esther had watched Logan beat Randolph at the game more than once. He loved animals and Randolph had bought him an aquarium, a hamster and a rabbit that were lodged at Naomi's. Esther kept Logan clean, drilled him on his manners. But rare was the surprise toy brought home for no reason, the longing to touch him or hug him just because he was hers. He was a pleasant, obedient child and Esther knew that Logan hoped with his goodness to purchase, over time, a more willing display of her concern.

One by one Esther's girlfriends married and passed, by virtue of a ring on their fingers, into a world of domesticity and broken dreams, in-laws and casserole dinners, BVD's left on the bedroom floor, arguments, hands groping over flesh in the dark, baby showers, censored shortened phone conversations because "Joe just walked in the door." Within six months her married friends assured Esther, "Girl, you not missing a thing" and "I sure do envy your freedom." Yet gone were the invitations to dinner, the shopping trips on Saturdays to Lerner's and one woman told Esther point-blank, when Esther asked why she hadn't called, "Honey, I got a husband of my own now. You messing with a man that don't belong to you. How I know you won't try to steal mine?"

"That never mattered before," Esther reminded her.

"I didn't have no husband before," the woman reminded Esther fiercely, as though her husband was fifty acres of land or a hundred thousand dollars in the bank.

In time, the secrets circled Esther's life like a noose. She lay in bed day after day, immobilized by anger and a co-lossal sense of loss. The sounds of Logan dressing, pouring cereal, preparing his lunch drifted into her bedroom, spark-ing only a mild curiosity. In response to Esther's apathy, Logan had quietly mastered a self-sufficiency practiced with uncomplaining stoicism. He would order groceries to be de-livered from the neighborhood store, make his bed, take the clothes to the basement Laundromat and cook Esther and himself a dinner of Campbell's soup and bologna sand-wiches. Logan approached Esther on these mornings with small uncertain steps, asking if she needed anything, if she'd be OK. Like dead skin, his childhood innocence peeled away, exposing the stance of the man-child before Esther's eyes. And she was both grateful and afraid. On the morn-ings she was most frightened by what had become of her life, Logan kissed Esther goodbye on the cheek, a light, in-tangible kiss that engulfed her with familiar, wrenching guilt.

As she lay in bed, the day was merely a backdrop for Esther's despair. She sat dredging up the past, combing through memories for moments to remind and convince herself of her worthlessness. The vivid, continuous images were easy to produce, a nightmare unraveling in her brain. Esther salvaged and stoked a sense of wickedness from ordinary failings, banal mistakes. And by the time Logan returned from school, she sat as he had left her, in bed, only now her face and eyes puffed from crying. A demented, satisfied smile unfurled across her face.

There had been two affairs—with men she didn't even like, but with whom she became involved simply because they weren't Randolph. He had either forgiven or ignored her transgressions. She imagined some days that he could look right through her, so inured to her had he become. To Esther, their relationship had crumbled into a series of time-worn reactions, a lifeless automatic emotion, as potentially lethal as a loaded pistol.

Some evenings she went out for walks alone, pacing the streets, oblivious and haunted, crossing on red lights, not hearing the screech of tires, the curses of angry drivers swerving to save her life. Esther returned home to find Logan asleep on the sofa, the TV on, the screen blank, and a plate of canned spaghetti or pork and beans that Logan had fixed for dinner, covered, sitting for her on the table.

In her dreams, on the nights she was able to sleep, Esther ran long distances down highways that had no end, tracked by a pursuer she could hear but not see. Or she walked down steps and skipped a stair, falling, falling, falling into the cavernous arms of an endless space on whose walls she glimpsed the face of her father, Randolph's wife or herself as a child. She woke from the running dreams, the sheet damp, her pillow soaked. The falling dreams made her toss and scratch in her sleep, gasping for breath and salvation so that she woke at daylight, the sheets draping her as though she'd been mummified.

I I I

Spring arrived, drenching the world in sunlight, blanketing the city with skies of a gently, impossibly perfect blue. The blossoming of flowers, the pungent smell of growth and living things plunged Esther into a self-doubt as fierce and undeniable as a full moon. Days passed without Esther bathing or combing her hair and she burst into ironic, mocking smiles of vindication at the sight of herself in the mirror—haggard and sleepless.

One day Naomi called and moments after Esther said hello, Naomi heard her daughter's sobs, dredged from someplace within her so deep that Naomi instantly heard the madness. Naomi, who spoke with Esther several times a week, had sensed her daughter's discontent. But she had thought that she merely needed a new job or a new man. Until this moment Naomi had not suspected Esther required a new life. Her daughter was inarticulate with grief, mute with despair. When Naomi arrived at the apartment, Logan opened the door. He wore mismatched socks and a wrinkled, unironed shirt. Wordlessly, Logan hugged Naomi around the waist. Standing in the doorway, her grandson clutching her with a determination that informed her of everything she needed to know, Naomi surveyed the living room. Piles of dirty clothes were stationed like sentries around the room. Empty Coke bottles and TV dinner trays littered the coffee table. Cigarette butts had been stubbed out on the furniture, ground into the carpet. Gently unlocking Logan's grip, Naomi went into the kitchen, where she saw a sinkful of dirty dishes and pots, several half-finished plates of food on the table and a stove littered with burnt-up pots and pans.

In the bedroom Esther sat on the floor, thumbing through a photo album, her cheeks streaked with tears as she cried silently, continuously, her voice shuddering with defeat.

Chilled by what she saw, nevertheless, Naomi walked to her daughter and asked gently, "What you doing, Esther?"

"I'm bad, Mama. Always have been. I'm bad," Esther said, speaking to the pictures. Naomi lifted Esther from the floor, held her, stroked Esther's foul-smelling, lint-filled hair and let her daughter weep on her shoulder.

"You not bad, Esther, you my baby." As she held Esther, Naomi asked gently, "Where's Randolph?"

"We had a fight, Mama, I haven't seen him two weeks."

Naomi undressed Esther and led her into the bathroom, where she ran a tub full of water and helped Esther get in. Stooping down on her painful, arthritic knees, Naomi bathed her daughter, gasping inwardly at the sight of the weight Esther had lost, how flabby were her thighs, how her collarbone jutted out like sticks and the dull pallor of her face.

Esther gave herself over to her mother, the steam of the water making her sweat as she stared into space at nothing Naomi could see, but the sight of which etched a look of horror on Esther's face. Naomi dried Esther off and helped her into a gown, gave her two aspirins and made her get into bed. Together, Naomi and Logan cleaned the apartment while Esther lay, tossing and turning, in her bed. That night, when Naomi put Logan to bed, he asked, "What's wrong with my mama?"

"I don't know, Logan, she's just not feeling right."

"Is it something I did? Is that why she's sick?"

"Uh-uh, honey. It's nothing you did."

"Is she gonna be all right?"

"Sure she is."

"Will she get better?"

"Sure she will."

"Will she love me then?"

"She loves you now, honey."

"No, she don't. Not like you do. Not like my daddy."

"Hush that. Stop saying that, Logan," Naomi warned the boy. "Go on and say your prayers," she commanded him. But Naomi sat on the edge of her grandson's bed in the dark, watching over him until he fell asleep.

The next day Naomi had Esther's doctor examine her. He found no physical ailment, only depression, and prescribed a sedative for Esther and wrote out a letter that would gain Esther medical leave from her job. Naomi spent two weeks with her daughter, discovering her like someone she had once known well. Her presence seemed to calm Esther and each day she was less dispirited and morose. One afternoon they sat watching "The Edge of Night" on television and while Naomi sat on the sofa, Esther sat between her mother's legs on the floor as Naomi braided her daughter's hair. Randolph had called and Naomi told him Esther had a bad cold. He was going to New Jersey on business and told Naomi he'd call when he returned.

Naomi had searched the apartment for clues to what had happened to Esther and found none. Naomi found no material evidence but sensed her daughter's loneliness, could nearly smell the doubt plaguing her, felt herself constricted as Esther must have been, by the rooms' smallness—a box for Esther, a box for Logan, a box to eat in. Naomi didn't know how people lived in apartments. Only the urgency of Esther's condition had enabled her to survive the small space this long. She parted Esther's hair on the side and asked, "Tell me what's wrong, Esther."

"I don't know, Mama. Sometimes I just feel like I'm the worst person alive. Like I don't even deserve to live."

"Now, don't think like that. I've felt like life was too much for me sometimes too. But I kept going. I want you to do the same thing."

"I feel, sometimes, like nobody loves me. And I love me least of all."

"I love you. You know that," Naomi said, stung by Esther's honesty.

"But right now I can't *feel* anybody's love, no matter how much it is. There's something inside me keeping it out. Driving it away."

"What about Randolph?"

"I'm so mad with him I can't hardly talk to him."

"Why, honey?"

" 'Cause I want him and he'll never be mine. 'Cause wanting him keeps me from reaching for something better."

"He's been a good man."

"Not as good as you think. Not as good as he thinks. Logan and me are convenient. He cares for us when he can, when we don't get in the way."

Naomi grew afraid as Esther's voice shook with an awful bitterness, a sense of denial profound enough, Naomi knew, to make Esther cry or to kill. "Why don't you all come and stay with me for a while?" Naomi asked hopefully.

"No, Mama," Esther said firmly. "I want to stay here."

Soon Esther healed, becoming not her old self but a new self in the waning days of spring. She returned to work. And on his return Randolph found little evidence of Esther's illness. Esther even managed some days to make her son feel as though she did indeed love him.

Then, the week after the Fourth of July, Esther didn't go to work and, for the first of several times, she went to a bar and brought a man home. Logan was away at summer camp and in his absence Esther shared her bed with a succession of strangers whose anonymity liberated her, whose contempt she found a challenge. She asked the men to do things to her that had uneasily stalked the corners of her mind, acts so filled with ecstasy and pain she was certain if she survived she would never die. And she did anything they asked, becoming in those moments invincible, convinced she would never again know guilt, that she would rise like a phoenix in the moment of orgasm above judgment or question.

Esther refused to see Randolph and quit her job. Cashing the U.S. Savings Bonds Randolph had given her over the years, she was certain she would get a new job and spent much of the money on new clothes.

One evening two weeks later Esther leaned out her window and watched Logan and the other children, playing tag. Logan was "it" and he leaned on an oak tree in front of the apartment, his eyes covered as he counted to ten. The sounds of the children's laughter plunged Esther into an abyss of self-hate so final that she was gripped by a sudden and perfect curiosity about death. She walked into the kitchen and stood at the counter, staring at the butcher knife she had used to cut up a chicken for dinner. The metal blade was still smeared with soft fatty blobs of chicken flesh and the odor was, in Esther's mind, more enticing than repulsive. She reached for the knife, but at the same moment felt the need to speak to Randolph. He had been there for her. Randolph reminded Esther of this again and again, but rarely was he there for her in the ways she needed most. She needed him in the unexpected dark, daring moments of a night's sleep derailed. She needed him to sit watching her cook dinner, he leisurely, comfortable with no place else to go as he savored her performance of this mundane yet honorable task. Esther needed more than the white envelopes with crisp tens and twenties inside that made her feel like she was being purchased and Randolph had never figured out the correct price. She needed Randolph to do what he could not—convince her that she was more than a parenthesis in the scope of his life. Esther needed to, but could not find a way to charge headlong into her dreams, independent and unbound. Fear of holding her life in her own hands was making her sick. Esther's fingers trembled as she dialed his number. After the seventh ring, he finally answered the phone. Esther heard laughter and voices in the background, but begged him to come to see her. Randolph whispered into the receiver that he and his wife were in the middle of a party. "I can't promise, but I'll try," he said, hanging up, brushing her aside as quickly as swatting a fly.

Later that night when Randolph arrived he saw the wild dissatisfaction gleaming in Esther's eyes and he took Esther in his arms and rocked her like a baby, wondering if she had it in her to hurt Logan.

They sat down and Esther launched into a long disjointed speech, her voice high-pitched and rambling, she talked about Logan, Marilyn Monroe, Naomi, her old supervisor at work, the need for a new dress, Sputnik, her sinfulness, the death of a cousin last year, the end of the world.

Randolph coaxed Esther into the bedroom and got her to sit on the bed, a process that took fifteen minutes, for she would not stop talking and accused him of wanting to hurt her. And yet, when they lay on the bed together, Randolph hoping to make Esther relax, she suddenly sat bolt upright and pulled a length of rope from beneath the mattress. She whispered an obscenity in his ear, told him to tie her to the bed and she began to yank off her clothes. Randolph stopped her and convinced Esther to take a sleeping pill. While Esther slept, Randolph packed a small suitcase with Logan's clothes and took the boy to Naomi's.

Randolph returned to the apartment and lay down beside Esther. While Randolph lay beside her, Esther felt the falling dream unfold her like a kiss and when she woke she knew that she had to stop the dream. She took the butcher knife she had hidden beneath the mattress with the rope and jabbed herself in the right side. But the pain did not last long enough, touch her deeply enough. Life oozed out of her body too slowly. There wasn't enough blood. Esther felt the dream returning so she stabbed her other side, holding her breath as she twisted the knife, hard, deep and fast. Finally the pain was enough. The blood was too much and she felt life flying out of her loins. Esther slumped onto the now sodden sheets, the smell of her blood filling the room. And Randolph's hoarse, awful man-scream rose just as she drifted into what she hoped was death, waiting for the dream to end.

St. Elizabeth's Hospital had been built on a three-hundred-and-thirty-acre stretch of land by slaves and patients in the early 1850s. During the Civil War, the institution, then called the U.S. Government Hospital for the Insane in the District of Columbia, served as a general hospital for wounded soldiers. Artificial limbs were manufactured on the grounds of the hospital for the thousands of men maimed by rebel artillery. Over one hundred soldiers were interred in a Civil War cemetery erected on the grounds.

White oak trees flanked the main entrance road leading to the hospital, located just off Nichols Avenue in Southeast Washington, "across the river" from the rest of the city. At first glance, the green beauty of the grounds gave the institution an atmosphere of a beaucolic sanctuary that promised more than most ever found in the institution.

Once, Randolph had told Esther about how he died for an instant and then came back to life. Now Esther lay on the cot in her small room at St. Elizabeth's and willed her body to turn on her, to release her from life, with no success. Hour after hour she lay, trying to slow her heartbeat down to nothing, praying to empty her mind completely. The pills she was given had relieved her of the running and the falling dreams. But Esther missed their fierce, blood-curdling embrace, for now her sleep was heavy and flat, pushing down on her like a boulder, and she woke up each morning stiff with fatigue.

They left her alone, gave her drugs twice a day and food that had no taste. Twice a week she saw a psychiatrist whom she refused to speak to because he had yet to ask her the right questions. He was a white man who interrogated her about her mother, her father and sex.

On Mondays Esther sat for two hours in a drab, cheerless room with other patients, weaving baskets and painting pictures with cheap, watery paint. An old woman as tiny as a hummingbird shunned the basket before her and sat counting matchsticks over and over, placing them gently in an empty shoe box, then carefully removing the sticks, counting again. The woman's tiny brown eyes darted constantly around her, as she huddled protectively over the stack of matchsticks that trembled in her yellowed palm, which had the longest lifeline Esther had ever seen.

Beside the woman a middle-aged man, with a shaved head and a massive beard that stretched down to the middle of his chest, sat rocking back and forth in his chair, talking to a host of unseen companions whom he had informed Esther were his personal angels. "I don't make a move without consulting them first," he'd told Esther. He asked her one day, as they sat weaving baskets, if she was in touch with *her* angels. Esther told him she wasn't.

"Then that's why you're here," he said.

"What about you?"

"I'm doing undercover work. Recruiting people like you to listen to what their angels tell them."

The patients appeared quite sane to Esther, their fears and obsessions mere exaggerations of what raged in the hearts of everyone. It was the staff that struck her as crazy. Large, overgrown men who roughly handled the patients, causing as much violence as the demons stalking the inmates' souls. The nurses gazed at the patients with pity and disgust, the lack of love in their lives, the frustration with their work giving them eyes that saw only a kaleidoscope of madness where a person, individual and noble, stood before them, seeking help.

Two days before Christmas Logan saw his mother for the first time since her hospitalization. In the backseat of Randolph's car, Logan had measured the uneasy silence between his father and grandmother during the long drive to Anacostia. The silence of the two adults had muzzled the questions throbbing in Logan's mind. As Randolph drove along the winding paths of the hospital, Logan saw streets with names like Golden Raintree Drive and Cedar Street. The buildings were built of old dingy red brick and made him think of a prison, though he'd only seen prisons on television or in the movies. Now and then they passed people who Randolph called *inmates*, staring straight ahead, moving slowly, sometimes with a nurse at their side. Logan was astonished by what he saw—a fire station and a cemetery. Passing the cemetery, he wondered if his mother died if she would be buried there.

In the visitors' lounge Esther sat before them, as still and elegant as a statue. She had entered the room with a nurse and sat on the leather sofa as if she had no idea what she was expected to do. Logan watched his father's eyes poring over every inch of Esther's body and face, searching for what he could not find. Naomi began to talk to Esther as though she was holding a normal conversation, except that she was talking for both of them. Esther looked younger now, like she had in pictures Logan had seen in Naomi's scrapbook of when his mother was in high school. The madness was gone from his mother's eyes, replaced by a still dullness. Esther had lost weight and the print dress she wore hung from her like a sack. When Naomi tried to give Esther the gift she'd brought her, she had to pry Esther's tightly coiled fingers open and wrap them around the box.

The sight of Esther drove Randolph from his chair, where he had sat transfixed and silenced, to the room's single window. There he stood, staring outside at the grounds—anything but to look at Esther. Before they left, Naomi pushed Logan toward Esther, urging him, "Go on, kiss your mama goodbye." Beneath Logan's lips, Esther's cheeks were cold and unpromising, even as her eyes flickered in a bright hot flash of recognition.

During Esther's hospitalization, Randolph came to visit Logan often and over time he and Naomi became allies. "I just don't understand what happened to her," Naomi said bitterly as she and Randolph sat in the living room one night. "I've been depressed, but not so bad I wanted to die. I don't understand this generation. We didn't have time to get this crazy."

"She's not crazy," Randolph said wearily. "I never knew what she wanted."

"You knew what she wanted."

"Would having me prevented this?"

"Maybe. Who knows? I just know she was unhappy."

"Name somebody who isn't. I gave her as much as I could," Randolph said.

"When you belong to somebody else, no matter what you give, it's never enough."

Naomi looked at Randolph and noticed the gray sprouting around the edges of his hairline, the bags beneath his eyes. She had known Randolph long enough to watch him begin to age and this suddenly surprised her.

"Logan was too much for her," Naomi said.

"Too much? With him over here on the weekends and me seeing him twice a week? Too much? You know, I think she don't even love the boy."

"It's not that. She don't love herself yet. So she can't love Logan like she should."

"I don't understand."

"A woman's got to know who she is. Being a mama is like being eaten alive. You give up everything and the child wants what's left. I've felt it sometimes too, though with me it was only a passing thing, a mood, a feeling I could throw off or forget. I had enough of me for me and Esther. Esther don't know yet what she's made of. She's been scared all this time the boy'll keep her from finding out."

"My son drove her to this?" Randolph asked incredulously, angered as much by the precision of Naomi's explanation as by its implication.

"I didn't say that."

"What kind of woman could?"

"Any woman. Hell, any man. You've done well by Logan. I'll give you that credit, Randolph, but it was Esther got up in the middle of the night when he was sick. It was Esther on Christmas or Thanksgiving, his birthday, with no excuses, when you had to be home with your family. It was Esther saw him every day, couldn't *decide* whether or not she was gonna be his mama. It was Esther who fed him, bought his clothes, spanked him, loved him. It was Esther did all that, not knowing how, wondering if she was doing it right, my baby did all that."

"I still love her."

"I don't know that that matters right now, Randolph. I don't know as that matters at all."

In the spring Esther was allowed to go outside for short periods alone. The grounds were lovely, with strong sturdy trees—silver maple, American holly, Atlas cedar, white oak—creating a fecund world. Esther worked in the greenhouse, sun filtering through the tiny windows, restoring and nourishing row after row of geraniums, coleus and carnations. The groundskeeper, a grizzled eighty-five-year-old white man who had once been a patient himself, gave Esther several potted plants, shriveled and dry, tossing them at her, saying, "See what you can do with these."

The plants were philodendrons and a beautiful yellow tropical flower called alamanden. Esther repotted the flowers with new soil, the feel of the cool dirt on her fingers assuring her in some sense, more than anything else had, that her particular life was indeed worth living. She tended those salvaged flowers as she had few other things. Week after week she watched, with eyes suddenly attuned to the microscopic, how they grew. The philodendrons grew vines slender and hearty, the leaves curling in glory. The alamanden sprouted, flirting with the sun, and made Esther recall, each time she gazed at it, moments she had felt herself to be happy.

One day Esther decided she wanted to put the plants in her room. On her way back to her building, Esther stopped at "The Point" a small secluded area where there were benches and picnic tables. "The Point" loomed high over the city, providing a view of the Washington Monument, the Capitol, the Anacostia and Potomac rivers. The city sat beneath a canopy of billowing majestic clouds, as in a vision inspired by religious ecstasy. Esther clutched the plants to her chest and knew she wanted to be well and that she was ready to go home.

In May Esther was released on the weekends for visits home. "Home" was once again her mother's house and she slept at night in the room she had known as a child. She looked at her son and she did not recognize him. He had sprouted into a gangly preteen, his body consisting, it seemed, simply of arms and legs. They had never talked much and they did not talk now. In the evenings, they sat playing Monopoly and checkers, the moves they made, whether they won or lost, informing them of what they needed to know. Esther watched Logan shun his friends, excursions to the movies, simply to sit in the same room with her.

Yet no one asked Esther what she had seen in the hospital or what she had suffered. And she felt that until the ones who loved her could bear to know this, they all would merely circle one another in a meaningless, corrupt dance. Naomi assured Esther, "It's all behind you now." Randolph spoke only of their future. The part of her that had been ill but not crazy, anguished but always worth saving, that was the part of her they all refused to touch.

"You'll never get well till what we have gets straightened out," Randolph told Esther one afternoon, as they sat looking out the window of her bedroom, waiting for Logan to come home from school.

"What are you saying?"

"I'm saying maybe I made you sick. Being with me all these years and not having anything or anybody you could really count on."

"That's not all I need."

"It's a part of it. Will you ever be the same?" he asked hopefully.

"The same as what?"

"As before."

"I don't think so."

"I feel like you're not even here."

"That's because I'm not. Part of me is already gone."

"Where?"

"To find something to live for."

"What you got here ain't enough?"

"I don't know what it is yet. That's why I can't hold it."

"You're a strange woman." He shook his head.

"That's why you want me."

"I'm a strange man," he conceded with a laugh.

"No, you're not. You're a greedy man. Me, I'm just figuring out my appetites."

Randolph now knew that he would lose Esther and each time he looked at her he tried to drink in everything she was to last him all the time she would be gone. When they made love, Esther distant, accepting his passion with vague disinterest, Randolph slumped upon her at the end, unashamed to release tears on her naked shoulders that said goodbye.

This was the summer when Negro demands for freedom and equality ruptured the complacent soul of the nation. Governor George Wallace of Alabama blocked the entrance to the University of Alabama so two Negro students could not register to attend classes. Watching the tense yet ludicrous melodrama replayed on the evening news, Esther laughed at the vanity of this tiny little white man who thought he could freeze history in its tracks. And the next day Medgar Evers, field director of the NAACP in Mississippi, was assassinated as he got out of his car in the driveway before his house. The young Irish Catholic President, forced by Negro demands to adopt an almost militant defense of the Constitution, promised in a televised speech to lead or push the nation into extending its most timeless promise to its most dishonored citizens.

This was the summer preceded by a spring in which the jails of Birmingham, Alabama, overflowed with so many protesting segregation that the city established temporary prison camps. Police dogs and water cannons vainly attempted to douse the drive for freedom and the protestors vowed, their hands clapping and bloodied, determined and wounded, "Ain't gonna let nobody turn me around."

That summer at night, in the same bed she had slept in as a child, Esther received visits from her father. He returned this time, as in the past, because he was needed. Esther had begun to read every account she could find of what was happening in the South. Weekly, she sent Logan to a newsstand downtown to buy *Life*, *Look*, *Jet*, *Ebony*, the *Afro*, the *New York Times* and all the Southern Negro papers he could find. Television took the temperature of the country.

And to Naomi's displeasure it stayed on nearly all day and much of the evening, so fearful was Esther that she would miss news of the "movement" as it happened.

Her father returned and told Esther what she had to do. In one dream Rayford Johnson told his daughter that she had tried, up to now, to be small, but she was his child and so she was born to be brave. In another dream he asked Esther why she had ignored her fate. In the last dream Esther told her father, "But I am afraid." Rayford Johnson assured Esther, "That simply means you are alive."

Near the end of August, Esther, Naomi and Logan joined two hundred fifty thousand people at the Washington Mall in a March for Jobs and Freedom.

Esther had never seen so many Negroes gathered in one place before. People had come all the way from California —Blacks and whites. Signs declaring EQUAL RIGHTS NOW!, AN END TO BIAS NOW! and what seemed like millions of tiny American flags were stationed among the mammoth crowd. The flags, ironic emblems of freedom, sprouted like fierce, life-giving vegetation. People crowded along the edges of the massive Reflecting Pool, soaking weary march-worn feet, in a mood almost jubilant, so certain were they that this grand gesture assured "Freedom Now."

The speech was like no sermon Esther had ever heard. For that's what it was—a sermon preached to a congregation that was the world. The words drifted over their heads and vibrated across the Reflecting Pool upon which Lincoln gazed—peaceful and free at last. The words condemned, challenged and made history, all in one perfect poetic blast. But to Esther, all those people, gathered in homage to what her people were owed, meant more than the leader's words. Without them, the leader roamed in the dark, without them, the leader was jailed for naught, conferred with no presidents, influenced no public opinion. Esther did not know if King knew it, but he owed his followers all he possessed.

Two days later Esther rose at 5 A.M. and dressed quickly in the room's hushed, expectant darkness. She slipped a note under Naomi's door and went to Logan's room, where he lay asleep. Esther kneeled beside her son's bed, wondering what he was dreaming, lodging the serenity of his face at this moment in her mind forever. She kissed Logan lightly on his cheek, which was humid and damp with sweat. He would turn thirteen in two weeks and she would not be here to see it. Still, as she gazed at her son, Esther finally knew what to say and she whispered, "I know I am alive."

Chapter Fourteen

N A O M I

The day Esther walked out of the house I knew she was going out to find some part of her soul. I knew that would take time and that she'd take the time she needed. This house, big as it is, seemed too small for her. She'd roam from room to room, cleaning up, looking around like it was the first time she'd seen it. Sometimes she'd stare out the windows, pulling back the curtain, squinching up her eyes like she was looking at something far off and she wanted to see it better. She'd dust the same table and chairs over and over again or sometimes just stand in the middle of the room like she was waiting for something or somebody to come and get her. I asked her one day, after she'd been home awhile, what she thought she might like to do now that she was well and feeling better. She told me, "I look around, Mama, and I don't see a thing made for me. Nothing cut to fit. I guess I'll have to invent something, do like you did, just make myself up." The morning Esther left she wrote me a note that said, "Daddy told me what to do."

I'd pretty much accepted by now that there wasn't much I could do with Esther. I didn't know whether to feel like I'd failed her, she'd failed me or God had somehow failed us both. Her spirit was restless and searching and she was hungrier for life than I had ever been. And determined! Nothing could stop Esther from doing what she wanted—not me, not her man, not her child. There'd never been nobody in my family that mad or that brave. And I felt afraid and proud at the same time. She didn't always know where she was going, but she refused to stand still. Even when she left like that, just disappearing, I didn't think she'd gone off anywhere to hurt herself. But I was pretty sure that the rest of us would end up hurting and someday even Esther, though I didn't wish it, was gonna pay.

I called the police and reported her as a missing person. But I could tell from the way they talked to me they wasn't gonna look too hard for one lost colored woman. I didn't know how to tell Logan I felt ashamed of Esther and, there weren't words, no matter how hard I tried, to make sense of what she'd done. So I lied. Lied like grown-ups always figure they can to a child. And he saw right through me. "She's not coming back," he said. And he didn't say it like a question, but like it was a fact. Even though he knew the truth, I still tried to hold onto the lie, like it was the only thing that could save us both. "She wouldn't just run off like that. Esther's your mother. She loves you."

"How come she had me anyway?" he shouted, stamping his feet. "Why'd she have me?"

Logan's face was so full of anger it nearly made my heart break. And in my arms all I could feel was bones and muscle, all I could hear was him breathing hard and deep and fast, nearly choking on the tears he couldn't let go of. So I told him what I felt, along with all the sadness and confusion. I pulled him even closer and whispered, "Boy, every goodbye ain't gone. We ain't heard the last of your mama. She's gone, but not to stay. Remember, she didn't say goodbye so that means she's coming back."

Well, Esther wrote me two weeks later, said she was in Birmingham, working with one of the civil rights groups, organizing, and that she was happier than she'd been in a long time. I know why she didn't call 'cause she'd have had to talk to Logan. She ended the letter by telling me to tell Logan she loved him, even though it didn't always seem like it, and that I should be glad for her 'cause she'd finally found something that fit.

hen Randolph parked in front of his house, he saw the yellowish mournful light in his wife's bedroom. He didn't see Wayne's car, so he figured he was still out chasing girls or trouble. It was eleven-thirty and Randolph could visualize his younger son Marshall, his muscular, broadly built fifteen-year-old frame beneath the blankets of his bed. Randolph sat in

the car and lit a cigarette and turned the radio to WUST and the voice of Nancy Wilson filled the car, asking "Guess Who I Saw Today?" Madeline Henderson was out walking her dog, a mutt who shared her four-bedroom house with her.

There weren't many lights on in the other houses on the street. His neighbors were mostly government workers who had to get up early in the morning to sit behind desks at the Pentagon, the Treasury Department or some other federal agency. And they were as proud of their jobs as of their children. Those jobs had enabled them to buy homes in this section of Northeast, Riggs Park. They made Randolph laugh, for they fought litter and enforced a strict code of how and where cars could be parked and when clothes could be hung out to dry with a passion few could imagine giving to any other endeavor. Their spacious ranch houses had made them proper Negroes, worthy of the social integration that was inevitable, but which the whites still fought tooth and nail. They were not dangerous, they were merely ordinary, attending church on Sunday mornings, committing their sins with discretion and more than a little fear, counting the years until they were eligible for their pensions, joyfully building up enough debts to give them financial credibility but not to endanger the lives they had created.

Most of them had come up from nothing and nowhere and now their government jobs gave them a feeling of security and a sense of self-worth. Some of the women acted like they didn't know what a pig's foot was and spoke so properly, contorting their mouths to imitate what they thought was white speech, as to be indecipherable.

There were a few businessmen among them, the kind who had married light-skinned beauties from "good" Negro families to endow them with the kind of social legitimacy there was not enough money to buy. They were men who dreamed at night of coming back in another life as J. P. Morgan or Henry Ford. Randolph was neighborly, now and then exchanging the pleasantries produced by mutual home owner-ship, but he kept his distance. He didn't want what they had to rub off on him. He had done well in his business the last few years and now owned two liquor stores and two dry cleaners. The liquor stores were not easy for a Negro to get, but the profit was tremendous. Some old Southerner had marketed fried chicken like it was a new invention and folks, black and white, were flocking to his drive-ins. Randolph had decided he was going to be the first Negro to own a drive-in fried chicken franchise and was in the process of negotiations.

When he entered his house, Randolph decided to stay downstairs. He wasn't up to going upstairs just yet. He went to the kitchen and got a beer out of the refrigerator and sat down in the living room, then he sat in the semidarkness and listened to his wife's footsteps overhead.

He had not slept with Mary in over a year. His two sons warred with him, defying and ignoring him, their contempt fed by his betrayal of their mother. Randolph now knew that he had expected and asked too much. The price of his sons' respect was the denial of Logan and Esther. No one in his family thought him honorable or brave for acknowledging his child, they looked at him and saw a liar and a cheat because he was claimed willingly by his wife and his mistress.

Randolph wondered what Logan's assessment would be when he grew old enough to hate as well as to love. Mary had never asked for a divorce and he had never considered leaving her. They were bound by flesh and despair. Still, Mary had never forgiven him. He had seen her on her knees beside their bed in the early days, praying with fervor and belief for a forgiving heart, for a way to love the husband who had shattered her life. Mary prayed for years, became active in the church, even though she was never able to get Randolph to attend, tithed generously, gave of her time to orphans. She prayed, Randolph knew as well, for him to forsake Esther.

But her prayers were not answered. And after years of belief unrewarded, Mary gave up her faith and she gave up on him.

They had gone through a period when they tried, simply and purposely, to kill one another, launching at the slightest provocation into fights that left them bloodied and bruised. They stopped fighting the night Wayne came at Randolph with a hammer to pull him off of Mary, whose arm Randolph had twisted behind her back as he pressed her against the kitchen floor.

The year before Mary told him that she was pregnant but that she wasn't going to have his child. "I'm going to have an abortion. And you can't stop me," she told Randolph. His first response was rage and he shook her, slapped her, trying to make her change her mind. But she didn't, she sat limp, emotionless and told him in a dreadful whisper, "You have no rights in this house until you leave that whore."

The next day, when Randolph woke up, Mary was gone. She came back three days later and she began sleeping in the spare bedroom. Randolph had not touched her since then. They had convinced themselves on one level that they stayed together for the sake of their sons. But they both knew they could not live without each other. Misery gave Mary a sense of purpose, enabled her to martyr her emotions for something larger than herself. Randolph was determined to win respect and he could only do that in the home he had made for his family.

He loved his sons, but could not say for certain that they knew it. Marshall, the youngest, suffered from dyslexia and he was in a special school. He was a large, hulking kid, self-conscious about his size and his inability to read well. For years his teachers had simply labeled him slow or dumb and kept him back, which increased his frustration and made him a behavior problem as he took out his anger on classmates. But Mary, from the start, had known something was wrong, had worked with him night after night on the alphabet. It was only after she took him to the fifth doctor that the dyslexia was diagnosed. Marshall had Mary's big heart and he was quiet and shy and his greatest happiness seemed to be when Randolph took him fishing. Marshall could sink a line and sit waiting for a bite with the patience of Job.

But Wayne, because he was so much like him, filled Randolph with the greatest anger. It was Wayne who told Randolph after the incident with the hammer, "If you ever hit my mother again, I'll kill you." He was fourteen at the time. And it was Wayne who asked Randolph, "How could you treat Mama the way you have?"

"Your mother and I have an understanding," Randolph said weakly.

"I'll never understand what you've done."

"When you grow up."

"I won't be like you."

His firstborn, his oldest son, simply hated him and in Wayne's presence Randolph could never escape his guilt.

Randolph heard the front door open and saw his oldest son come through the door.

"Hi," Wayne said warily, his face a harsh defensive mask that still could not hide his father's wide-set eyes and broad lips—evidence of their bond starkly etched on his face.

"It's almost midnight, where you been?"

"Nowhere. I just went out for a drive."

"A drive? Didn't I tell you about driving around on school nights, hanging in the streets?"

"Ma said."

"I don't care what she said."

"She knew where I was."

"Well, I didn't."

"You weren't here."

"That doesn't matter. What I say rules whether I'm here or not."

"All right, all right," Wayne snapped impatiently, hunching his shoulders.

"And you watch your mouth. You're almost in trouble," Randolph warned the boy, aware that he was going on for his own sake and not Wayne's, aware that his threats were hollow. "Go on to bed," Randolph muttered angrily, more disgruntled with himself than with Wayne. The boy walked away and as he neared the stairs he stopped, turned back and said, "Goodnight."

Chapter Sixteen

N A O M I

W as the funniest thing. After Esther had been gone about a year, me and Randolph become, in time, pretty good friends. We both felt we had to work extra hard with Logan to make up for Esther not being there. And though he never said nothing about it, I got the feeling his marriage was just about over. He came to the house regular and he'd eat dinner with me and

Logan at least once a week. Got so he was always taking Logan someplace with him. Saturdays they'd be gone all day, Randolph driving Logan around, taking care of business for all those shops and such that he had. I remember the time I figured I'd never give Randolph Spenser credit for nothing. But he turned out to be OK. One Sunday I'd fixed my usual fried chicken dinner and Randolph had dropped by. Logan was in his room, doing his homework. And we sat, picking over what was left of the mashed potatoes and biscuits and watching "The Ed Sullivan Show."

"I got another letter from Esther," I told him, watching him real close to read him as best I could.

"Where is she now?" he asked, bunching up his lips and his face, looking madder than I'd seen him in a long time.

"Selma."

"Selma! She's gonna get killed."

"No, she's not. I got a feeling Esther's safer now than she's ever been."

"Down there in the lion's den?"

"Look at what happened to Daniel."

"Naomi, this ain't the Bible, this is real life."

"You the only person I know think they ain't the same thing."

"She ask about me?"

"Didn't say a word."

"Wonder how come she don't write me?"

"How come you men always think a woman got to be thinking about y'all *all* the time?"

"I'll bet she fell in love with one of them civil rights workers."

"You act like she's on a holiday."

"She's acting like she's a leader, a Martin Luther King or somebody. She's a woman." Randolph got so mad he could hardly sit still. "Down there, going to jail to integrate. Hell, integration'll put me outta business. Once Negroes start going downtown, the Eden Bar and Grill won't last a year. We begging for a gun to kill ourselves with and can't even see it. Now, this Malcolm X, he's kinda way-out, but he's talking my talk."

"You *would* follow those old hate-filled Muslims. Like hating the white man is the answer."

"Naomi, they don't hate the white man. They love the Negro."

"Love? Love? I don't hear them talking nothing 'bout love, just stirring up more trouble for the rest of us."

"You just like most Negroes, scared of freedom. So scared of it you don't even know what it is."

"Randolph Spenser, I think you better quit while you ahead."

"Naw, I mean it. What's Esther trying to prove?"

"Only thing she told me before she left was that nothing fit, that she was gonna have to make something up for herself."

"Long time ago, when we first met, she told me one day she was gonna just take off and not look back."

"She couldn't have known then," I said, "what her future looked like."

"You know like I do, it ain't everybody that *has* a future. If you can't imagine doing something, no way it can possibly happen. Esther always had more imagination than she let on." Randolph said this like it was something he'd just now discovered. His face that had once looked so strong, made of stone, had started to sag, got soft and flabby like all the disappointments was just too much. He was getting old and wasn't fighting back.

"I got a visit from the FBI last week," I told him.

"About Esther?"

"Yeah. Two men come to the door. One white, one Negro. Showed their badges like that was supposed to put the fear of God in me. I almost didn't let them come in."

"What did they want to know?"

"When I'd last heard from her. Where she was. Had she been involved in this kinda stuff before. I told them since they was representing the government I figured they'd know more about Esther than me. Naturally they didn't like that too much. And the colored one, well, he just showed off something awful. Acted real nasty, threatened to put me in jail if I didn't tell them what they wanted to know. Well, I just let him go on. Like they say, *No master like the former slave.* And when he got through, I asked him if his folks knew he was going around, trying to put colored folks in jail for fighting for freedom. That little rascal shut right up. Shut right up. And let the white man do all the talking. And by that time all *he* could do was apologize."

"I think they bugged your phone."

"Bugged, what you mean?"

"Put something in it so they can listen in on conversations in case she calls."

"Well, I'll be. This is the United States and . . ."

"This sure is, Naomi. It sure is," Randolph said, real bitter.

"And you not the least bit proud of her?" I asked him finally, asking what I'd wanted to since Esther left.

He just sat there, looking at the TV screen, but I could tell he wasn't seeing a thing.

"Proud? Why should I be proud?" he said, turning to me. "It would've took just as much courage for her to stay here and raise Logan. Naomi, there's all kinds of courage. So far Esther ain't showed me but one kind, the kind that's easy 'cause you give it to strangers."

"Well, *I'm* proud of her." I said, trying to beat back his words, that hurt of her so bad I felt like I'd been hit. Watching Randolph drumming on the table, his face as stern as a warning sign, and I realized how Esther had hurt him and how much he cared. "She just wants to make a better world," I told him, feeling like I had to keep on defending Esther.

"She coulda stayed here and give us a chance for a better life. When she got out of the hospital, I thought real serious about leaving my wife and us getting married. But everything about Esther was temporary, impermanent. I'd hold her and it would feel like I was hugging a ghost. I knew she wasn't ready to stay. She didn't want to be mine."

"Not at that moment. Not then."

"Well, when?" Randolph shouted, like a child demanding some treat he'd been denied. "When? Naomi, you think life's just overflowing with second chances?"

"If Esther didn't believe in second chances, she wouldn't have gone down South."

"And not a single note, not a call all this time," he moaned.

"What you feel weighs too much, Randolph, right now she can't carry it."

He lit up a cigarette and slumped back in his chair, sat there, blowing smoke rings and watching them evaporate, and every time one of the rings would disappear he'd look like he missed it. "And I'll be right here when she comes back," he said with a laugh—the kind that comes from way down deep and makes you feel ashamed 'cause it lets on how weak you feel.

"Then I'll be right here," he said again. "I've got to see how strong she is when she comes back and if she can carry what I got to give her."

Chapter Seventeen

The longer Esther was away, the more Logan became positively and totally Esther's child. At seventeen he possessed her beguiling face that seemed to promise that it would never betray. This face, masculine yet gentle and at the same time impenetrable, seemed at odds with the strong, compact body he had inherited from his father. Logan was more like his mother than he knew or would ever knowingly admit and he had not told anyone how much he missed her. He had removed a picture of Esther from Naomi's scrapbook, a picture taken of Esther sitting on the front porch, holding him in her arms. In the photo Logan was two years old and now he slept with this picture beneath his pillow and sometimes let the snapshot rest on his palms, closed his eyes and tried to *feel* where Esther was at that moment, what she was doing. In the photo, Esther was a young girl and the dreamy, hungry eyes of mother and child gazed longingly at the camera as if seeking a confession. Esther was smiling and Logan convinced himself that she was smiling because he was her child.

For each of his birthdays in the four years she was away, Esther had sent Logan a card signed simply, "Love, your mother." And twice she had sent him photographs of the woman she had become—blue-jeaned, determined, her skin dark and burnished by the Southern sun, her hair cut short, rebelliously framing a face that Logan simply refused to believe. Those pictures he placed in his drawer and never looked at again.

Loneliness drove Logan—easily, naturally—to the pursuit of knowledge and of dreams. Books gave him answers—neat and unequivocal—that buttressed his conviction that life could be managed with more skill than he had seen his parents use.

He was at heart his mother's child, but to become his own man Logan made choices that required an adherence to conformity his mother could not now imagine. He and Naomi ate dinner while watching footage on the evening news of riots in Watts, New York and other cities. The fire and destruction of the uprisings singed the present, burned a path into the future. Black anger and anguish were spreading like a fault line across the land. One evening Naomi gazed across the dinner table at Logan, turning the news off in disgust, and said wearily, "Boy, you gonna have to make the world all over from scratch." Logan thought, but did not say, "Maybe we'll do it right this time."

At seventeen, Logan's friends were other studious, often shy young men who, driven by doubt or loneliness, believed in great expectation. They secretly assumed they would achieve as no one else in their family had and thereby win more love than even they thought they deserved. They were bookwormish, eyeglass-wearing, awkward-with-girls young boys, who would grow into suave, disarming men, willing themselves into personal charm with the same doggedness that characterized all their pursuits.

In the summer of his junior year in high school, Logan broke his leg when he fell off the diving board at the neighborhood swimming pool. He was treated by a Black doctor at Freedmen's Hospital, who, by his mastery of the art and science of medicine, defied a host of expectations about Black achievement that Logan secretly harbored. Dr. Melvin Hopkins was a few years younger than Randolph, Logan guessed, and during his visit for initial treatment Logan assessed the complex yet simple nature of the man's job. Dr. Hopkins spent a great deal of time just talking to Logan, asking how he had broken his leg, teasing him mildly about his lack of swimming prowess, getting Logan to talk about school and hobbies, distracting him from the sound and feel of his bones being set.

Logan watched the meticulous application of the cast and thought he had never seen anything more impressive than the long-fingered, competent and caring hands of Dr. Melvin Hopkins as they set his leg in plaster. The doctor's mind, Logan knew, teemed with terminologies that were scientific, biological and puzzling to the uninitiated. And it was that sacred healing code that endowed the doctor's hands with the firmness and compassion that sculpted the cast. On other visits Logan saw the deferential yet comradely relationship between the doctor and his nursing assistant. His eyes scanned the office bulletin board, where photos of younger patients and cards and letters from older ones were posted. And Logan listened, curious and awed, as the doctor shifted between the specialized, dense jargon of medicine and the less intimidating language he used to tell people how he would make them well.

By the time the cast was removed six weeks later, Logan knew that he wanted to be a doctor so that the same gratitude he felt toward Dr. Hopkins would somehow always be his.

His father intrigued him. Logan was never sure that he was the son that his father would have wanted. He only knew he was the son that his father loved.

One day Randolph drove Logan to his properties, showed him the two liquor stores and the dry cleaners. Then Randolph took Logan to a Hot Shoppes restaurant for lunch. "I want you to know what I've got and what I'm worth. When I die, some of what I have is going to you," Randolph said as they waited for their order.

"You rich?" Logan teased.

"Wish I was." Randolph laughed. "You got to have a whole lot more than the little I've got to be rich. But I'm not hurting."

"I'd like to be rich one day," Logan said wistfully.

"Long as you never say you want to be white."

"I'd never say that."

"Saying it ain't the worst part. Feeling it is."

"You hate white people," Logan accused him.

"Naw, I don't hate them. They're cowards, that's all. And I want you to always know that. Know that and you got the secret to everything they do. Just last week I got into an argument with a white man downtown over a parking space. Was over near George Washington University. I think he was a professor or something. He ended up getting all mad and calling me stupid. Stupid! Only reason he called me that is 'cause I'm a Negro and he figured I had no real education and he was carrying a briefcase and I wasn't. They'll always use that on you, boy. And what brains you got, they'll try to convince you they're in your penis or your muscles. Anywhere and everywhere but your head." Randolph's voice was rich with sarcasm.

His father's words unsettled Logan. And it was in this mood of agitation that Logan felt an unfamiliar courage rise like a fever within him and inspire him to engage his father in a bold glance that asked for an accounting of his life.

Never once had Logan asked Randolph about his wife or sons. Logan wanted at that moment, more than anything else, to speak his brothers' names. "Tell me about Wayne and Marshall," he demanded quietly, then took a large bite from his tuna sandwich.

"What? What'd you say?" Randolph blustered in angry surprise designed to extinguish Logan's curiosity, shame him into meekness. But Logan looked at his father, pretending for a moment that they were equals, and said, "I want to know about your sons. Tell me about my brothers."

The question's simplicity and the fact that he had waited all of Logan's life to hear it quelled the defensiveness that had surged into Randolph's mind.

"They're good boys. They really are," he began slowly. "Wayne, the oldest, he's in the navy now. On a ship over in Europe. I'd wanted him to go to college, but he didn't even apply. You see, I'd kind of hoped he might take an interest in business and build on what I've got. Liquor stores and apartment buildings, that's nothing and I know it. But somebody with some business education could build on what I have and turn it into something with class. But he never expressed an interest, no matter what I said or how much I talked to him about it," Randolph shrugged. "He just didn't care."

"How come?"

"Oh, I think it was to spite me. Because of you and your mama. Ever since I can remember, seemed like Wayne's been mad with the world and I think it's mostly because of the things he saw me do. Got so he wouldn't listen to a word from me."

"Why'd you never leave your wife and marry my mother? Why'd you keep her as your whore?" The anger stung Randolph, who countered, "She wasn't my whore. Never was she that, boy, and I'll let you get away with that tone and that word 'cause I know you got a right to be mad with me too." Randolph looked away and spoke more to himself now than to his son. "If I'd been a real man, I'd have let her go way back when, before it got this far. She could've had a real life, not the one I gave her." He braved a look at Logan, saying, "And since I didn't let her go, I don't even know how to tell you to be a man. You can look at me and see how hard it is. But I just tried to do the right thing, even when it looked like the wrong thing. You try to do the same."

Logan turned away from Randolph and stared out the window of the restaurant. Randolph reached across the table and put his hand on his son's shoulder and said simply, "I tried to do right."

"And what about Marshall?" Logan asked.

"He's a little like you—quiet sometimes. But he didn't do too well in school, so he's worried now about what kind of job he can get. You'll be graduating soon. You thought about what you want to do?"

"I'm thinking about going into medicine, maybe becoming a doctor."

"I'm proud of you, boy. Real proud." Randolph smiled for the first time that day and thought how miraculous was this son, whom he had not really wanted but whom he had never thought *not* to love.

The news aroused Harvard Street, set it lurching into action like a giant unceremoniously roused from sleep. A light, harmless rain had fallen intermittently all evening, yet each time the showers ceased, the front stoops filled once again with people seeking relief from stuffy, humid rented rooms. It was early April, cherry blossoms had lavishly unfolded on the Mall, tourists had begun the first leg of their spring invasion of the city. And on Harvard Street third-graders jumped double-dutch after school, counting the days till June. Half a dozen houses on the street had given up sons to serve in Vietnam. And among the young men who escaped Uncle Sam's grasp, dashikis, beards and dark glasses had begun to sprout as camouflage and declaration.

That night, drawn by some mutual instinct, people streamed out of the houses toward the main thoroughfare, Fourteenth Street. On Fourteenth Street stood the stores that housed the clothes they coveted to transform them into women of beauty and men of substance, the record shops that sold them the sound of their dreams and their breaking hearts, the cheap easy-credit furniture and appliance stores that furnished their homes, the big national chains, where they spent their money but could rise no higher than clerk in the store's chain of command, the Negro-owned barber shops, where they went for haircuts and to be rejuvenated by the gossip, tall tales and outright lies that filled the air like music, and Riggs Bank, where they could store their money but rarely got a loan. Swarming, restless and anguished, the people ran toward Fourteenth Street because the street determined the quality of their lives even more than the houses and rooms where they made love and babies and returned to at the end of the day. Fourteenth Street determined the size of their lives, the perimeters of their hopes in ways that they honored yet despised.

At nine-thirty that night Logan heard a howl, let loose from the lungs of a young boy running past Naomi's house. "They killed King! Damn them, they killed King!" Moments later Logan heard the first sound of glass shattering and it beckoned him from his room where he sat, paralyzed by anger, after Naomi told him of the murder of Martin Luther King, Jr.

Logan ran out of the house, past Naomi's bedroom, where, behind her closed door, she sat reading the Twenty-Third Psalm. He was one of hundreds streaming from the houses on all the adjacent streets, running to Fourteenth Street to gather in clusters that milled, testy and impatient, awaiting the courage of one of their number to commit some act they all yearned to complete, and by that, invest themselves with a temporary bravado they would remember all their lives.

Logan looked among the crowd. He had seen all their faces before. This was his neighborhood and his home. And these people standing with him beneath the darkness and a sky that hung heavily with the promise of still more rain, sprang from him as surely as he contained the best and the worst of them within his soul.

Helmeted, gas-masked policemen armed with rifles and tear-gas canisters stood in the streets, like sentries dropped from another planet. The street was ominously empty of traffic and young people in groups of twenty to thirty fanned out along the commercial corridor like soldiers on a search-and-destroy mission. At the head of one group, Logan spotted Butch Jenkins. Butch had dropped out of Cardoza Senior High School the year before and now, on his way home from school, Logan often saw Butch shooting baskets in the play-ground near the school or smoking cigarettes and hanging on the corner in front of the neighborhood liquor store. It was Butch who had taught Logan how to fight. Butch had ambushed Logan on his way home from school when they both were in junior high and Logan had proved so ineffective at defending himself that Butch, while straddling Logan in the alley and punching him in the chest, had told him in exasperation, "It ain't even no fun kicking your ass."

Soon Butch began to come to Naomi's house after school and take Logan out to the garage, where he taught Logan how to bob and weave, how to jab and punch and turn his fists into instruments to be feared. Butch had eight brothers and sisters and his father worked three jobs to support his family. He was a strapping, muscular youth whose bulk inspired ridicule and fright. His classmates turned into bullies at the sight of Butch's frame and his teachers assumed that a body of that size left no room for much of a brain and so proceeded to ignore him with a consistency that informed Butch that he simply did not count. Logan had seen Butch alternate between two emotions, anger and fear. After Butch taught Logan how to fight, Logan began to help Butch with his homework after school. No one at school knew of their unexpected alliance and in public Logan and Butch, with differing constituencies to please, barely acknowledged each other.

Yet by the time the two boys entered high school, Butch had been drawn irrevocably to the streets.

Now Logan saw Butch smash the window of an appliance store with his fist, the breaking glass filling the night like gunfire. This action set the other youths to action, as they poured through store windows, which they broke with rocks, sticks and fists, and grabbed radios, portable television sets, electric fans and toasters. At the sight of Butch leading the youths in a hit-and-run strategy up Fourteenth Street, Logan began to run with another group of youths, their minds bursting with rage and betrayal, their hearts gluttonous and vengeful. Logan ran with the young men, some who sat next to him in classes at school, others who had chiseled out their destiny in the alleys and on street corners. Logan's heart pumped with excitement that released the anger, with an anticipation that quenched the sorrow.

Tear gas hung in the air, the smell threatening to choke them, unable to vanquish them. Other youths stood in the middle of the streets, throwing rocks and bottles at the few passing cars and buses, heckling the police with taunts and jeers.

As Logan's group stopped at the corner of Fourteenth and

Fairmont Street, policemen rushed them, their nightsticks flailing wildly, scattering the youths, bruising them and leaving a few bloodied. The boys scattered, only to regroup a few yards away.

By midnight both the Central Market and the Pleasant Hill Market on opposite corners of Fourteenth and Fairmont were ablaze, the fires igniting the grieving sky with a glorious, awful presence. The people were stunned by the fires. They stood, their arms filled with dresses, food and appliances looted from stores they had shopped in earlier that day. Numb, they gazed in silence at the flames that both cleansed their bitterness and inflicted wounds beneath their skin.

A Molotov cocktail had provided the first attack on Murphy's five-and-dime and as Logan ran toward it the white mannequins that had smiled haughtily from the front windows only hours ago lay armless, legless, naked in the entrance, their bodies part of a general carnage overflowing into the streets.

Logan entered a store, drawn by the people inside clamoring over the counters, coming to blows over the most precious items, by the flickering fluorescence of the lights, by the celebratory mood—even as fire raged in the back. Logan walked down the aisles littered with loud springtime colors of inexpensive women's dresses, children's sneakers, goldfish squirming for life in a puddle at his feet, blankets, crushed lampshades, torn paperback books. Logan looked at the destruction around him and knew there was nothing that he wanted. Yet the sight of a man's Timex watch, untouched, still in its case on a counter near the front, made his heart beat momentarily with desire. And amid the din surrounding him, Logan allowed himself to touch the watch, then to remove it from the box and hold it in his hand. He started to slip the expanding band easily over his wrist, but Logan thought of Esther, wondered where she was at that moment, if she knew King was dead, and he could feel, as he had not been able to at any moment before, that she was coming back. Logan dropped the watch as though holding it would delay his mother's return and he turned to see the flames moving closer to the front of the store as he ran to the exit.

From across the street Logan watched G. C. Murphy's crumble in on itself, the flames spreading across the roof, traveling to the lower part of the building. And in a final awesome burst, the store collapsed. Logan stood watching the firemen vainly try to defeat the flames. He stood even after the firemen gave up, boarded their trucks and roared away to put out other fires hungrily devouring the length of the street, leaving the charred, smoldering ruins of the five-and-dime for Logan's eyes to witness but not believe.

Three months after the riots Esther walked back into her mother's house as carefully as she had fled five years earlier. King's words had drawn her, like a clarion call, to the South. His murder, which killed the man and the idealism of a generation, propelled her back home. During the twenty-two-hour bus ride from Selma, Alabama, to Washington, D.C., Esther relived every moment of her time in the South, the land that had nurtured her kin, and then spat them out like a mutinous taste in the mouth into the arms of the North. And yet the South, its cadence its promise and betrayal, flourished inside all of them, as strong as a heartbeat. Esther had ventured into that seething terrifying land to change it and, in the end, submitted to its more willful touch, felt the South mold and shape her, momentarily break her. A small cardboard suitcase in the overhead compartment held all that she owned in the world—blue jeans, work shirts, underwear she had bought at the Goodwill in Montgomery, a Bible and a diary she had kept. The diary overflowed with words she had denied her mother and son—names of men and women she had walked to courthouses to register to vote, of a woman beaten to death with a whip in the basement of a jail as a warning to other Black women not to leave the kitchens of whites to protest segregation, of the two lovers she had had—one driven mad by the sight of a friend dredged from the Mississippi River, the other who drove her to the bus station in silence the day she left the South and told her, as they sat together in his car, "The stakes are higher now than ever. If I didn't leave before, I sure as hell ain't leaving now." The book held dreams of her own death—a white man's hands around her neck or a bullet wound setting her on fire with pain. Into the diary Esther had poured the words that were too heavy, too monumental to enfold in a dutiful letter home.

Beneath a translucent full moon, occupying the Mississippi night sky with an opulent beauty, the tents stretched—crowding the field, dotting the landscape, their tops jutting like steeples filled with uncertain yet persistent hope.

It was almost 11 P.M. and the kerosene lamps in most of the tents had been extinguished. Earlier in the evening the dim lights had lit more tents. All over "Tent City" reflections had danced on the sturdy canvas cloth, as women poked the insufficient wood stoves, men layered cardboard on the tent floors to keep out mud and the November frost and children sucked thumbs in their sleep, tossing on slender army cots.

For three hundred families "Tent City" was now home. Over a thousand people had been evicted from plantations in McComb, Mississippi, for registering to vote and a third of those people had taken refuge here.

Esther kicked dirt over the remaining embers of a small fire that several women had used to cook evening meals. They were women who had started picking cotton at four, had their first child at fourteen, women whose hands were callused, bruised, as hard as the lives they lived. Women who had seen a doctor maybe once in their lives, a dentist never, who, if they could read at all, hid that fact from the bosses who owned the land they toiled. The bosses were men and women whose families had owned the dark rich soil for generations and who had held these women in hock, at bay, who demanded their respect, subservience, who could deny them food, shoes, dignity and life. Esther escorted these women to the courthouse, women who had marched through the main streets protesting segregation, women who had reclaimed what their bosses told them they had never had.

Pouring a tin cup of water over the soil to completely douse the fire, Esther heard the men's voices—flexing and oddly triumphant in the darkness, scattered among the trees surrounding the field. The men sat on the edges of the camp in small groups, their eyes wide and searching for danger, ears cocked and their rifles loaded. The men had ignored the bosses who told them that Esther and all the civil rights workers like her were agitators, Communists. They had dressed in their best overalls or suit the day they went to the courthouse seeking vindication and freedom. They had turned aside pleas of cautious relatives and wives, begging them to "leave well enough alone" and not to risk the little they had. They were men who could have hopped a train North, freeloaded, hoboed their way off the land that enslaved them. But they stayed, wedded to the soil, the plantations, the bosses, by women and children they loved, families they could not live without. They were men who knew they were men because of what they owed to others and what was owed to them.

Esther stood up and wrapped her poncho, made from an army surplus blanket, closer around her arms. A car, its headlights off, cruised past the field, tracking the sounds of life on the campground.

People and families had been arriving at the camp all day, as word had spread of its existence. People had arrived in ramshackle trucks, loaded with beds, cookware, furniture. Some had walked, carrying what they valued most wrapped in knapsacks on their backs, teenagers pulling crumbling wagons burdened with tattered secondhand possessions. The people had ended up in "Tent City" because of the risks they had taken to be free. They had taken risks urged on them by people like Esther.

For over six months, the civil rights workers had walked and driven along the back roads, broken bread with these people over skimpy meals and worked to persuade them to brave their bosses and their deepest fears and register to vote. And when the sharecroppers had taken what was, for some, the longest walk of their lives, they returned to plantations from which they had, by their actions, set themselves free. They returned to face the wrath of people who thought they owned them and who thought these people could be destroyed by forced separation from the land that they did not own and that had always—somehow—betrayed them. The plantation owners, in league with the White Citizens' Councils, had pledged to stamp out "the movement" and so the people were driven off the land.

Luta Mae Allen and her husband Sam and their five children were amongst the throng that had arrived that day. Esther was the first person Sam saw when they entered the camp. She was giving out blankets and sleeping bags to a line of people. "I don't mean to be interrupting nothing here, Miss," Sam began, removing his cap and gazing at the ground in that automatic gesture of deference Esther had seen the people adopt in the presence of whites or those they felt were their "betters." This was the etiquette of oppression, ground in over generations. Esther and all the others had come South to bring these people's gazes up from the ground.

"You'll have to go to the back of the line," Esther told him.

"It ain't a blanket I'm asking for right now. It's a favor," Sam said, daring a full glance at Esther. "You come out to the McKessin plantation a few weeks back. It was you and a man come out, talking to the folks about registering. You probably don't remember us, but we was in the crowd gathered at old Uncle Bob's place that night. Well, I went on down with one of the workers and registered and now I ain't got no place to stay. But I got a few dollars and I'm going to Hattiesburg to see if my folks'll take us in. I'm asking you to keep an eye out for my family here while I'm gone."

Luta Mae Allen stood beside her husband, her belly protruding in what, Esther guessed, was the eighth month of pregnancy. She stood beside her husband as fragile as a flower, as sturdy as a tree, old woman's age lines marring her still-young face. The children, in ill-fitting clothes covered with dust and grime gathered on the trip to the camp, stared openly at Esther and at the activity around them—people arriving, stations set up to give out clothing donated by people in the North, firewood, canned and surplus dried goods and tents.

"I'll be back in a day or so," Sam said. "Will you just watch over them? And see that they get everything they need?"

Esther promised she would and Sam told the oldest boy to do what he was told and to "take care of your mama."

The Allen family became Esther's charge. She got someone else to give out the blankets while she found a tent where Luta Mae could get off her feet. Luta Mae took slow, painful steps and sat down and accepted a glass of water gratefully. The oldest boy, Ben, who possessed his father's spry combination of hustle and self-effacement, managed to keep an eye on the other children while getting the supplies and help they required to set up while Esther continued working with other families. Later, she ate a dinner of cornbread and pork and beans with Luta Mae and her children. As they ate, Luta Mae said, "I'd be right grateful if you'd share our tent with us tonight. This baby feels like it might come any minute and having you nearby would be a blessing. We got two beds. You take one. The children'll make pallets on the floor. Sam'll be back soon, then we won't ask nothing more of you."

When Esther entered Luta Mae's tent that night, she stepped over several feet. The children slept on blankets on the cardboard floor, their aggressive, contented snores warming the tent like a smoldering fire. Esther removed her shoes and lay on the cot, pulling her poncho tighter around her shoulders. Her body smelled old and unwashed. The demands of the past two days had sunk into her muscles and congealed into a fatigue that, after all this time, still could defeat her. And yet she knew it would be an hour or more before she slept. Fear, anxiety, apprehension formed like a cloud over her each night, making her wakeful and strangely excited. Even as she lay in repose, her heart beat as if she were pursued, her eyes fearfully scanning the darkness. "Maybe us getting throwed off McKessin's place was a good thing." Luta Mae said lazily, as though continuing a conversation.

"Well, registering to vote was a good thing, no matter what the price," Esther replied, grateful for the woman's voice.

"Sam's folks and my folks been on that land long as we could remember. And no matter how much cotton we planted or growed, we never got outta McKessin's debt. Sam says now we can start over. We ain't got much. Just what we brung with us."

"Luta Mae, that's all you need."

"You got a man? A husband up North?" she inquired, her voice melting with a warm familiarity.

"Yes, there's somebody I love."

"How'd you leave him to come down here?" Luta Mae wondered, surprise raising her voice.

"You know, Luta Mae, sometimes I don't know. But I had to come here. When I left, there was nothing else I could do," Esther said, thinking of Randolph, really thinking of him for the first time in months. He lived in her memory, bold, inescapable. She never had to think of him. He was simply always there.

"You got kids?" Luta Mae asked.

"One. A boy. He's a little older than Ben," Esther confided softly.

"You miss him?"

"Sure. But I'm doing this for him too, Luta Mae. It's hard to see it, but I'm here for both of us."

This is what Esther told herself every day. And there were even days when it worked. Days when her inability to "mother" her own son and her willingness to lay her life, sanity, and tranquillity on the line for people who were strangers seemed less of the obscene contradiction she felt it to be in her heart. He would never forgive her, that is what Esther feared most when she thought of Logan. And Randolph would never again love her. Yet Naomi's embrace soothed Esther into sleep each night, no matter where she slept. She had tutored youngsters the age of her son in Freedom Schools across the South, yet had not seen Logan's report card in four years. She had lain in bed beside men with whom she had shared terror and bravery and clung to them as lovers. Yet she had not once written to Randolph, the man whose measure she had yet to find. But soon, very soon, she knew, there would be dues to pay. She wanted to pay her debts, collect what was owed her. And she had begun to feel the stirrings of a need for home—the face of her son, the sound of Randolph's voice, her mother's love. She was a prodigal, selfish and shameless, yet she was a woman larger now than even she knew. It would be a while, but soon she would go home, to see if she still had one, to build one if she did not.

"Y'alls some brave folks to come down here," Luta Mae said sleepily.

"You're the brave ones," Esther said.

Luta Mae yawned and turned on her side, the springs of the army cot squeaking, as she concluded, "I think maybe we's all brave."

The battlegrounds of the movement were plantations, classrooms, bus stations, swimming pools, lunch counters, libraries, courthouses, department stores, churches and jail cells. In southwest Georgia, Esther and twenty-five others were jailed in a cell made for four people for leading a prayer vigil. Outside the jail hundreds were being arrested in waves. Inside the cell humanity, packed as tightly as in a slave coffin, persevered, overcame. Freedom songs rang through the jail —pure, righteous, undefeated. Breakfast and dinner were cold grits and fatback on a tin plate. The toilet backed up after one day. At night the cell trembled with the sounds of fear and bad dreams rising like a fever from troubled, uneasy sleep. Esther wrote messages on scraps of toilet paper to movement workers in other cells and watched the orderlies smuggle the words across the hall. She spent fourteen days in the cell, watched as others were bailed out one by one.

Esther and the other workers remained, in solidarity with those who could not make bail.

For years after that jailing, those fourteen days when her life was confined and determined by the borders of a cell haunted Esther in nightmares and loomed behind her when she left the jail cell. The word *freedom*, sung or chanted or shouted, swelled in her mouth and in her imagination with a fervor so intense, uttering the word could choke her with tears. At unexpected moments—once when she lay in the arms of a lover in a small house in Hattiesburg, Mississippi, once as she sat teaching a man to read—the bars of the cell flashed before her eyes, as gruesome as the unexpected sight of blood, and yanked her back behind their steely, desolate embrace. Both times Esther ran, ran as far as she could go from the cell's grasp, ran to feel the wind against her skin, the sun on her arms and the feel of freedom all around her.

How would she ever be normal again, when the abnormal and the extraordinary had scarred her so deep? Esther had witnessed cowardice that made her mute and courage of the kind that made her want to live forever, just to witness it again. And yet it was over. It was done. There was no more for her to do. Others stayed because they were shaped to run the long distance life in a manner that did not belong to her. Esther left the South because she knew it was simply time to come home.

Though she was only sixty-two, Naomi's hair was now prematurely, solidly white. Awaiting Esther's return, praying for her safety had driven the rich black color from her hair. The sight of her mother's hair and the crevicelike worry lines across Naomi's forehead informed Esther, as did nothing else, of the price her family had paid for what she had chosen to do. Naomi said nothing the evening she saw Esther get out of a taxi in front of the house, for she had seen her daughter's return in a dream a week earlier. Naomi was not surprised, yet she was limp with gratitude. As she watched Esther get out of the taxi and turn to look at Naomi and the house, Naomi stood up from the metal folding chair she sat in and shouted to Esther, "Come on up here, gal. I knew you was coming home tonight and I got a sweet potato pie in the house with your name on it." Esther ascended the stairs, walking with an assurance, a resoluteness that she flaunted like a prize she had won. She was heavier and there was a bright tremor of sadness in her eyes—a clue to what she had seen—that Naomi knew would always be there. The sight of Esther had started Naomi's heart beating so fast she thought she might faint and so she held on tighter to the banister, clutching it to calm her overexcited spirit. And when Esther reached the top step and gazed into her mother's face, she could only say what she had wanted, through her love of Randolph, the birth of her child, her flight from them all, to say: "Mama, I'm home."

That night Esther sat up with her mother and son until 3 A.M. Logan, now nearly as tall as Randolph, muscular, his face both boyish and restlessly masculine, held Esther in his arms in silent, total possession when he bounded into the living room, summoned from next door by a phone call from Naomi. Esther felt in her son's embrace everything he expected of her, all he had ever asked and would now demand. And she felt his tears against her neck and for the first time she held him as he held her, unconditionally, fiercely. Esther lay Logan's head on her suddenly strong shoulder and stroked him, stroked the child he would never be again, stroked the man he was becoming. But finally she had to break Logan's grip, for he held her for the five years she had missed. And Esther knew what her son refused to believe—they would never get those years back.

They all sat up until early morning, Naomi plying Esther with food, Logan alternating between moments when he looked at his mother as if he did not believe what he saw and nonstop questions about what she had done.

The next morning Naomi brought Esther her breakfast in bed. She entered the bedroom and found Esther awake, staring out the window, gazing at the street. "I brought you two strips of bacon, two eggs, grits and toast, just like you like them," Naomi said, placing the tray on Esther's lap.

"Oh, Mama, after all that food last night," Esther groaned.

"That's why I didn't fix much. Just go on and eat. It'll be good for you." Naomi shushed her.

Watching Esther eat slowly, Naomi said, "I'm not gonna ask you no whole lot about what you seen and did down there, I can look at your face and get my answer. I just want you to know I was always praying and I was always proud of you. I don't know if I could've done what you did."

"Mama, you had no road map when you left down there and came up here and you found your way pretty good. I learned to read signs by watching you." Esther looked at Naomi as the sun filtered through the curtains.

"Mama, your hair. I know that's from me. You were praying. And maybe you were proud, but I know you were worried. I made you old."

"You turned me gray," Naomi said primly. "That's not the same thing as getting old. I ain't decided yet to get old. Don't know when I'll get around to doing that."

"Mama!"

"Don't start apologizing. I might just put you on a bus and send you back on down there. You made your bed. You chose your life. It's not mine, its yours. Don't apologize to nobody."

"What do I tell Logan?" Esther asked, letting her fork fall from her hand with a sigh.

"Tell him the same thing you told me, *I'm home!* That's what a man would say and everybody'd feel like they'd been blessed. And wouldn't nobody dare mention the time he'd been away. He was your son while you was gone. Just like I was your mama."

"How do I explain?"

"You can't," Naomi assured her daughter, as if these words explained everything. "Baby, you can't."

When she finished eating, Esther bundled herself beneath the spread. She lay looking out on the sidewalk, too full of the pain and triumph of what she had seen on her mother's face and in her son's eyes to imagine a way to fashion answers to Logan's questions. And yet he was on the threshold of entering the world that Esther had helped to shape and so he would insist on answers as neither Naomi nor Randolph would. At this thought, so heavy and burdensome, Esther fell asleep. When she woke up two hours later, she saw Logan sitting in a wicker chair in the corner of the room, watching her. Logan gazed at his mother so full of love that Esther allowed herself to believe that the demands she had felt in his embrace might go unacknowledged. Instead Logan came and sat on the bed and asked Esther, "Why did you come back?"

Esther stretched and then let her hand rest on Logan's cheek and said, "I'd done as much as I could do."

He hoped she would say, "I came back to see you. Because I missed you more than I could stand." But she had denied him those hallowed words, which had been the music of his dreams.

"What was it like down there?" he pressed on. Esther closed her eyes and threw her arm across her face, as if to block out the question.

Finally she said, "It was too much. Too much of everything—the good and the bad."

"Was it worth it?" At the solemnity of the question Esther opened her eyes.

"If I didn't think it was worth it, I couldn't have come

back to face any of you. Not with the price I asked you to pay."

Logan sat—still, unsatisfied—savoring the sight of Esther. The tiny, almost indistinguishable threads of gray in her thick wild Afro, the feel of her hands, callused and tough now, not soft as he remembered them. There was simply so much more of her now. Logan wondered if she was as amazed by the sight of him as he was by the sight of her.

"Mama says you're off to Columbia University in September."

"Yes, ma'am."

"They give you a scholarship?"

"Uh-huh."

Esther sat up and held Logan's head tightly against her breast. And she thought of the illiterate sharecroppers, the bulging-bellied children and the shacks she had left behind. There were no words to tell her son about that and so she simply repeated what Naomi had told her, "All the time, Logan, please believe me, every day I prayed for you and every day I was proud."

Logan had lived on the memory of his mother. And the glow of memory transformed Esther into an obedient cooperative phantom, too intangible to possess but too elusive to disappoint. Now Esther had returned and this real-life mother —flesh and blood, tears and smiles—was more immune to his love than she had ever been lodged in his memory. Esther had stolen five years of his life and Logan felt the absence of those years like an object he had hoarded and then lost. Logan felt he was owed an accounting. Had she squandered the years, frittered them away, lavished them on someone else now resident in her heart? Had those years been better to her than they were to him? What had she done with those years that were not only hers but his as well? What had she done with their life?

One afternoon when Esther was out, Logan went into her room and rummaged through her bureau drawers. She was easing out of the blue jeans and men's work shirts and into skirts and dresses again. And, rummaging through the clothes from Esther's past, Logan found the diary. It was a dark brown leatherbound book, its cover ravaged and worn. Logan felt no shame, no sense of impropriety as he held the book in his hand, felt, in fact, that what he was about to do was his right. Even Esther's handwriting had changed—the first entries were written in a neat, meticulous script that was self-conscious and restricted. As the dates progressed, from 1963 to '65, '66, '67, the script grew bolder, the lines longer and wider, in some places indecipherable, as though she sought both to hide and reveal, as if the words, their very formation, was a code only the initiated could break. And yet Logan understood everything. Reading the words— evolving, retreating, changing before his eyes—he heard the gallant rhythm and majesty of freedom songs and the shouts of defeat and praise at the funerals that filled so many pages of the book and he saw hate and fear and pride and yet, even though he now knew that Esther had used those years, *their* years, in ways that were inevitable and necessary, the book still did not reveal enough. He had finished reading the diary and sat on Esther's bed with it in his lap, unable to move, when he heard Naomi and Esther enter the house. When he heard Esther come up the stairs, he sat perfectly still, patiently awaiting discovery.

Esther entered the room and the smile that started across her face froze at the sight of the diary.

"Oh, Logan, why'd you do it this way?" she asked plaintively. "I'd have told you about it one day. I'd have told you everything you wanted to know. I can't now. It's too soon.

It's still too fresh." Esther reached for the diary. "You didn't have to do it this way."

"Sure, I could've waited another five years to find out about the *first* five," Logan shouted, rising from the bed. He stood up and found himself, to his surprise, a few feet taller than Esther. "You walk in just the way you walked out. No excuses. No answers. No questions. You owe me," he shouted. "I'm your son. You're my mother. You owe me. I want those years back."

Esther watched her son transformed by a rage she feared might move him to strike her. When she reached to touch him, Logan moved out of her reach.

"All right," Esther told him. "You're a man and this is your first lesson as a man. I can't give you those years back. And you'll have to forgive me. You'll have to, in order to be my son or your father's son. If you don't forgive me, Logan, it's you who'll be hurting from now on. I carved out my share of suffering a long time ago. You're late, kid. You can't shame me no more than I've shamed myself in my thoughts. I'll never forgive myself for leaving you like I did. But you're my son, Logan, you've got to."

The next day Esther decided to go see Randolph. She had been back a week. Bruised by Logan's anger, Esther looked forward to Randolph as though he was her last possible source of redemption. She found herself hungry for him, her desire sparked as much by curiosity as by longing. Naomi had told Esther that Randolph was now divorced and was living in a house by himself and she had told Esther, as well, that he still loved her.

Walking along Fourteenth Street, Esther was stunned by the damage and loss inflicted by the uprising. Whole buildings had collapsed into a mere pile of bricks and debris. The charred, hulking frames of several stores rose like beasts in a nightmare, hovering over the street. She passed a dark, stench-filled alley and saw a young man hunched beside a garbage can, sticking a needle into his arm. It was two-thirty in the afternoon, yet the destruction lent an eerie, otherworld quality to the once-bustling corridor. Some stores had somehow escaped damage, their survival seeming more serendipitous than resulting from the SOUL BROTHER signs that remained in some windows. DIE WHITEY had been spray-painted on the brick side of a building and a photo of Martin Luther King, Jr., lay among a small mountain of trash on a corner.

The Eden Bar and Grill and the stores immediately surrounding it stood intact, unscathed. From the inside of the Eden Bar and Grill, Esther heard the sound of Aretha's ecstatic, mournful, confession "Since You've Been Gone." As she opened the door, Aretha's voice pleaded, "Take me back ..." The restaurant was empty and Aretha's voice echoed, cavernous and lonely. The shock of sunlight entered the room with Esther. She heard the whir of overhead fans. Somehow she'd expected to see Forty Carats and even Geraldine, but she saw first, in the afternoon darkness, posters along the walls, advertising the Temptations, Gladys Knight and the Pips, photos of James Brown, Jimi Hendrix, Marvin Gaye.

But what surprised Esther most was the emptiness of the place. The decor had been changed to a color that was a harsh fluorescent mix of brilliant shades. Overhead, a ball twirled and threw a shimmering cascade of stars onto the floor. A wall-high drawing of a go-go dancer claimed an entire wall. And the area that once had mostly been for dining had been turned into a dance floor. At the bar a young man in a sweatshirt that read NATION TIME stood before the wall-length mirror and picked out his hair with a plastic Afro comb. Esther walked up to the bar and when the young man had finished with his hair she asked, "Is Randolph Spenser here?"

"Yeah, he's in the back. You want to see him, sister?"

"I'm a friend of his. Just tell me where he is."

"In his office."

A side exit by the kitchen led to a narrow hallway. Esther knocked on the door.

"Who is it?"

She didn't know what to say so she merely opened the door and walked inside.

"Well I'll be damned!" Randolph shouted, throwing down the pen he'd been using to go over his books and covering his face in surprise. "Come on in. Come on in," he told her, standing up and pulling Esther from the doorway into the office. Randolph gazed at Esther uncertainly, eagerness competing with control. "Sit down. Sit down," he said finally, straightening up the small sofa cluttered with papers and books and a jacket. "When did you get back?" he asked.

"Just the other day," Esther lied. She did not want him to know that she had waited a week to see him.

"You look . . ." he said, assessing her, his eyes roaming from her face to her legs.

"I put on some weight."

"Didn't do you no harm."

"The place looks different."

"Times changed. I had to keep up with them."

"How'd this place escape the riots?"

"I was sitting at home, watching it on TV. I was seeing stores owned by friends go up in flames. I got in my car and came over here with my shotgun. Stood out front and dared anybody to even think about throwing a rock or a Molotov cocktail at the place. They got the message and ran past me up the street."

"How's business?"

"How do you think? Slow, real slow. The riots killed business. Just killed it. Who wants to spend Saturday night in an area that looks like Hiroshima? Folks trickle in on Friday and Saturday nights. I got a go-go dancer comes in and shakes her stuff around. But it'll never again be like it was. Those days are gone. I'm even thinking about getting the place off my hands. I just don't know who'd buy it now. Overnight, the location cut the value in half."

The sound of his voice—its rhythm, intensity—set Esther at ease and she sat back against the sofa.

"You finished up down there?" he asked slowly, looking at Esther as though there was no way he'd ever get enough of what he saw.

"I'm finished. Mama told me all you did for Logan."

"You forget? I'm his daddy. I did no more than when you were here."

"What made you get a divorce?"

"After the boys left home, it just seemed there was no more reason to stay. We both knew that. I let her have the house. I'm still paying the last of the mortgage."

"Blood money?"

"She deserved it."

Esther saw Randolph's slight paunch, the receding hairline, the patient eyes and knew she still loved him. Randolph stubbed out a cigarette in an ashtray and said simply, "Girl, I ain't done nothing since you left but wait for you to come back." Esther reached for his hand and gave herself up to him with a glance. Randolph said in a husky, low whisper, "Come on, let's go."

Quiet, agitated with desire, they drove to Randolph's house—a small home on a quiet tree-lined street in Northeast, not far from where he had lived with Mary. When he parked before the house he told Esther, "I thought about moving into an apartment but then I kept thinking about you coming back one day and I wanted a place big enough for all of us. I swore to myself we'd be a real family before it was over and that's what I aim for us to be."

Inside the house filled with nondescript furniture that felt as though it was yet to be fully possessed, a house that was as lonely as the man who called it home, Randolph led Esther upstairs to his bedroom. He quickly closed the door behind him, as if to prevent her escape. Esther sat on the bed in a pink blouse, under which she wore no bra, and a blue skirt, beneath which her thighs awaited Randolph's touch. Randolph knelt on the floor beside the bed and kissed Esther, his tongue unearthing her mouth, his hands roughly massaging her hair, her neck and shoulders. He unbuttoned her blouse, his hands so eager they fumbled like a careless child's. Randolph let his hands rest on her breasts, which, like the rest of her, were fuller, more radiant than before. He held her breasts in his palms and leaned forward with a groan to suckle them hard, his hands breaking the button at the back of her skirt, palms sliding into the thin sliver of cloth of her panties. Esther fell back on the bed and raised her hips, guiding Randolph's hands as he pulled off her skirt and panties. And now he saw all of her, the parts he had missed and yearned for, and he looked at her so full of desire he wondered why he did not explode. There was her dark brown skin and her ass—a full, high-riding Black woman's ass—that he leaned over to kiss, so grateful was he for the sight of it. Randolph gazed in wonder at her vagina, covered by tufts of hair as unruly and stubborn as she. He buried his face in her and she smelled of some gentle cologne and sweat and Ivory soap and longing for him and she tasted better than she used to and there was her hand inside his pants, releasing him, and he wanted to kiss her, there, forever, and there was her mouth on him, a perfect fit, loving him as he loved her, had always loved her, had never stopped loving her and he cried, "Never stop. Never stop," releasing so fast, so full she could not take all of him, let him go, yet let her fingertips discover him again as he shriveled, satisfied and happy, against her neck.

Randolph knew that Esther would not believe that he had

dreamed of this moment while she was away, dreamed of it even as some other woman, some woman he was just marking time with, lay beside him. He was almost fifty and yet the years had taught him the meaning of dreams. He knew she would not believe him if he told her how he could hardly remember the names or faces of the other women, so little had they meant to him. Nobody believed men had hearts, not even the women who loved them. So they lay in bed the rest of the day and that night, sleeping in each other's arms, stirred periodically by a precise, perfect passion. And for the first time since he'd moved into it, that night Randolph's house sheltered him like home.

A month after her return, Esther moved in with Randolph. Together they gloried in the mundane, went bowling on Saturday nights, turned grocery shopping into an adventure. They made friends with other couples, visited Naomi for Sunday dinner. Logan, however, insisted on remaining with Naomi, overwhelmed and confused by the sudden intense domesticity of his parents. Still, Esther was happy. There were days when she felt light-headed, so complete was her pleasure. And she felt that it was only a matter of time before Logan would bestow forgiveness and acceptance upon her by choosing to live in his father's house.

In September Logan entered Columbia University. The day before Randolph drove Logan to New York, Esther came to Naomi's house to talk to her son. Since their verbal showdown and her reconciliation with Randolph, Esther and Logan had alternated between wary appreciation and befuddlement over the etiquette that would shape and control their feelings. Begrudgingly, Logan had come to respect Esther's sacrifices and to acknowledge, though not accept, that they could never retrieve the years they had lost. Imprisoned by contradictory emotions he did not know how to express and refused again to unleash, Logan waited for a miracle.

Although he and Randolph would not leave until 5 A.M.

the next morning, Esther found Logan in his room, his suit-
cases packed, boxes of books and records lined up beside his
desk.

When Esther entered the room, Logan looked up, surprised
to see her. And as she often did now, before saying a word,
Esther reached for Logan and held him tightly. She held him
as if his journey symbolized a conclusion that she would
reverse by the pressure of her embrace. And Logan never
resisted Esther's touch now. He looked at her sometimes
when she came upon him with a childlike stare that somehow
fit his young man's face, sprouting the beginnings of a beard.

When she released him, Esther said, "You think they'll let
you keep that beard up there?"

"Why not?"

"I guess you're right," Esther conceded. "Short skirts, long
hair, anything goes now." As they sat on Logan's bed, she
told him, "I don't have any profound words of wisdom for
you. Just go and do your best. You scared?"

"Nope."

"Not even a little?"

"Why should I be?"

"I don't know. I think I'd be scared and I want you to
know there's nothing wrong with feeling that way sometimes."

"I knew that already."

"You know, this education you're going off to get would
be a wonder to most people I worked with in the South.
There's still plenty of people can't read down there—I've met
whole families in some cases. But you know, even not knowing how to read, those people are still smart. They understand
human nature in a manner as sophisticated as a psychologist,
almost like forest animals whose senses are so sharp and fine
they can hear or smell danger coming miles off. Living always
on the edge of things, not never having much and knowing
what they had could be taken away simply because some

white man or woman changed their mind, didn't like how they looked or was in a evil mood, gave them a kind of second sight, a gift for seeing deeper than just on the surface."

"You make illiteracy sound noble."

"I don't mean to. Their worlds are small. And so much of what they need to know is written and hidden in books. Law books in libraries they couldn't use kept secret the fact that all their rights were already there to be enforced. Since they couldn't read, they couldn't get their hands on the kind of information that would allow them to design their lives rather than endure them.

"I taught a ninety-three-year-old woman on a tenant farm to read and write. She told me she wanted to learn so she could write with her own hands what she wanted put on her tombstone. We started out reading funeral home calendars, then moved to a church hymnal, then the Bible. I tried to get her to read the newspapers but she said she wasn't interested in the news 'cause it was all things she'd heard before. So I got her to reading and writing pretty well and a few months later we sat up one night and she wrote her will and epitaph. She got in bed that night and she didn't say goodnight. She said goodbye. And when I came around the next day, the whole family was crying. She'd died in her sleep. I went into her room and pulled back the sheets and that old woman had died with a small, crooked smile on her face. She hadn't had much say about her life, but she'd managed to have the last word about her death."

Esther rested her arm on Logan's shoulder and said, "Take that old lady's spirit with you in every classroom you go into."

Logan had waited for a miracle. And it had arrived as miracles do, with so much simplicity that not until Esther removed her arm from his shoulder was he aware of what he had received.

▮ ▮ ▮

The quiet cold January morning entered the bedroom carried on rays of muted sun. Randolph lay on his elbow, watching Esther, her body still, wrapped in a slumber that remained as poised and undefinable as she.

They had made love during the night, waking simultaneously from a light, fanciful sleep to reach for each other with confident arms. Esther lay naked beside him and Randolph watched and measured her body as he had done, without her knowledge, every morning that she had lain beside him since her return. He had always known that she would come back. But that he would easily construct a new life with her had been beyond his imagination. When he had thought of her return, Randolph's daydreams began and ended with them merely saying hello.

Esther had told him after dinner the night before that she was pregnant, that she wanted to have their child and that she wanted, more than anything else, for them to marry. Randolph had been content to age steadily, predictably. Yet the thought of a child made him realize, as few other things had, that he did not really want to grow old, that he did not want to die.

He had three sons and each one had chiseled out a life that was in some way a rebuke to him. Wayne had been discharged dishonorably from the navy and, the last he'd heard from Mary, Wayne was working as a security guard and got into a fight with his boss and was fired. He couldn't seem to keep a job or a woman, reaching for both with a grasp so defiant that it spurned all that it sought to claim. And every time he talked to Mary, she made Randolph feel that if he'd been a better father, a more honorable man, Wayne's life would have turned out differently. He'd run into Wayne at a gas station a month ago and they'd stood before each other, shuffling their feet, avoiding each other's eyes, rescued from the painful reunion by the girl in Wayne's car, who honked the horn and bellowed his name so impatiently that Wayne fled from Randolph's sight without explanation. And yet he'd thought about the boy for days after and thought to call him, though he never did.

Marshall was a clerk in a hardware store in Southeast. He was so placid, his life so uneventful and calm, that Randolph wondered sometimes if he was indeed his son. It was Marshall—big, strapping, still clumsy, so quiet he made you nervous—who remembered his birthday and every Father's Day gave him a tie. It was Marshall who, yes, loved him despite who he'd been, what he'd done. And in his heart Randolph would've given anything for even half of that love to come from Wayne. Marshall was engaged to marry a young Jehovah's Witness, a severe young woman whose face was etched in permanent disdain and who, when Randolph met her in Marshall's apartment, had looked at him as though she instinctively knew all his sins. The girl talked to Marshall like he was a child and Randolph was still figuring out how he could get out of going to the wedding.

Not one of his sons would know how to handle his businesses. Logan, smart, too sensitive, kept his head in books. Wayne was too mean, Marshall too oblivious to carry his businesses into the future. He had worked thirty years for it to end like this. To end with him. There had been times he was so angry at his sons' lack of commitment to his enterprises that he thought of torching every property to spite them all.

But now he had another chance. That's what children were. And they'd get married this time, do it right. All the young folks were running around, splitting the world wide open, the white kids telling their parents they'd made a mess of things and they might as well go on to hell and the Black kids telling the white man to move over and all of them flaunting sex like it was a toy. They ran around talking about *free love*. Hell, that's how you knew they were kids—they hadn't learned yet how much love cost, thought desire alone was gonna buy them a free ride. No, he didn't want nothing for free. Not a thing. Randolph moved closer to Esther and she moaned gently in her sleep. He felt her stomach, wondered how large his child was, if he had eyes, a nose, could he laugh, cry, was he equipped to pay his price.

When Esther moved into the house with him, Randolph had seen her stacking her things on the dresser and that's when he saw the birth control pills. She had left them up there, right where he could see them. And that night he'd told her, "I don't want you to use no pills. I don't want a thing to come between us."

"You ready to handle what that means?" she asked.

"You know I am."

"You sound like one of those *Birth control is genocide against Black people* folks," she'd laughed nervously.

"Ain't nobody in this bed but you and me. The white man ain't under the sheets with us. But I waited too long for you to come back. And I don't plan to hold out on you. Don't you hold out on me."

Soon the pills were gone and Esther began to give herself to Randolph with a startling grace and gratitude that sometimes made Randolph so happy he was almost afraid. It seemed to Randolph that Esther had grown up in his arms. For in his arms she had become a woman, conceived a child, gone mad, denied him, planned her flight to the South. She had come back, knowing that his arms awaited her and that they contained even more challenges than before. His arms —resting place, prison, inspiration.

The sun had risen fully now and with it Esther's smell seemed to fill the room as well—the musky, humid smell that he loved. Randolph turned on his back. God had given him another day and all the others, he felt sure now, were guaranteed.

This child, Esther was certain, would redeem her. The in-difference that had characterized her first pregnancy had been replaced by a heart-stopping happiness and anticipation that was reflected in her skin, clearer and softer than she could ever recall, her hair, which suddenly began to grow massive and thick, and a sturdy sense of well-being so powerful she wondered if it could possibly last. She was thirty-nine years old and felt at last self-aware, bristling with the knowledge that women wait for to transform and save their lives. Her intense desire for this child, the blossoming of her maternal instincts, was merely one of the ways Esther had designed as a method to discover herself.

It had never occurred to her not to give birth to Logan, even in the face of Naomi's suggestion of an abortion. At nineteen, Esther's vision of womanhood encompassed only the narrowest range of choices. At nineteen, Esther could not imagine painting a landscape for her life drenched in as many tones, riddled by as many contours as her life now possessed. Guilt-ridden, afraid, she had returned home to find love in-tact, worn at the edges, still possible. She had returned, brim-ming with a knowledge too exacting to share yet that inspired respect and wonder in the hearts of those who mattered most. And now she loved herself as she never had before. She loved herself and jealously guarded that love, savored the thought of it at times when she was alone, laughed aloud at the pleasure of it, hoarded it, felt it possess and define her.

For the first time, Esther was prepared to allow herself to be happy.

N A O M I

Well, I just sat back and watched. Watched my daughter enjoy the peace she'd found. They say the only reason we know how good it feels to be happy is 'cause we've been sad. I don't think I've ever seen two people happier than Randolph and Esther once they got together again. Randolph lost weight, got rid of that stomach he'd been letting himself get out of sheer laziness. And by the time Esther had been back two months, I swear he looked ten years younger. And Esther'd come over to the house after she moved in with Randolph and we'd talk like we were trying to make up for all we couldn't say the years she was in the South. And she told me stories about what she'd seen and done that made my heart break. And even then I knew she wasn't telling it all. She didn't say much, but I think it was easier for her to tell me all that stuff than Randolph and Logan 'cause it was their hearts she broke. She knew that since I'm her mama, short of her going out and robbing and killing, if she did anything halfway in the realm of reason, I'd find a way to understand. I think me raising Esther all those years by my-self, with it just being the two of us, gave us something deeper than just being mother and daughter. I had to be her mama, her daddy and, yes, even her friend sometimes. And that girl witnessed more of my mistakes and sorrows up close than anybody except Rayford. With it being just the two of us all those years, we had to learn to get along with each other, no matter what. She was my daughter, so I couldn't just get mad and stomp out like a husband or boyfriend would have, I couldn't try to get back at her, spite her 'cause she hurt me, the way a child would when he feels left out or unloved. All flowers don't grow at the same speed beneath the same sun. Esther bloomed when she was ready. I'm just glad I never stopped tilling the soil.

Chapter Twenty-One

Lor Logan, the sight of his parents now was as satisfying as gazing upon some delicate object of art. He had spent his childhood yearning for what Randolph and Esther now possessed, yet the arrival of this nuclear community of love caught him off-guard, unprepared to render himself up into its grasp. Randolph was the most comfortable of the three of them, loving Esther and Logan as though the roles of husband and father were ones that he had merely waited to play, with a good humor and generosity that surpassed all their expectations. With her son Esther acted more as friend than mother, assessing Logan with a detachment rooted in respect that he found occasionally more valuable than unbiased maternal devotion. Yet Logan had not yet learned to take his parents for granted, he was afraid to.

One spring weekend Logan came home from Columbia and stayed with Esther and Randolph. He arrived home wearing an Afro and carrying a copy of *The Autobiography of Malcolm X*. He was dubious yet excited about Esther's pregnancy. After dinner, while Esther washed dishes in the kitchen, Randolph told Logan, "Your mama and me decided on the date for the wedding, the third Sunday in May. And I want you to be my best man."

"What do I have to do?"

"Stand beside me. Make sure I don't make a fool of myself." With a nod of his head toward the kitchen, Randolph asked, "How does it feel to have her back?"

"There's times I'm still afraid she'll walk away," Logan admitted.

"You too?" Randolph laughed. "I waited for this for a long time. And I don't want to blow it."

"Are you scared?"

"Sure. I don't want her to know it, though. I made a mess of my first marriage and although I want to get married again there's moments I'm not sure I'm qualified. And Esther, she's been free so long I don't know if she can stand the reining in us being together will require. You know what I'd like you to give us as a wedding present?"

"What?"

"Forgive us. Me for never giving you a real home before now and your mama for leaving the home you had." Logan traced the water rings his glass had left on the tablecloth, avoiding his father's gaze.

"Will you think about it?" Randolph asked.

"That's all I've ever thought about," Logan told him. "It's all I ever really wanted to do."

A week later Randolph went upstairs after dinner to take a nap. He had slept for half an hour and dreamed about Esther, who seemed, in the dream, to be very far away. In the dream, he could hear her voice, but he could not see her. Suddenly in the darkness, Randolph was startled into wakefulness by the sound of his own breathing. He heard Esther and Logan talking in the living room, their voices floating up the stairs and down the hallway as from the other side of the world. He heard Esther's deep, melodic laughter and Randolph sat up and felt his heart turn over, contract with a pain so severe his throat jammed with pain. Esther's voice seeped through the blanket of pain, but already it sounded like a memory. His heart clenched—viselike, tight—pushed against his chest and Randolph tried to call Esther but his lungs made no sound. Pain had pushed all sound from his throat. He was sweating, drenched and clammy, trying to get off the bed, he thought, to crawl downstairs, the fear pumping him more full of death than the betrayal of his heart. Randolph's right arm was limp, paralyzed, and his heart seemed steadily to devour every part of him. And since he could not say Esther's name, Randolph thought it, let the letters blaze like a neon sign in this feeble final consciousness. And the last thing he thought was that she had made him think life was wonderful, convinced him you could win when it was really all a bitch, really, always a bitch, to die when he finally had every reason to live.

INHERITANCE

Chapter Twenty-Two

N A O M I

A coupla days after the funeral, Logan asked me how God could take his daddy away from him like that, just as Esther and Randolph was fixing to do the one thing they'd never had the courage to do before. And then he asked me how the Lord could take Randolph away before he graduated from college, his only son to do such a thing. I didn't have an answer for the boy. He didn't know it, but

I was as shook up by Randolph's death as him and Esther. So I just sat in my rocking chair and kept my peace. We were sitting in front of the fireplace that day. Two days after Randolph died, a blizzard come, seem like out of nowhere, and just covered the city. But sitting in front of the fireplace, I was chilled down to the bone, looking at my grandson with no words to say. We sat there for a while, listening to the crackling of the fire, Logan all twisted and mad and no way to let go of all he felt.

Then, just like that blizzard come unexpected, the quieter and more still I sat there, with Logan, the more I could feel a answer forming. And so I says, "You know, Logan, we always put all the blame on the Lord. Wondering why things go wrong. How come life's not perfect and just the way we want it to be. And I've done it plenty times myself, got mad with God 'cause He did things His way 'stead of mine. Well, I don't have no special pipeline to heaven but I *do* know that the question's not really *Why did God do this to me?* The question you got to ask is *How do I find what God give me, to get through it?* Then open up your eyes and look around you like you looking for money somebody told you was hid where you live, like you looking for love been promised and you can feel it coming to you. Look like that for the answer, Logan, and you can't help but find it."

That's all I said and just saying that little bit 'bout wore me out. And then Logan comes over to me and hugs me real hard and real tight. And I feel a little bit of that madness with God coming out as he's holding me. And the boy is holding on like he's trying to get rid of something he's got and take something of mine. When he's through, he sits back down in the chair facing me and wipes his eyes and says, "But I hate God. Right now I hate Him. And I'm scared I always will."

"Don't you worry 'bout that, boy," I told him. "The important thing is, God loves you and what you feeling now's got no effect on that love. That's the promise, Logan, and that's the answer you got to find."

Randolph dying like that, kinda set Logan free. Randolph had give that boy what he needed to find and make a way. So when Logan came home for the summer that year, I told him he had to go on and live with Esther. I told him she needed him and he needed her. Oh, he put up a big fuss, arguing, complaining, give a whole speech about the years she was away. And I just listened and told him, "You got a mama and soon you gonna have a baby brother or sister. And if you don't get your butt over there where you belong, you got no right to carry your daddy's name. And you leaving this house tonight 'cause if you don't pack your bags, I'll pack them for you."

So I drove him over to Esther's house and the two of them were skittish and awkward around each other. I didn't stay long, just long enough to tell them both that Randolph was dead but he wasn't gone so they better watch they steps and if they didn't find some way to love one another, Randolph and me both was gonna come back to haunt them.

ogan's last years at Columbia became a time to be endured. He performed with efficiency but with little passion. He made the dean's list and watched the campus protests against everything from war to sexism, racism, the university's expansion into Harlem, germ warfare and military research on college campuses. Logan had concluded that the world's threshold for peace and justice was miserably low and, moreover, that the world would never be much better than it was then. Professors returned Logan's papers and reports with comments applauding the suppleness of his mind, his cerebral passion for analysis. Yet Logan felt that his father's death had taught him everything he really needed to know.

When Logan entered Tufts Medical School, one of fifteen Blacks out of one hundred and fifty students in that year's class, the optimism that he had held at bay as an undergraduate engulfed him and invested his pursuit of medicine with an urgency that was both unfamiliar and welcome. He became a member of the Black Medical Students Caucus, which pushed for the development of more community health programs and the recruitment of more Black students. The camaraderie Logan shared with his fellow Black students endowed them all with weapons to survive the white patients who refused to be examined by a Black doctor, white professors who implied that Blacks were ill-equipped to be surgeons and the Black patients who asked white interns to assure them that the Black student doctor knew what he was doing.

The simplicity of the profession amazed him, for his task was primarily talking to people, analyzing what was wrong and helping to fix it. This combination of the mundane and the miraculous retained Logan's loyalty to a profession that he had not chosen but that had claimed him.

The demands of medical school and then his internship distanced Logan from his family in ways that he felt he would pay for someday. Esther gave birth, six months after Randolph's death, to a boy that they had decided to name Nathaniel. Like Logan, Nathaniel shared Randolph's high-cheekboned face, yet, just as Logan bore the stamp of Esther's solemnity, Nathaniel, even as a child, strode amongst them with a vigor that conjured echoes of Randolph. Esther, Naomi and Logan were grateful for the memory, yet each shivered at the thought of what it could portend.

They had become a family that gathered at Thanksgiving, Christmas and Easter and then only if Logan's rotation at the hospital allowed it. Yet even during these visits, Logan could see in Esther the latent talent for motherhood in full bloom. On each visit Esther handed Logan a new stack of photos she had taken of Nathaniel, gushing with pride over the color snapshots. She bought clothes for Nathaniel and read to the boy at bedtime and engaged the child in long conversations about everything around him with such patience and unabashed interest that Logan, at the age of twenty-six, was gripped by a burgeoning envy of his seven-year-old sibling.

One Easter Logan journeyed home and as he stood beside Esther at the kitchen sink, drying dinner dishes, listening to Naomi and Nathaniel in the living room singing some childish song as they watched "Sesame Street," he heard himself ask, "It really fits you this time—motherhood, I mean?"

"I *decided* it would fit me," Esther said emphatically, placing one of the good china dishes carefully in the drainer.

"Why didn't it fit you before? Was it so hard? Was I so different?" Logan asked, ashamed of the pleading sound of his voice.

"I was different, Logan. I was still a child myself," Esther said, casting her gaze staunchly into the soapy water. "I was nineteen years old when I had you."

"Why'd you have me?" It was the one question he always wanted to ask.

"Because I thought all the questions, all the doubts I had about being a grown-up, becoming a woman, would be answered," Esther said, drying her hands on her apron and leaning against the counter.

"It seemed so easy, you know, loving another person, taking care of them. What was living if it wasn't that? And then, when I had you, I got scared. And, Logan, I was scared for so many years and nobody knew. Scared that having you meant I couldn't have anything else, so I just *took* what I was scared I wouldn't have—something grand and big, something I could lose myself in and hide from what I feared—and I walked away from you. Not because I didn't love you. It was never that. I was afraid I couldn't love us both. And, Logan, I'll never be able to love you as much as I can if you don't let me. And you're still trying to decide whether you will."

Esther's awareness of the awful fragility of his affection stunned Logan. She was his mother and so she saw him with eyes telescopic with understanding. And in that very examination were the seeds of love, in that quest the proof.

A year into his residency at Boston City Hospital Logan married. He had been dating Sylvia Braithwaite for over two years and the prospect of setting up his practice and edging each day closer to the age of thirty inspired in Logan a need for predictability that allowed him to ignore the absence of a riveting desire for the woman he chose to be his wife.

When she was eleven, Sylvia's parents and two brothers were killed in a fire that destroyed the family's Roxbury double-decker house. Subsequently, Sylvia was raised by an older, childless aunt and uncle who enforced a decorum and rectitude upon her childhood that Sylvia gratefully accepted, as a way of absolving her guilt for surviving. She was a woman who camouflaged her liveliness behind glasses she did not need, a matronly hairstyle and an air of self-effacement that appeared, to the casual observer, as a singular form of piety. Sylvia sang in the church choir with a gusty abandon that, Logan was certain, could stop angels in their tracks, yet she rarely even hummed outside the walls of her church. Once Sylvia showed Logan a children's book she had written and illustrated. Despite the urging of one of Logan's friends, who thought a publisher should look at the manuscript, Sylvia kept the book and several others she had started hidden in her trunk at the foot of her bed.

It was this rejection of the extraordinary that drew Logan to Sylvia. On their first date she told him, "In all fairness, I have to tell you that I'm looking to get married and have babies. I want to make up for everything I lost when I was a child and everything I'll do with you I'll do with serious intent."

"Is that supposed to scare me away or trap me?"

"I don't know. I haven't had a whole lot of joy in my life and I woke up the morning of my twenty-first birthday and decided I was going to find some."

"What do men usually say when you tell them all this?"

"You're the first one I ever felt like I could speak my mind and my heart to."

"Would it surprise you if I told you I was lonely?" Logan asked.

"Not one bit. Why do you think I said yes when you asked me out?"

Sylvia was a secretary in the Engineering Department at MIT. Over dinners in her apartment, Logan told her stories about his patients and revealed the Machiavellian world of internal politics in the hospital. Sylvia drew Logan into a perfect-fit world of domesticity that he could not imagine himself leaving. Sylvia extinguished so much of herself that when they were together he glowed for them both, effectively hiding herself from view. Sylvia prepared dinners each time he came, as though he was a special guest. There were movies on the weekends, drives in the summer to the Cape and occasional uncomfortable visits to the aunt and uncle who raised her, with Sylvia presenting Logan like a trophy she had won despite a disdainful, mocking world. But mostly, she made a kind of home for Logan, turned her apartment into a place that offered the certainty of her presence. Sylvia's loyalty to the conventional, the tried and true, tapped a need in Logan for borders that were small yet occupied by splendid everyday miracles. The ambiguity of his father's presence made him eager to have children of his own, whom he imagined fathering with a precise and satisfying simplicity. And so when Logan asked Sylvia to marry him it was because he was sure of her, utterly convinced that *he* was as much as she would ever need.

Logan established his practice in Roxbury and purchased a brownstone in the South End. Sylvia supervised the remodeling of their house with zeal and a competence that Logan had suspected she possessed but which amazed him nonetheless. Sylvia quit her job and a year after they were married she was pregnant. They gave dinner parties and spent time with other young couples like themselves, first- or second-generation Black success stories, who knew they were symbols to whites of how far Blacks had come and proof to other Blacks of how much still remained to be done. Their friends taught at Boston University, were reporters for the *Globe*, political activists doing research at Harvard. And in their midst Sylvia remained a bedrock of domestic commitment, shunning the temptations of the world beyond their door. They had a second child and Logan gazed at his life, overwhelmed with satisfaction at the conventional domesticity he saw.

But by the fourth year of their marriage Logan had simply and completely begun to disdain his wife for the very qualities that had initially won his heart. They no longer shared a tiny apartment, as they had in the early days of their marriage, but lived in a house that contained twenty thousand dollars' worth of original artwork and that they had spent forty thousand dollars to refurbish. She ran their home with military-like efficiency that drove Logan from the home he had built as a monument to his delayed domestic fantasies. Most nights, by the time Logan arrived home, Tiambe and Amir were already in bed. Sylvia was so afraid that the children would not get the exact amount of sleep they needed that she rarely kept them up to await Logan's arrival. One night, when Logan suggested that Sylvia take some classes or consider getting her degree, she told him, "I've got all the education I'll need for the next eighteen years asleep upstairs."

Sylvia did not appear to be happy, but rather, militantly determined to create in their home what fate had stripped her of in her own childhood. She had mapped out a circumference for her life—and, by extension, all their lives—that Logan began to feel was a premeditated betrayal of his hopes.

He began a halfhearted affair with a former girlfriend, but being a man of whole not half measures, he could neither commit adultery nor remain with his wife with any real sense of passion. This realization drove Logan into a depression that culminated in his first heart attack, a mild yet convincing seizure that kept him away from his practice for three weeks. Recuperating at home, Logan lay in bed, wondering how to tell Sylvia he wanted a divorce.

One afternoon Sylvia brought him lunch in the bedroom, placing the tray with a light meal on Logan's lap. The teak tray, which they had bought on a trip to the Bahamas, held a bowl of homemade soup on a rattan place mat, surrounded by a linen napkin, a tall glass of orange juice and a vase with a single rose. Sylvia sat at the foot of the bed and watched Logan eat. When he finished the meal, she told him, "Don't worry, I'll let you go."

"What do you mean?"

"I know you want a divorce. And I won't try to stop you."

Logan looked at the woman who was his wife and saw the child surprised and dismayed by her mere survival, the young woman summoning the courage to seek a safe haven in the pursuit of marriage rather than love and the woman she had become, more timorous and untrusting in the midst of her bounty than when all she possessed was a hidden daydream.

"God, Sylvia, I wish you would try to stop me. Why don't you?"

"All I ever wanted, Logan, is what I have now. That's enough for me. I know it's not enough for you."

"I thought this was all I wanted, Sylvia."

"I just wish, in a way, that it had been something terrible, unbearable, then I could understand. Then I could explain."

"It was getting that way for me," he told her.

"What did I do wrong?" Sylvia asked.

"Nothing you *did* was wrong. You were a perfect wife and mother. Just look at this house. Look at it. But I need you to be someone you can't be."

"Why can't we just stay together for the children?" Sylvia asked.

"If you'd had my parents, you'd know why that's impossible for me to do."

"If you'd had my life, you'd know why *this* is the worst moment I've known."

"We could just separate for a while, see if things work out," Logan heard himself saying.

"You just said you didn't want to lie."

"I told you I *can't* lie, not to my children."

"Why not? Isn't that all happiness is anyway? A bunch of lies? Anyway, they'll find out sooner or later." Sylvia sounded bitter, tossing the words like stones at him.

"Sylvia, this isn't getting us anywhere." Logan moved the tray and reached for Sylvia, pulling her beside him.

"What will I do without you, Logan?" Sylvia sobbed into his chest.

Logan pulled back the covers and Sylvia climbed into bed beside him. He kissed her and removed her clothes and made love to his wife for what he knew would be the last time, felt Sylvia cling to him, kissing him fiercely, hard. And when they were through in the afternoon quiet that filled the room, Logan lay next to Sylvia and wondered what it took to be happy, what it meant to be brave. They were questions that filled him with a sense of his father, who had found the answer by holding on to everything, by not letting anything go.

Logan moved out of his house and into an apartment in Jamaica Plain. On Saturday afternoons he went back to his house to pick up his six-year-old daughter Tiambe and his three-year-old son Amir. Nothing that he had ever done up to the night he left his wife and children had filled Logan with as cavernous a sense of failure. Logan had sworn when he married that he would erase the memory of his part-time absentee father by being there for his own children full-time. Anger at what his life had become surfaced in persistent migraine headaches that he could cure only by forgiving himself for leaving his family—which he was unable to do.

Because they were so young, the separation and divorce stunned and confused the children. They lacked the language to express their anger and found the new shape of their universe utterly frightening. Tiambe, who was as assured and self-possessed as a miniature adult, lapsed into temper tantrums and bed-wetting. And Amir, who had once chatted gaily and nonstop, was seized by recurrent, morose silences that Sylvia could not penetrate.

Logan spent Saturdays with his children, playing ball with them on Boston Common or driving them to the Children's Museum or eating at McDonald's, but he despised the almost ceremonial nature of the time they shared. He longed to take them to his apartment and watch them do "nothing"—argue over who could turn on the television, lapse into unexpected moments of cooperation, play aimlessly with toys he brought them nearly each week. Logan longed for the simple, unhurried mundane acts that were the real measure of childhood. Instead he crammed every moment of their Saturday afternoons with activities that left Amir cranky and exhausted before the day was half over. Tiambe, inspired by the activity, begged for more. He felt cheated and unsatisfied because of the need to *do* something with his children rather than merely be their father. Anger swelled inside him, growing like a tumor, and then, burdened by the increasing load of his practice, the emptiness of the apartment he returned to each night, Logan sank into a depression that he walked through with zombielike steadfastness for nearly a year— performing every required task dutifully but with little love, for it was love that had betrayed him. Three weeks after his divorce was final, Logan received a call from a former colleague at Tufts who was heading a research project at Georgetown University School of Medicine in Washington. He asked Logan if he knew a doctor who would be interested in a two-year appointment to do research and teach. Logan told him he was.

When Logan returned to Washington, after an absence of over a decade, he was determined to rediscover the family that made him who he was.

He found a city riveted by change, yet sublime in a familiar sameness. On his occasional visits to Esther and Naomi, Logan had rarely looked closely at the face of the city. Change was all around him, but he'd been too busy to notice. The young Black mayor who ran Washington now had traded dashikis for three-piece suits. He managed the nation's capital with the approval of the city's working class, who counted him as one of their own, with the grudging assent of the Black upper class and the city's white business interests, whose real control over the city he had never challenged. Washington, D.C., had once been dubbed "Chocolate City" because of its overwhelming Black presence. But by the early eighties the city was home to a sprawling population of Asians and Hispanics, some clustered in an energetic melting pot neighborhood being gentrified into WASPish conformity by real estate magnates. Yet the area ravaged by the riots remained scarred—only a few newly erected buildings making the dankness and debris around them all the more stark.

Several years earlier Naomi had moved out of the house on Harvard Street and into a small one-bedroom apartment. She was almost eighty now, but the calm generosity of her spirit made her seem ageless, as if she were both very young and very old, simultaneously possessing both curiosity and wisdom. Her days were quiet, blessedly uneventful. Each morning she woke at 5 A.M. and spent an hour in prayer. After breakfast she listened to the radio—one of the "All Talk" stations, marveling as she listened at the anger and sadness that gripped the world, thankful that she had lived, had been a wife, long before surrogate mothers and mass murders and people going to psychiatrists instead of God. Afternoons, she'd go for a short walk if the weather was good. Then she'd get on the telephone and call the friends who remained, the three or four who hadn't yet died. There had been a year when she had buried five friends and there were times when the loneliness Naomi felt as her generation passed on was greater than any burden she'd ever known. And Naomi now knew that real loneliness was not being without someone to love you, but losing those who looked at the world with a vision you shared.

One afternoon Logan drove Naomi to look at the house Randolph had left him in Columbia Heights. They sat in Logan's car, looking across the street at the three-story boarded-up pale brown Victorian structure.

"Don't let the outside fool you," Naomi told him. "Esther and me have been in there and the building is sound."

"I'll need a lot to renovate it," Logan sighed with a dubious shake of his head.

"This neighborhood don't look like it did when I lived

here, but you can believe they're gonna fix it up," she assured him. "Subway's coming through. Whites gonna follow."

A somber pall hung over the neighborhood now, as though the houses and the people in them were utterly exhausted by the pursuit of a fickle, unworthy promise. Although there were colorful murals, a gleaming municipal building, a few trendy upscale shops and restaurants paving the way for the impending white invasion, none of it camouflaged the absence of a coherent, vibrant core of concern, the kind that had once safeguarded and honored the same streets. The old people who remained were merely waiting to die. The young people felt no allegiance strong enough to change the streets into a community. And yet Logan had decided when his tenure at Georgetown was up he would repair his father's house and establish his practice here, where the halfheartedness that was everywhere he looked informed him that he was needed.

"Everything I ever got from him I had to earn."

"That's not hardly true and, even if it was, so what? That way at least you know you deserve it. You ever think about him?" Naomi asked.

"All the time. I don't feel him like a person who's dead, but rather like a presence that's alive, as long as I am. Whenever I've come down for visits, you know I've always gone to his grave. I think I was looking for answers, I'd even stand there and talk to him. The only advice he ever gave me was to go on back to my life and keep on searching the way he did."

"I sometimes wonder what would've happened if he'd lived long enough for him and Esther to get married."

"Life would've happened," Logan assured her, starting the engine.

"And that would've been more than enough."

When Logan returned to Washington, he had the first real

opportunity to spend time with his brother. Logan longed to love Nathaniel unequivocally, to shape a bond that would erase everything that had separated them. Logan embarked on a flurry of regular activities with his fourteen-year-old brother—taking him to basketball games, bowling, talking to him about school and careers. Still, age and the radically different ways in which Esther had been a mother to them made Logan feel perpetually exiled from his brother's love.

Because Logan had been unable to take Esther's love for granted, he could hardly conceive of committing an act that would endanger it. Yet Esther had spoiled Nathaniel, rarely saying no to him, because she had found it so hard to say yes to Logan. And so Esther's unchecked, bountiful love enhanced and encouraged Nathaniel's vulnerabilities. Esther had not looked on Nathaniel both as her son and as a stranger. Both visions were required—the one to nuture, the other to warn and advise.

Increasingly, Logan feared that he could not be the mentor his brother required. Logan could sense the boy's need for Randolph, the questions he felt unable to ask, producing anxieties and doubts that swelled within him. How would Nathaniel punish himself or spite Randolph for his premature demise? No one knew. His family, like everyone's, had shaped a net of platitudes and secrets around their existence to forgive and deny the past. Only occasionally did truth storm the gates.

Nathaniel's room was filled with gadgets and material objects designed to entertain and, Logan felt, keep Nathaniel from learning how to think. He had a small television set, a radio, stacks of computer games, a stereo. Yet repeatedly, Logan had watched Nathaniel survey this bounty in complete, utter boredom. On the occasions Logan had tried to talk with Nathaniel about Randolph, the boy had flinched, his body turned rigid, his eyes drifted away from Logan, as if Logan's words promised fulfillment he could not bear, threatened knowledge too dangerous to touch. "I'm not ready to talk about that. I just don't feel like it." Nathaniel would shrug morosely in response to Logan's offer, then, in one agile move, reach for a basketball and toss it to Logan, saying, "Let's play, man, *that*'s more fun."

ers was the first face Logan saw when he entered the apartment, which was crowded with people, dense with cigarette smoke and music. Her eyes—brash, wondering, locked with his and invited him across the room. Logan removed his coat and handed it to the hostess, a friend of his partner, Joe Barnes, all the time afraid and in some sense unable to look away from her.

She stood in a corner of the room, holding a drink, and while Logan studied her she studied everything and everyone around her as if she were taking notes. The sight of her had set him on edge with an excitement he hadn't felt in years. She was wearing turquoise—a bright vivid slash filling her part of the room. She wore huge round earrings. And she was the only woman in the room with a natural—a close-cropped haircut, that thrust her busy careful eyes and her high cheekbones into full view. Just looking at her filled Logan with so much satisfaction he almost didn't want to move. But then she moved, walked out of her corner, her eyes on his as she gracefully nudged her way through the crowd. Her movements activated him and Logan felt himself circling through the crowd toward her. The sleek and sultry saxophone of Grover Washington, Jr., poured into the room like a spring shower, enticing couples onto the floor. Halfway across the room, she made a detour into the kitchen, turning, when caught between two dancers, to look back as if to be sure he was still on her trail. When Logan made it to the kitchen, she stood leaning against the sink, her arms casually folded across her chest.

"Hello," Logan said, slightly breathless, feeling soiled and rumpled because of the crush of bodies he had plowed through to reach her.

"Hi," she said, grinning with a smugness that was more inviting than Logan had ever thought overconfidence could be. A woman entered the tiny kitchen, shoving Logan closer to her, and he took that moment to ask, "Who are you?"

"My name is Felicia Kincaid."

"Are you a spy?" Logan asked, reclaiming the space where he had stood before being pushed.

"A spy?"

"I mean, the way you're casing the joint. I took one look at you and I couldn't stop. I felt like I'd been kidnapped."

"Who are *you*?" she countered.

"Logan Spenser."

She reached for the paper cup on the counter beside her and said, "It was fun looking at you too."

"I didn't say it was fun. I said it was strange, a little scary."

"Most interesting things are," she told him, taking a bite from a black olive on a toothpick.

"You know Lynn?" he asked.

"We went to high school together. That's how far back we go."

In order to move closer to her, Logan poured some white wine into a cup and said, "I hate to say this, but you're very attractive."

"Why do you hate to say it?"

"Because I'm sure you've heard it so many times before."

"Not so often. It's such a shameless cliché, few men bother to use it."

Then she laughed, long and loud, melting into a fit of giggles. Logan felt himself blushing, his hands pulsing with so much excitement he couldn't keep his glass from shaking.

"You must admit," Felicia said graciously after her laughter had subsided, "that a comment like that in an environment like this one is like asking, 'And what do you do?' "

"I hate to be asked that," Logan said.

"So, I won't ask you," she promised.

"I've always wanted to reply, 'I'm an ex-militant, seeking funds to run for public office.' "

Felicia laughed, making her even more attractive, her face becoming fuller, more complex, less guarded. He wanted to stand before her the rest of the evening, just saying things that would make her smile.

The sound of a slow and silken melody drifted into the kitchen and she told him, "I'd like to dance."

She was about an inch taller than Logan, but she fit into his arms as though carved for that space. And she held him, her arms wrapped around his waist as though she had been waiting just for him. He was full of her—her warm musky scent, the feelings she inspired.

When the record was over, Logan did not let her go. And Felicia held him, her breath warm against his cheek as she hummed the final notes of the song. They were the last ones on the dance floor. Felicia lifted her head and told Logan, "Let's go someplace where there's food and a semblance of quiet." And then she kissed him, smooth, slow, soft on his lips, then held his hand, leading him to the closet to get their coats.

They went to a nearby café, where they ate pasta and drank wine.

"All I know about you is your name," Logan said. "I want to know everything else."

"How much are *you* willing to reveal?" Felicia asked, raising her wineglass, as if hiding behind it as she took a sip.

"I'm a doctor," he told her.

"Are you a good one?"

"I try to be. A partner and I just opened our offices a few weeks ago."

"What's it like being a doctor?"

"Every day I go to work and I listen to people tell me a story. Who could resist that?"

"Why'd you go into medicine?"

"I wanted to have an endless supply of approval for the things I did. Really, I just always wanted, very much, to be loved," Logan said, proud of his eloquence, shaken by the honesty she provoked.

"Approval. Is that important to you?" Felicia asked, listening with a nervey concentration for his answer.

"For most of my life it has been, but the older I get, the less it matters."

"The right thing," she mused gently. "Approval meant everything in my family and almost none of us ended up getting it. I think I've always fought it tooth and nail as a way to distinguish myself." Felicia confided this in gentle, quiet tones, almost as if talking to herself. "What kind of doctor are you?"

"An internist—a family physician."

"Why family practice?" Logan was awed by the sturdiness of her inquisitive mind.

"Working with families reminds me how normal the abnormal is, how blessed and ordinary, in the end, my family was. I deliver babies, I treat illnesses related to old age and everything in between."

"But how do you absorb all that pain, all that misery? Where do you put it?" she insisted, her eyes appearing as if she were suddenly infused with the pain his patients felt.

"Dump it on your family, drown it in booze or pills. After a while you learn to leave as much of it as you can in your office. I've got kids from a previous marriage so I simply won't do fourteen-hour days anymore."

"I'm a freelance photographer."

"So you're pretty busy then," Logan concluded warily, as if this information portended their future.

"I don't say yes to everything," she told him pointedly.

"Can freelancers afford to say no?"

"Anyone can afford to say no, once they decide how much they're worth."

"What's that like, taking pictures?"

In answer, she told him how she'd gotten started. Through a former lover she'd lived with in New York, she had gotten a few jobs as a model, mostly for catalogues and now and then the Sunday supplements. But the anonymous, amorphous feeling that suffused her, standing before the camera, threatened sometimes to kill her.

A hundred times a day she was ordered to *smile*, but the smile the photographer wanted had to possess the genial seductiveness of a robot. She watched the other models come in for ten- or twelve-hour days before the camera, high on pills or grass when they arrived, and Felicia quickly realized that she was not hungry enough to do what had to be done to get on the cover of *Vogue*. Soon it was the photographers who intrigued her most, for they were the ones in control, energetic and inspired. She bought a cheap Kodak in a Woolworth's and started taking pictures. Photography allowed her to forget herself. She could hide behind the camera as well as *become* behind the lens. She got some freelance assignments, but wasn't making enough to even pay the rent, so while Steve, her lover, waitered between acting jobs, Felicia was a secretary for a Village-based newspaper. And then she got an assignment to take pictures to accompany a profile of a prominent Black politician for a cover story in *Newsweek*. That was her break.

"It's hard work," she concluded.

"Do you do portraits?" Logan asked.

"Not often. I don't meet many people willing to have a picture taken that reveals the face they've earned instead of the face they wish they had. People come to me all the time and ask me to take portraits that will take ten years or twenty pounds off. Sure, I can perform all kinds of tricks in the darkroom, but some tricks I'd rather not do for a living. So I do a lot of news photos, a fire or the face of a mourner at a funeral—things that can't be staged. I like animals and nature shots too. I used to work with *National Geographic*, but the traveling was just too much. But I made enough money with them to live for a while and do what I want and that was nice."

He liked her openness, the way she listened with her eyes.

"So, you've got kids."

"Yes."

"Where are they?"

"In Boston."

"That must be hard."

"It is. All this bullshit about quality time is just that—

bullshit. I miss them. I hope I never accept the way we live because that means I've accepted being a footnote."

"You know that politician I photographed?" Felicia asked casually.

"What about him?"

"We were married for three years."

"What happened?"

"I realized I couldn't be a political wife. I wasn't devoted to his career. And the fact that I cared for him wasn't enough. I had to be too discreet, too careful, and I've always found that a bore." Logan watched as Felicia attacked the slice of cheesecake the waiter had placed before her. "And no matter what he did," she said, pushing the plate aside and wiping her mouth with a napkin, "it was like he was always performing, waiting for me to applaud."

"Aren't we all in some way waiting for the world to applaud?" Logan asked gently. "Hoping, praying it will anyway? If not the world, at least those closest to us?"

"In a sense, yet," she admitted, sipping her wine, her mood mellow, subdued.

"I want to see you again." Logan said.

Felicia set down her wineglass and clapped her hands, the sound of her poised, energetic applause inspiring Logan to recall moments when he had been this happy before.

"I think that's a great idea," Felicia told him, stopping her applause, to reach out for Logan's hands across the table.

"Why did you applaud?" he asked quizzically.

"I wanted to start practicing early. I think you deserve it and it's a talent I'm ready to develop."

"What about standing ovations?" Logan asked.

"Don't get greedy." She laughed huskily.

"Why not? Just tell me why not." Logan asked.

Felicia Kincaid was the daughter of the city's Black elite, descended on both sides of her family from mulattoes who had for generations inbred their white blood like a sacred inheritance. Felicia was born with a light tan coloring that, nevertheless, made her the darkest member of her family, a fact for which she was secretly pitied by aunts and openly chided by cousins. Personal history was important among the Kincaid clan and the house Felicia grew up in was filled with sepia-tinted photos on the walls and mantelpiece of the illustrious ancestors of whom her parents often spoke. On her father's side were men like Preston Kincaid, who was a surgeon for a colored regiment during the Civil War and who served as a conductor on the Underground Railroad on the Washington, D.C., leg, meeting boats at the wharf in Southwest and assisting fugitive slaves from the Deep South. Felicia's grandfather was one of the first Negro deans at Howard University and his sister was active in the National Council of Negro Women. On her mother's side there was Josiah Blakely, a freedman who had worked twelve years to purchase the freedom of his slave wife and two daughters owned by a Virginia tobacco farmer. Blakely labored as a blacksmith and visited his wife once a week until she was free. And the year after he bought his family's freedom and they came to live with him in Washington, he died during a smallpox epidemic. Felicia's great-grandmother was among the first colored women to enter Howard University and the great-grandmother's sister had run off to New York City to star in *Blackbirds of 1917*, a musical revue by Noble Sissle.

Felicia's father, William Kincaid, was a lawyer for many years with the NAACP on some of the most important cases relating to segregation. A slender, elegant man who resembled a slightly tan version of Errol Flynn, William Kincaid's ambition was relentless and single-minded and he passed over the lives of his children like a heavy cloud of authority, exacting but unreachable. William Kincaid chose his wife Dorothy because her qualities of devotion and discretion promised never to subvert or overshadow him. There were five children and the Kincaid family lived a comfortable life in the days of Felicia's adolescence, in LeDroit Park, the upper Northeast neighborhood that nestled in the shadow of Howard University.

Paul Laurence Dunbar and Duke Ellington had once lived in LeDroit Park, originally conceived as an exclusive suburb of Washington. In 1873 Amzi L. Barber, one of the white founders of Howard University, purchased forty acres of university land for one hundred and fifteen thousand dollars. With the help of his father-in-law, real estate broker LeDroit Langdon, Barber employed an army of creative stonecutters, fresco painters and slate workers, who spent four years producing a neighborhood of unique elegance and grace. Sumptuous cream-colored Italian villas, dignified brick fortresses, pristine Swiss chateaux stood opposite medieval stone mansions and gothic cottages. Archways, mansard roofs, leaded glass or gingerbread woodwork enabled each home to flaunt its architectural individuality. By 1887 LeDroit Park was an exclusive enclave for white congressmen, professors and high-ranking military men. So exclusive was the neighborhood that it was considered a county with its own government. But LeDroit Park was also surrounded by a fortified fence with posted guards, an affront to the Black residents of nearby "Howard Town," who eventually tore the fence down. By 1888 Negro families were settling in the area and by World War I the area was almost completely Black.

These genteel well-bred colored folk created a world of afternoon concerts, lawn parties, church socials and fireside chats about the most pressing issues affecting the race. Felicia's parents had grown up in LeDroit Park near the "hilltop" campus of Howard University, Freedmen's Hospital, Dunbar and Armstrong high schools, once the two best "colored" schools in the city. This placid, gracious world was passed on to the children of William Kincaid, who played jacks, hopscotch, went to Saturday afternoon matinees at the Republic and Booker-T theaters with the sons and daughters of Negro judges, social workers and professors. This was a world where money mattered less than achievement, breeding and "taste." And while the Negro lower classes were sometimes disdained, a sense of noblesse oblige among the Negro middle class nurtured bonds between the varying Negro societies that strengthened both.

In the months after John F. Kennedy's election as President, William Kincaid was appointed a lawyer with the Justice Department. This rise in fortunes inspired a move from LeDroit Park to the nearby "Gold Coast" along Sixteenth Street, then just beginning to be integrated by a few Negro families. The axis of the city, Sixteenth Street was a seven-mile-long stretch of some of the city's prime real estate. Towers, turrets, steeples and circular drives enhanced the mansions and embassies and the roomy private residences that endowed the street with an overwhelming and nearly palpable aura of prestige and power.

In the early 1900s Mary Henderson, a wealthy eccentric and wife of the senator from Missouri, owned much of the property along Sixteenth Street. Henderson pressured congressional friends and allies in 1913 to rename Sixteenth Street "Avenue of the Presidents," a change that, to the chagrin of Mrs. Henderson, lasted only a year. At the turn of the century the White House occupied one end of Sixteenth street, Mrs. Henderson's residence the other—and everyone who ever saw the Henderson estate agreed that it was fit for a king. Over forty churches, cathedrals and religious temples along Sixteenth Street consolidated the street's aura of power.

The move to Sixteenth Street seemed a precursor of the future for the Kincaid family, whose children had actually been touched by President Kennedy during a reception at the White House. But then the idealism of 1960 became the grief of 1963, when Kennedy was assassinated. William Kincaid remained in government, working with the Justice Department eight years as a civil rights lawyer, traveling the country, tracking the wave of unrest and protest that was the new political language being shaped by those voiceless and powerless for generations.

In William Kincaid's absence, his wife Dorothy lapsed into a genteel alcoholism that became increasingly difficult to hide. The Kincaid family lived in a huge, rambling cottage-style house with five bedrooms, two garages, a winding staircase that connected the spacious first floor to the upstairs. Yet in time this house became the setting for the demise of a host of long cherished, jealously guarded hopes. They had been a close family, bound as much by memories of collective family achievement as by expectations for the future. Yet the sixties were nothing less than horrible. The oldest of the children, Eric, as handsome and ambitious as his father, graduated from West Point and was killed a year later in Vietnam. The youngest, Olivia, the family poet, who had wanted to be a painter but whose diary was filled with dark brooding premonitions of early death, died of sickle-cell anemia two years into her studies at Radcliffe. Therese, whose biting wit, sarcasm and energy had suited her, everyone thought, to follow in her father's footsteps, went to London to study at Oxford and met a young lawyer from Ghana whom she married. Therese returned to Ghana with her husband, who had been appointed to a position in the civilian government. Three years later her husband was killed when the army took over in a coup. And, to the family's dismay, Therese and her three children elected to remain in Ghana, calling it the only home they now knew. By 1968 only two of the children remained in reach—Vaughn went to New York to study theater and Felicia was studying at Spelman.

After leaving the Justice Department in the wake of the election of Richard Nixon, William Kincaid taught at Georgetown Law School and soon left his wife who, racked by the deaths of Eric and Olivia, spent months in and out of private hospitals, battling depression. Kincaid married a woman twenty years his junior and Felicia had not spoken to her father since.

Felicia Kincaid had started smoking at the age of twelve and didn't quit till she was thirty. Her virginity was shed at fifteen like a gift someone had given her that was the wrong color and size. She dropped out of Spelman in her junior year and married the son of the dean of the School of Medicine at Meharry, an earnest, innocent young man who had fantasies of a political career one day in the "New South" and whom Felicia had married because she'd begun to find her classes boring and thought marriage, if not fulfilling, would at least be interesting. A year later she left her husband, immune to his tear-stained face and the loud grumbling of his father in the living room that "I told you she was crazy. She's a devil. Not a woman. Love don't mean a thing to somebody like her." Fleeing the South, Felicia hitchhiked to New York City and on her arrival felt, for the first time in her life, that she had found something that would refuse to leave her exactly as she had been found.

Felicia told Logan her story one night in his apartment, as an early Miles Davis piece played on the stereo like a score for the unfolding of her life.

"Where's your father now?" he asked.

"He has some distinguished chair at Brown University. They funded it a few years ago and basically rent a Negro scholar every few years to sit in it."

"You're cruel."

"His wife is my age. I have a five-year-old stepsister I've never seen. And my mother lives in a rooming house six blocks down from where we used to live on Sixteenth Street."

"Rooming houses on Sixteenth Street?"

"Sure. Discrete, genteel ones. Those houses are so big you could cut a house up into a dozen rooms."

"What's she doing now?"

"Oh, she takes classes at UDC and Howard, she's studying for her doctorate."

"Who pays for all this?"

"My brother and me. Between the two of us, we keep her afloat. My mother refused to accept alimony from my father. She let him off scot-free. Said she wouldn't allow money to taint what they'd had. Her definition of what they'd had was different than mine. When my father left her, my mother was a former teacher who hadn't worked outside her house in twenty years, a woman who to this day refuses to use the word *Black* or *Afro-American* and who has never forgiven me for refusing to have a cotillion."

"Y'all are the kind of colored folk my mama warned me about," Logan said with a laugh.

"We're the kind of colored folk *everybody* got warned about."

One evening on their way to a concert, Felicia and Logan stopped by to see Dorothy Kincaid. Felicia was, if nothing else, most definitely her mother's daughter, for Dorothy Kincaid sat on her bed facing Logan and Felicia and bluntly asked Logan what his intentions were.

"Mama!" Felicia groaned.

"Oh, that's OK," Logan protested nobly. "To answer your question, Mrs. Kincaid, they're completely honorable."

Dorothy Kincaid reached for the teapot that sat on a small bedside table. The teapot was made of Limoges china in a pink floral pattern and she poured tea for the three of them. Felicia had come by to drop off a paper she had typed for her mother. Despite Felicia's protests that they really couldn't stay long, Dorothy had laid a setting for tea.

When Felicia and Logan had first entered the house, they saw an elderly white-haired woman sitting at a piano in the huge carpeted sitting room, playing a sonata. Eyes closed, her humpbacked body absorbing and absorbed by the music, the woman played as if possessed. As they walked up the first flight of stairs, an elderly Black man with aged, bloodshot eyes opened his door as their footsteps neared and stared at them, then quickly closed the door.

Dorothy Kincaid's apartment was on the third floor. Her skin was nearly translucent and light blue veins ran along her neck. Her large gray eyes were intelligent and eager and her nose and lips were turned up, it seemed, in permanent judgment. And yet she was fragile too. Dark brown age spots littered her hands and she wore a pale green dress whose colors were fading. The ravages of alcoholism and depression had marred a once beautiful face. The spacious room contained a bed and a desk. A small kitchenette and books filled one corner and there were dozens of boxes filled with books, souvenirs and mementos. On the desk were pictures of each of her children and a photo of Dorothy and William Kincaid shaking hands with President Kennedy. And over her bed was a portrait of Dorothy that had been painted when she was twenty-one.

In the portrait she was dressed formally, her slender shoulders draped by a silk dress, and she wore an expression that revealed the smug expectation of permanent happiness as her due. Still, the artist had captured the fault lines that widened as she grew older and that haunted the confidence of her face.

Dorothy now sat sipping her tea, assessing Logan with impatient curiosity.

"Spenser, Spenser. Are you related to Margaret Spenser from Baltimore? The Baltimore Spensers, Margaret Spenser's son is a congressman?"

"No, ma'am. My people are all from D.C. I'm a native, in fact."

"What's your father's name? I might know him," she asked

excitedly, certain now that she would find out who and what Logan really was. "I'm a sixth-generation Washingtonian myself."

"He's dead now."

"I'm so sorry," Dorothy said with genuine concern.

"His name was Randolph Spenser and he owned a restaurant called the Eden Bar and Grill."

"The Eden Bar and Grill?" Dorothy asked, her eyes bulging with disbelief. "I don't think I ever heard of it." She took an agitated sip of tea, then added, "And your mother?"

"She's a consultant for the city schools."

"But what's her name?"

"Esther Johnson."

"Johnson, Johnson," Dorothy said, squinting her eyes, her spindly index finger jabbing the air. "Is she related to the Atlanta Johnson's?"

"Mother, we've got to be going," Felicia said abruptly, looking at her watch and draining her teacup.

"She never wants me to meet any of her friends," Dorothy complained. "My daughter is very headstrong, Mr. Spenser. She's a modern woman. Her brother Vaughn only thinks about making money and says he doesn't have time to get married. She's had two husbands and I still don't have a grandchild, don't you think that's the least I could expect?"

Felicia stood up and sat on the bed beside her mother and hugged her tightly, closed her eyes and sighed, "Oh, Mama."

Dorothy patted her daughter's hand and said, "You don't want to be like me. To end up like me. But, oh, Felicia, it wasn't so bad."

Six months into their affair, Logan looked at Felicia and knew he was looking at the woman who would be his wife. He was in her apartment lying on the sofa, listening to a Charles Mingus album. She had been out taking pictures all day and was in the darkroom developing film. They had picked up some barbecued ribs on the way to her apartment.

Logan hated dating, figured he was simply too old for it. He was a man born to be a husband. And in this he was his father's son.

"You ever think of getting married again?" he asked Felicia when she came out of the darkroom and settled on the sofa beside him.

"Rarely," she said.

"Why not?"

"I'm scared."

"*You* scared?" he teased.

"Sure, you can't imagine how much like a failure I feel with *two* marriages behind me."

"Marriage isn't like taking the SAT's," Logan protested.

"Sometimes that's exactly what it's like," Felicia told him seriously. "I was too young the first time, too cynical the second time."

"And now?"

She did not answer him.

"And what about you?" she asked. "Do you think about getting married again?"

"All the time."

"For convenience, I'll bet."

"Marriage is a lot less of a convenience than people think."

"I don't know." Felicia shook her head. "I just want to get it right next time."

"Don't worry," Logan promised her, reaching to hold her in his arms. "You will."

Chapter Twenty-Five

The birthday presents lay scattered on the blue-and-gold madras-covered sofa, haphazard, yet serious as evidence of some exquisite moment of revelry, flaunted as a way of sharing its grace. A cashmere sweater from Esther and several pairs of corduroy slacks, an Apple computer purchased jointly by Naomi and Logan, a Sony clock radio given to Nathaniel by his girlfriend, Bridgette. Boxes and tissue paper lay at Logan and Nathaniel's feet as the brothers sat eyeing one another with casual appreciation. Full of the well-planned meal Esther had prepared and capped with a home-made coconut birthday cake, Logan and Nathaniel sat as if overwhelmed by contentment, too stunned by its presence to move.

Nathaniel had turned sixteen and the evening possessed a mood that was both celebratory and momentous. For as they all had sat before plates and saucers littered only with crumbs and limp, cast-off reminders of the meal and half-full cups of coffee, Logan reached for Felicia's hand and, gazing at the faces of all those gathered—as if for approval that, if denied, he would not contest—he announced that they had decided to get married. Logan made the announcement with more relief than relish, feeling that it ended a campaign more tenacious and willful than any he had ever undertaken. It took eight months for him to convince Felicia to marry him. She had argued that they were a "modern" couple and, as such, marriage was no longer necessary, that they could merely live together and hold on to a respect for one another that marriage seemed guaranteed to extinguish. But Logan had unashamedly argued, as they lay in bed watching Johnny Carson, driving to the theater, showering together, in the middle of phone conversations, that marriage was for him and for them both, the most necessary of all acts to perform.

"I want to make a pact with you," he'd told Felicia, "one that will be witnessed by everyone in my life who counts. A pact that's legal, moral and sanctioned in ways that seem like a prison to you, but are bridges to me. If I wanted a roommate, it wouldn't be you I'd choose. And I sure don't want just a 'woman.' I want a wife, old-fashioned as that sounds. And I want a mother of my children, the other ones I want to have."

For several months Logan said nothing, chastened by Felicia's resistance. Then a week ago she had met him at his office and taken him to lunch. As they parted, promising to talk that evening, Felicia smiled, a grim vanquished smile and said,

"I'll marry you."

"Why the change of heart?"

"I'm an overachiever with a merciless fear of failure. I'd also thought of marriage as just another of life's obstacle courses."

"It is," he warned her.

"But that's *all* I was thinking about. I'd almost forgotten how much I love you."

Felicia had gone with Esther to take Naomi home and Esther's house was resonant with the metallic silence that falls, upon the departure of voices eager for happiness.

"You made out pretty good," Logan observed with a nod of his head toward the sofa.

"Sure did." Nathaniel laughed sheepishly.

"Think you deserve it?"

"Sure I do."

At sixteen, Nathaniel was tall and strapping, sitting in the chair facing Logan, his body mature and placid, as though carved for the chair's embrace. Recently, they had guided Nathaniel through a rough year and a half of minor scrapes with the law and a burgeoning adolescent fury that had set Nathaniel on a potentially treacherous path. And yet he had come out all right. A lawyer friend helped Logan to get the incident removed from the police files so Nathaniel would not have a record and Esther and Nathaniel had undergone a period of counseling that appeared to set Nathaniel aright and to endow him with a sturdiness to resist the gale force winds of dead-end choices draped in a tempting, shiny façade. Now Nathaniel was doing well in school and had found a new set of friends. In response, Esther crossed her fingers, Naomi praised the Lord and Logan allowed his vigilance to momentarily relax. "You've only got another two years of high school. You thought about what you want to do?" Logan asked.

"Not yet." Nathaniel shrugged with a disinterest that Logan had witnessed in so many of the young people he knew. Test tube babies, moon shots, heart transplants and young people who had no idea what they wanted to do with their lives. Were they swallowed up by choices or so intimidated by the implications of the world they were to inherit that silence and a carefully honed nonchalance became their weapons for survival?

By the time he was sixteen, Logan recalled, he already knew that he wanted to save the world because he took its continued existence for granted. But now the idea of "progress" possessed a kinetic nuclear glow and hardly anyone he had encountered under the age of thirty took the world for granted.

"Do you know how dangerous it is for you as a young Black male, even at sixteen, not to know where you're headed?"

"I've got time," Nathaniel said defensively.

"Not as much as you think." Logan stifled the urge to lecture his brother. Nathaniel had heard enough lectures from them all the past year, lectures that, in an often harsh and demanding tongue, threatened and cajoled, promised and denied, over and over sought to make Nathaniel a man.

"All I'll say, Nate, is you carry a legacy, all the things Grandad did, our father accomplished and Mom's work in the movement. It all gets passed on, brother, from them to me to you. We're expecting you to do your share."

"Why can't I just be me?" Nathaniel asked with quizzical impatience. "Why do I have to be you or my father?"

"Because we're in you—like it or not, know it or not— and you've got to honor that."

Logan watched his brother's face, drawn and quartered by lines of doubt. Logan had encroached on the boy's still-fuzzy sense of individuality with the looming responsibility of family ties.

"But where do I fit in?"

"That's for you to decide. But you need to know what we expect."

Logan wondered how often Esther talked to Nathaniel about her time in the South. He guessed that she had rarely, if ever, discussed those years with her youngest son. The year before, Esther had journeyed to a three-day reunion of civil rights workers from all over the country held in upstate New York and when Logan asked her about the weekend she answered him with eyes luminous with tears and a choked, "It wasn't in vain. None of it was in vain." Logan gathered that his mother, like many of the other ex-movement activists, now lived lives of nearly blatant conventionality; they had mortgages, kids in college, jobs they hated, although most had tried to remain in the sphere of socially conscious activity and employment—education, social work, politics. Just as Esther had cheated him of that knowledge, Logan was certain she had cheated Nathaniel as well. And yet Esther had kept this house, chiseled out a successful career as an educational consultant and raised a son, each endeavor as political in its own way as a boycott or sit-in. Besides, years ago he had promised not to blame Esther ever again for love lost or the awkwardness of love regained. Logan stood up and placed the computer on the dining room table. Then he turned to Nathaniel and asked, "You ever been called nigger?"

"No, of course not." The boy laughed uneasily.

"Too bad."

"Why do you say that?"

"It helps you to know the score. I wasn't called *nigger* until I went to medical school. And, believe me, there's plenty of ways to do it. Ways so subtle, if you haven't been trained what to listen and look for, you'll sit there laughing with everybody else and not know they're laughing at you."

Logan sat at the table and cut a slice of cake and motioned to Nathaniel to join him. They sat eating cake and drinking sodas as Logan thought—of the Black man who ran for

President the year before, the professor at Howard University who told him that light skin was "in" again and that the students socialized and chose friends on campus on the basis of color as rigidly as at any time in the past. He flashed onto the image of the contact lenses in vogue that, according to the commercials, "turned brown eyes blue" and the young black high school girls he had witnessed wearing them, their hazel and green eyes shocking and sad, set against ebony skin; he thought of the article he'd read that included an anecdote about a group of Black college students at an Ivy League college who had called Malcolm X *Malcolm Ten* and had no idea who he was and who couldn't find Vietnam on any map. Where did it all go? he wondered. Why didn't anybody care? Why had his generation failed so miserably to pass the dream on, to institutionalize pride and power?

"We're counting on you," Logan heard himself saying, the ominous tones of his words shackling him to a sadness he hoped his voice did not betray.

"I know that," Nathaniel told him. "But I'm counting on me too." Nathaniel finished his cake and said, "It's scarry sometimes, that's all. Like, who knows if there'll *be* a world in ten years?" Nathaniel gazed at Logan, his eyes pleading for an answer no one could give. And Logan knew that was the ethic of his brother's generation, "Who knows?" And if nobody knew, nobody cared and if nobody cared . . .

"You're still a member of this family, Nate. Don't let the world's madness make you forget that."

But Logan watched his brother's eyes return to the cake and the three remaining candles and before Logan could demand or extract the promise he required he heard Esther and Felicia bustling in through the front door and Nathaniel had risen, as if in flight from the demand in Logan's eyes, to greet his mother.

Chapter Twenty-Six

The nervous energy of airports gave Logan a headache. Whenever he had to travel, he usually arrived an hour before the time of departure to avoid missing the flight and then headed for the bar, where he could easily down two or three shots of scotch that would numb him to the swirling chaos and movement around him. He sometimes wondered how an illiterate could successfully negotiate their way through an airport, cowering beneath the huge signs pointing to immediate and then final destinations. The cold clinical efficiency, the sheer size of airports, Logan felt, assumed a degree of confidence and educational proficiency that was a telling statement on the importance of status in the world of flight.

The Eastern Airlines flight that was bringing his children from Boston to spend the weekend with him was an hour and a half late. Thunderstorms all along the East Coast had clogged National Airport with more than its usual share of aggravated, disgruntled passengers.

Logan stood up and walked to the window and looked at the dark threatening clouds overhead. A stark vein of thunder lit up the darkness, a linear eye piercing the rain-drenched sky, and he remembered, as he often did, how nothing had turned out the way he had planned. How his life, like the thunderburst, had lurched and jolted to an inner rhythm often totally opposed to the beat that moved him from one dream or desire to the next.

His daughter Tiambe was pensive and intense. Tall and gangly, she had her mother's dark brown coloring and soft doelike face. But she was headstrong and willful too. And Logan could not overcome his ambivalent pride in her assurance and fear that it might be her downfall. She was fascinated by his work, plying him with questions about medicine, diseases, life and death.

Amir was gregarious and cheerful. The earlier scars the divorce had inflicted were beginning to fade. Amir picked up the phone every Sunday evening to talk sports with Logan, to ask for an increase in his monthly allowance and to tell him the latest joke he'd heard from his friends at school. Sylvia had remained in Boston and two years after the divorce married one of Boston's few—and the most successful— Black real estate investors.

His children had already acquired the kind of surface sophistication that he had not attained until he left college.

Sylvia had enrolled Amir and Tiambe in a mostly white private school in Newton, a suburb of Boston where Sylvia and
her husband now lived. It wan't until he entered college that
he had spent any significant time around whites. He liked to
recall the satisfying womblike atmosphere of Cardoza High
School, where the principal, most of his teachers, classmates,
the editor of the school newspaper and the valedictorian were
Black. Nobody at the school ever gave him the impression
that whites had anything of value on them. And that consciousness had enabled him to defend himself against the
subtle yet pervasive racism he encountered in the world beyond Cardoza's doors. Now his kids were growing up with
whites, assuming an intimacy that he was not totally comfortable with. Logan worried that the white world would
swallow them up. Their sheer ease in that world bothered
him more than he would ever admit openly. And yet wasn't
that what "the struggle" had been about?

He found himself interrogating them, questioning Tiambe
and Amir about their teachers and classmates and friends.
Listening closely to their accounts for slights and insults their
youth might blind them to. And it irritated him that when
he gave them books on the lives of Black heroes they accepted
them grudgingly, telling him with their eyes that they would
have preferred something else, something mechanical and
expensive. Had the struggle been about this too? Feeding
your kids their history like it was castor oil?

The orderly precision of the custody arrangement between
he and Sylvia guaranteed that the quicksilver nature of his
children's youth would never be his to witness. During some
holidays, most summers and an occasional long weekend,
Logan gauged and assessed them, searched for a reference
point more immediately relevant than his love for them, to
open their minds all over again, to discover how they thought.
They arrived each time as strangers, despite long distance

calls, in spite of blood. And by the time they retrieved and perfected, once again, a language to say everything but still not enough, they all sat in the car on the way to the airport, all three of them dazed by the arrival of the end, hushed and wondering why the last words they would say that day were *Goodbye*.

But when his children arrived, disembarking with the other passengers in a thin bedraggled stream, familiarity automatically charged Logan's brain and he knew he could pilot them to a safe landing in his heart. Amir was rumpled, disheveled as a pack rat from the flight, and Tiambe, with the vanity of the preteen embarrassed by a younger brother's presence, grabbed her father's arm as if to fly on it, like a magic carpet, away from Amir.

They were eating dinner and Tiambe had been telling Felicia and Logan about a science project when Logan finally realized the difference in her that was at once subtle and as militant as a flag. He had thought she had gotten taller. She had, but even realizing that, Logan knew there remained a difference that gave the braces she still wore and the neat yet childlike braids Sylvia imposed on Tiambe's short, coarse hair a contradictory, befuddled air. She had breasts. Staring across the dinner table at his daughter, Logan could not see the outline of a bra and so he assumed that she was wearing some kind of feminine sleeveless undershirt. And while Amir tapped him on his arm to get his attention, Logan wondered if Tiambe had had her first period. He listened to his daughter's confident, light-hearted voice and wondered what the boys at her school looked like. Wondered if she had been kissed. And the fact that he did not know the answers to these questions made Logan push his plate aside. Because he did not know how to ask, he rose in anguished, controlled anger from the table, his children and his wife gazing at him in puzzled surprise. Inspired by Logan's sudden movement, his year-old son Mugabe began to scream ecstatically while squirming for release in his high chair. "Daddy, wan' go! Daddy, wan' go." And Amir complained in a brooding, threat-filled voice, "I've been trying to tell you about the hockey team, but you won't listen." Felicia asked him with her eyes and he told her, "I'm going out for a walk."

Chapter Twenty-Seven

The street Logan lived on was tranquil, shaded by an impressive congregation of sturdy trees. In summer, the generous foliage cast protective arms over the houses on each block, houses which exuded, at their most impressive, an imperial air and, at their least, an attitude of smug conceit.

Each residence stood staunch in its individuality, disdainful of those in whose company it was found. Eloquent brownstones, their sloping lawns and steep steps inviting yet somehow admonishing passersby, held court beside homespun double-deckers, advertising their worth with a stolid handsomeness. Shutters, white-washed columns, portals were attractive but superfluous touches. The houses, like the trees, had witnessed the impermanence of the lives disclosed beneath their gaze and quite literally within their grasp.

Not even the obsession with "improving" and modernizing the houses, so prevalent among the homeowners on this block, counted for much. For the installation of a massive wooden door from Nigeria, carved with figures that spoke of the history of an entire race (as one man on the street had done), had more to do, the houses knew, with the eternal fight against anonymity than with architecture.

Autumn came and men obsessively raked muted yellow and fervent orange leaves from their lawns as though these singular smiles, shed stubbornly by the trees, defaced not just their lawns but their lives as well. And springtime witnessed gardens dug by the women, who planted seeds because, in their minds, backyards were where children should play and flowers should grow.

Twenty-four houses lined the street, all tended lovingly, all nurtured more carefully, sometimes, than the people who lived within.

The late November afternoon hung chilly yet ripe over the neighborhood. The air smelled of a faint promise of snow and the now barren trees clung, nevertheless, to a grace that made the street feel like a welcoming sanctuary. Esther parked before Logan's house and marveled again how far he had come. Her heart swelled with pride at Logan's prosperity, feeling, though she was not certain why, that some measure of his affluence belonged to her as well.

Esther turned off the engine and reached in her purse for her gloves, then she glanced at her face in the rearview mirror. Time had been benevolent, maturing her like a work of art whose real colors and true meaning are discovered years after first meeting the canvas. She wore makeup more often now than she had in the past, but the deftly applied lines and shadings merely enhanced a completeness, an assurance that sang in her flesh and, when she laughed, made her laughter sound like a quickened, expectant pulse. There were doubts etched on her face too, embedded in the tiny lines pricking her upper lip.

But as Esther gazed at herself in the mirror, smiling at herself, she liked what she saw.

As Esther walked up the steps to the front door, she quickly glanced at her watch. It was 12:05. She hoped she was not too early. She had promised Felicia to come over a few hours early to help her with Thanksgiving dinner. There was a time when she was nearly always late for appointments. Esther had perceived time and "tomorrow" as inalienable, guaranteed rights. But, with each passing year, she found herself more sensitive to what time meant and how she used it. To keep fit, she began an early-morning regime of aerobic walking through her neighborhood. And she loved the feel of 6:00 A.M.—uncluttered, sleepy yet auspicious and unblemished by disappointment. She had undergone a hysterectomy several years ago and during the month-long recuperation Esther learned to see and sense the passage of time with an eerie precision. And what had surprised her most during that month of novel-reading, game-show-watching and list-making was how quickly and resolutely the hours melded into one another, forming a morning, an afternoon, a day, a week. Illness, money, success, prayer—nothing stalled the onslaught of time. And Esther arose from her bed, recovered and determined to appreciate the force that she could not master but had, until then, failed to respect.

Only moments after Esther knocked on the front door Felicia ushered her into the house. She was armed with a huge spoon that smelled of turkey dressing and hugged

Esther lightly to avoid touching her with her grease-stained apron.

"Am I too early?" Esther asked, immediately buoyed by the presence of her daughter-in-law, who bristled with a competence and charm that Esther had at first suspected but now accepted, guilt-free and grateful.

"Oh no, you're just in time to taste the dressing and tell me what it needs."

Esther removed her coat and hung it in the hall closet.

"Do I smell pumpkin pie?"

"You sure do."

"Go on, girl. You mighty ambitious." Esther laughed.

"Well, with my mama, your mama and my husband's mama breaking bread with us today, I had to try to strut my stuff." Felicia grinned with a broad smile that trembled with the tiniest trace of anxiety at the mention of the female triumvirate she had cited.

"Well, strut on, honey. Strut on," Esther said, following Felicia through the huge living room, which was sparsely furnished with only a black leather sofa that seated eight, an oriental rug partially covering the gleaming hardwood floor and off-white desert-sand-colored curtains. The walls were filled with vivid prints and sketches by a host of Black artists, the colors filling the room with images of mourning and freedom. A huge yellow, green and red kente cloth hung like a blessing on one wall. And Esther noticed the slender, innocent necks of a bouquet of pussy willows arching from a huge clay pot on the floor.

In the kitchen Esther settled on a stool at a long rectangular wooden table that occupied the center of the space. Wine and champagne glasses hung from a wooden holder attached to the ceiling overhead.

"Logan and Mugabe drove over to the 7-Eleven to pick up a few things I forgot," Felicia told Esther as she offered her a spoonful of the dressing from a bowl on the table.

"A little more sage," Esther said after savoring the mixture.

"That's what I thought." Felicia measured a teaspoonful of sage and stirred it into the dressing.

"Where's Nate?"

"He's coming over around four o'clock."

"He didn't come in till almost five this morning," Esther said, tossing the spoon onto the table, as if the mention of her younger son had spoiled her appetite.

"It takes all night to have fun, sometimes, when you're twenty," Felicia offered weakly, hoping to stave off Esther's anger, which she could see swelling and distorting the carefully planned exterior Esther presented to the world.

"There's not that much fun anywhere," she said bitterly. "Ever since he dropped out of college it's been like living with somebody that I don't know, somebody who doesn't want me to know them."

"What do you think's going on?"

"I've no idea. And I'll be honest with you, Felicia, there are times I don't want to know."

"Is he hiding something?"

"He's hiding the boy he used to be."

"Maybe he's not hiding him. Maybe that boy's simply gone."

The two women shared a glance fraught with more knowing than either could bear and the sound of Logan coming through the door rescued them from a prolonged, silent testimony.

Four-year-old Mugabe bounded into the kitchen ahead of Logan. "Hi, Gramma," the boy said easily, standing before Esther and holding his arms up to her.

"Well, hello, Mister Man." Esther smiled, her discontent extinguished by one look at her grandson. She picked Mugabe up, settled him on her lap and rubbed his still-chilly hands and cheeks.

"We bought ice cream," the child informed Esther, gazing

at her staunchly, his stare as open and secure as his mother's. The child possessed Logan's studied, rapt demeanor, completed by the definitive impact of Felicia's questioning spirit. He could read already and count to twenty-five, although he had yet to start school. And Esther had watched the boy listen to adult conversations as though he was absorbing everything he heard for imminent future use.

"You must have arrived the moment we left," Logan said, giving Esther a light, perfunctory kiss on the cheek as he reached in the bowl for the last scoop of dressing while Felicia stuffed the turkey. Unlike Nathaniel, with whom she could improvise a vast range of emotional responses, with Logan, Esther's concern acknowledged the distance they had erased and the distance that still remained between them. Logan's lips lightly brushed Esther's cheeks, offering more than a casual observer would ever suspect.

"I haven't been here long," Esther told him, holding Mugabe tighter as he squirmed for release.

"And Felicia's got everything under control."

"It just looks that way," Felicia moaned. "My biscuits *always* fall flat and I wondered if . . ."

"Sure, bring on the flour," Esther said brightly. "And Mugabe'll help, won't you?"

Logan made a sandwich and wandered into the living room. Moments later the sounds of the Macy's Thanksgiving Day Parade drifted into the kitchen, where Esther sat rolling dough and watching Mugabe roll small balls of dough into tiny shapes.

"I'm going upstairs to take a bath," Felicia announced after she had washed the dishes that remained.

"Go ahead," Esther said. "Me and Mugabe will watch the turkey." Quietly and methodically, Mugabe sat making balls of dough, squishing them flat with his palm, his small body shaken by a gleeful, mocking laughter at the sight of the pancake-thin dough.

As Esther sat across from her grandson, she recalled how, after Randolph's death, the child she carried seemed to shrivel inside her. As if sensing her grief, absorbing the rage and terror that infected her spirit, the child lay in her womb, dormant, and still. The sudden movements that had fluttered beneath her breasts, filling Esther with flickering moments of happy anticipation, the sprightly somersaults that had made her imagine that the child was playing tag with his shadow all ceased. And there were no signs of life, save the child's heartbeat, until he was delivered in an intense, painful twelve-hour labor.

And yet, when Esther saw the shadows of Randolph that permeated Nathaniel's face, she felt full to bursting with the maternal affection that Logan had not inspired. As a baby, Nathaniel's small, chubby hands reached for what they desired with a tenacious will. He was playful, moody, changeable. Some nights Nathaniel cried for hours, although he was not wet, and refused Esther's breast. Hearty and determined, the child seemed content merely to exercise the miraculous sound of his lungs. It was when Nathaniel was sick or had to be taken to the doctor that Esther missed Randolph the most and at night, when she finally coaxed Nathaniel to sleep, she was restless as she cursed Randolph for leaving her, begging him to come back.

When Nathaniel was two, Esther decided to go back to school. The executor of Randolph's estate had, at his request, sold off much of his property and Esther and Logan and the baby had received a hefty amount. But Esther had invested much of the money for their collective futures. The colleges and universities in the area had developed many innovative programs to attract nontraditional students. So Esther enrolled at American University under a program that gave her college credit for her life experiences and she was awarded enough credits to put her a year away from her B.A. She decided to study education on the graduate level and received a full scholarship and attended school full-time.

When Esther received her master's degree, she went to work for a private philanthrophic agency that specialized in funding educational programs and projects. She started out as a program assistant—a glorified secretary—then rose to project director.

Esther had always feared loving Nathaniel too much. She was a woman of extremes and because she had given so little to Logan she tried to check her tendency to sacrifice everything for Nathaniel.

Nathaniel lacked Logan's single-mindedness, mastering subjects in school with ease, yet making poor grades that belied his abilities. He was easily gripped by enthusiasms—Boy Scouts, tennis, hockey—for which Esther spent small fortunes and watched in dismay as he grew bored with each one. Even now, the attic was filled to overflowing with evidence of Nathaniel's fickle, mercurial nature.

During the summer, Nathaniel had announced that he was dropping out of the University of Maryland, where he had managed to complete two years. Esther sat across from Nathaniel, his face, as he told her this, charged by a cocky, assertive grin, as if he had some plan in mind that was superior to college, and wondered if she was being punished for her own retreat from school at the same age. Just as Naomi must have felt, Esther saw some intangible yet splendid dream crumble, felt it as a pain in her heart. Nathaniel's apologetic, shamefaced monologue about jobs he could get, space he needed curdled into a vague, obscene music that hit Esther's ears like a dirge.

Mugabe's laughter pierced Esther's reverie and stalled the sudden spiral-like descent of her emotions. When she finished the biscuits, Esther suddenly found herself very tired and she lay down for a nap in the guest room. As she drifted off to sleep, Esther recalled how watching Nathaniel grow up had struck her as an experience that possessed all the qualities of a good drama. This time she was there for all of it and Esther marveled at how imperceptible yet totally obvious were the changes that occurred in Nathaniel. She had thought she could hold his childhood, but it passed through her grasp like sand through a sieve.

In his study Logan sat waiting for the arrvial of his brother, listening to the sturdy voices of the women below him. Esther had asked him when she came downstairs, after her nap, to talk to Nathaniel.

"What's up?" he had asked, turning from the football game on the TV screen to look at Esther.

"I don't know."

"What do you suspect?"

"I'm not sure."

"You've got to give me more information than that."

"He stays out late. Very late. Comes in at all hours of the morning. And he gets strange calls sometimes."

"From who?"

"People I never hear from anymore, people that sound like they're doing some sort of business with him."

Neither of them wanted to say more, although both shuddered at what they had revealed and what they feared. "I'll talk to him," Logan assured his mother and began watching the game again.

Now, as he sat waiting for Nathaniel, Logan marveled at the confidence with which he had promised to talk to his brother. He had always envied Nathaniel's ease, his handsomeness and nonchalance. The agony and doubt over choices, self-worth, career, family that plagued Logan, he could already see, would simply be foreign to Nathaniel. Although Nathaniel was still young, his approach to life was already established and his certitude seemed to ensure that his battles would be no less rigorous but perhaps less bloody than those Logan had waged. They talked often, but rarely with the serious intent Esther now requested. And lately, the closer Nathaniel drew to adulthood, the less fulfilled Logan was by their conversations. There was a tentative, halting quality to Nathaniel's revelations, an imprecise feel to Logan's requests. He longed to bestow upon Nathaniel assurances that were a sign of love and trust. Logan had hoped the way he had lived his own life would inform Nathaniel of the things that were important. Even when he had lost what was precious, Logan could always say he had tried. Never had they been a family for whom words came easily. The most necessary language was retrieved as a last resort, when predictable, comfortable yet ill-serving responses broke down and forced a dredging of honesty that could only be borne in small doses.

Logan was dismayed and confused by the ease with which Nathaniel had dropped out of college. Twenty-one was an age of brash arrogance, overconfidence and sheer ignorance. Logan knew that, with a steady concurrence, his brother was running out of time and had the rest of his life. What he did not know was which destiny appealed to Nathaniel more.

As Nathaniel entered the study, Logan thought that his brother had never looked more like their father. As Nathaniel had grown older, his face had seemed to flatten out, molded by the tautness, the edginess that had so defined Randolph. Nathaniel had the face of a tiger, stealthy and poised to attack or claim. His eyes were unsettled and luminous. They were the only two men in the house and Logan felt buttressed, despite the impending task Esther had charged him with.

"Hey, big brother," Nathaniel said, slapping palms in greeting to Logan.

Nathaniel sat down heavily in a lounge chair beside Logan's desk.

"I didn't hold up dinner, did I?"

"No, but we're about to eat."

Nathaniel sat, stretching out his legs, gazing around the book- and paper-filled room, the walls covered with prints by Henry Tanner and Horace Pippin.

Logan turned back to the desk, where he had sat putting photos in an album, pictures of all his children that he and Felicia had taken during the summer.

"You still doing that courier bit?"

"Yeah," Nathaniel said defensively.

"How long do you plan to waste your time?"

"I'm not wasting my time. I'm marking it." Nathaniel stood up and leaned over Logan's shoulders at the desk. He picked up one of the photo albums and leafed through it absently. "Hey, like, no *Hello*, no *How's it going?* Just jump all over me from Jump Street," Nathaniel fumed, placing the album back on the desk after a cursory glance at its pages.

"Mom's worried about you."

"What for?" Nathaniel had retreated to the lounge chair, where he sat, slumped and testy.

"Your habits. The company you keep."

"I've done nothing wrong."

"That we know of."

"You accusing me?"

"You got anything to hide?" Logan asked, closing the album, slamming it shut for emphasis.

"Look, man, I don't have to take this." Nathaniel rose from the chair.

"Sit down. Just sit the hell down."

"What'd she say?" Nathaniel warily asked as he slowly eased back into the chair.

"Don't use the house as a pit stop, someplace just to change your clothes and then hit the street. Did it ever occur to you to spend an evening at home with Mother?"

"At home? For what?"

"To show her you care. Or have you forgotten how to do that?"

"That's low, Logan. I don't deserve that."

"She deserves better too."

"All right. All right. I'll take her to a movie sometime."

"Maybe eat dinner at home now and then," Logan urged.

"You're pushing it, man," Nanthaniel said, holding up his hands in protest. "When was the last time you had Mom's cooking?"

He had done it again, Logan thought, as he grimly stifled a smile. Nathaniel had defused his anger, turned the tables, matched a storm of disapproval with charm. And Logan laughed in spite of himself, felt buoyed and uncomfortable, unfairly defeated.

Felicia called upstairs, "Logan, we're about to eat."

"Who cooked?" Nathaniel asked, extending his mastery of the moment, aware of how much he had won.

"Felicia."

"Well, come on, bro, what we waiting for?"

Chapter Twenty-Eight

He'd always felt like an outsider. Never like he "fit." And it appeared to Nathaniel that his brother Logan had never made a single mistake, never *blown* anything in his life. But what he held most against both Esther and Logan was their knowledge of his father. The death of Randolph six months before Nathaniel's birth had marked Nathaniel, in his eyes, as orphan and outcast. If Randolph had really loved him, Nathaniel was utterly convinced, his father would have lived. Esther had created a resilient mythology for Nathaniel that forgave his father far more than she ever had when he lived and invested Randolph with a wisdom that Randolph himself would have easily admitted that he lacked. Esther saw this legend as a gift to her youngest son, yet the tale of enduring love, unvanquished loyalty stoked Nathaniel's hunger and shaped it into an ache for his father that was indelible and complete. Nathaniel had searched for his father in the sepia-tinted photos in Esther's album, in the more honest yet still wrenching anecdotes Logan sometimes shared. But he had not found his father there. And the two or three times he had gone with Esther to lay a wreath on Randolph's grave Nathaniel lingered at the grave site as Esther walked back to the car. Nathaniel stood, erect and hopeful, and spoke, in a whisper, the single, blessed word *father* as his eyes grazed the name and dates on the headstone. And the word, dredged up from the canyon of longing inside him, landed gentle and insubstantial, on the air, hitting his ears like a shamefaced lie, not strong enough to echo, dying so fast that Nathaniel wondered if he had spoken the word at all. And his mother and grandmother were always telling him he was "just like his father." They told him this when he performed some act of bravado or daring, their eyes growing large, sparkling, as memory invaded their minds and filtered through their gaze. Approval and fear lodged in their voices, even as love gleamed in their eyes. Yet the words meant nothing to Nathaniel. He did not know his father. Had never seen him laugh, felt Randolph's hand punishing and hard against his face, had never seen him reach for Esther as if she was the best thing in the world, had never heard his father say what he, his son, was expected to be. Maybe he *was* just like his father, but it was up to him to decide what that meant.

He liked to think of himself as a freelance businessman. And he didn't care what other people called it—*pushing, dealing*—he was simply following the laws of supply and demand and doing it the American way. He sold cocaine and rarely lost a night's sleep over the implications and results of what he did. Sure, he heard the stories of overdoses and users getting so strung out they'd sell their ass and their mama, but that was *their* problem, not his. He'd been in it for a year and a half and had decided to give it one more year and then get out. Nobody got old doing this, either the drugs or the competitors caught up with you and blew you away. And he had no plans to wake up dead. Several doctors, a college professor, three police officers and an accountant with one of the city's largest law firms were among his steadiest customers. Thirty-five people knew the number of his telephone beeper. And he conducted business a few hours a day, usually in the evening, when he drove around the city, watching telephone numbers appear on his beeper. The deals were made on street corners, in living rooms, bars, anyplace his customers felt comfortable.

The gun was at home. Snookie bought it for him on order shortly after they started. And even if he never ended up using it, Nathaniel knew he had to have it. The .22 fit neatly into his hand, heavy yet light, and as he assessed the gun the first time, Nathaniel had admired the craftsmanship that had produced it. It was simply a beautiful piece of work, almost like a sculpture, except that it was designed to kill. And even when inert, the coldness of the steel, the sharpness of its edges hinted at the gun's intent. The .22 lay in a locked metal box on the top shelf of his closet. Sometimes, when he was home alone, he'd take the gun out and just hold it and watch his grip turn into a fondling action, nearly an embrace, so awed was he by the weapon's potential, so buoyed was he by the boost it gave to his concept of who he was. In the beginning he hadn't carried it much. But in the last year he had begun to travel with it when he had to buy from certain suppliers or travel through rough neighborhoods. There were sixteen-year-olds running around with Uzzis, ready to blow you away. And it didn't matter that he tried to be cool. A couple of thousand dollars went through his hands every month and that alone made him vulnerable, turned him into a target. He could never be sure who was aiming at him.

There'd been a few indulgences—he had bought a two-year-old Mercedes with cash and the look in the salesman's eyes had been worth it all. He kept the car in the garage of Ulysses, his other partner. He'd always wanted a sailboat and now he owned one, docked at the harbor in Southwest. And his wardrobe was a little flashier now. But he didn't flaunt any of it. Besides, just knowing that he had a small fortune stashed away in a hiding place no one would ever suspect was satisfaction enough. Nathaniel had created a small universe in which he set the rules. He could show up late for a meeting with a client and, if the guy was a heavy user, fuck up his whole nervous system. To some people in the city he was more important than wives, kids, girlfriends, parents. And some men looked at him and wanted everything he had.

When Esther got on his nerves, he thought about the money he had stashed away. When his girlfriend Trudy threatened to drive him crazy, he got into his Benz and went for a drive. Now he had an answer for everything. He snorted once or twice a month, mostly to be sociable with an especially favored customer, and in all of it he felt almost legitimate. But it was the illegitimacy of it all that gave him the rush, made the whole thing taste and feel so good.

He had thought a lot lately about joining the air force when this was over. Ever since he could remember, he'd wanted to fly. When he was a kid, he'd sit in his room, using up all his notebook paper to make paper airplanes. He liked the planes he made much better than the ones Esther bought him. When he aimed the lightweight paper plane through the air, the gliders especially, smooth and twisting, he could feel the curve inside his body. The dips, lifts, twirls spun vicariously inside his ten-year-old soul. As he grew older, the improbability of flight was what appealed to him most. The defiance of nature inherent in the act teased his imagination as few other options had. If he could learn how to fly, he'd feel like he could do just about anything. Sometimes he thought the only moments he was really alive were when he was nearly losing his life. Like when he bicycled through downtown traffic, sideswiping cars, the tires of his bike screeching to a halt at a red light, the unbearable pounding of his heart as he estimated how to be the first person in the intersection once the light changed.

When he was fourteen, he and two friends, Rodney and James, had become proficient but amateur shoplifters. Rather than specializing in the small neighborhood stores and shops where they would blend in and not be so easily noticed, the three boys took on the big department stores downtown. In Woodward & Lothrop and Hecht's the quality of merchandise was better (which interested Rodney and James) and the risk of getting caught greater (which intrigued Nathaniel). Entering the store, each of the boys would head in a different direction. And yet from the moment they entered they knew they were being watched, could feel the eyes of the conspicuous security guards following each step they took. Rodney was greedy, stuffing his pockets and the spaces beneath his jacket with so many items Nathaniel called him *Magnet Man*. James, cautious and joining in the adventure to gain the friendship of the other two, might come out with only one item, but it was always something, he would tell Nathaniel and Rodney, that he'd always wanted—be it a fishing pole, tennis racket or a leather briefcase—"for when I grow up." But Nathaniel swiped articles within a few feet of the security guards to test his luck and prowess. He'd lift anything, for there was nothing really that he wanted in the stores. Esther bought him anything he asked for. But his mother could not purchase the fleeting yet remarkable sensation of control that embraced him as he walked out of Woodward & Lothrop with a portable radio or a cashmere sweater beneath his coat. And he was caught one day because he had come to think he never would be.

Standing beside a rack of boys' slacks, looking for his size, Nathaniel felt a large, heavy hand on the collar of his coat. "Turn around, boy, and don't try to run," the dark, masculine voice ordered him. Naturally he ran, his arms nearly knocking down customers, his feet tripping over four displays. The men's cologne and the Sheaffer pen had clattered to the floor from the inside of his jacket with the first steps. Bounding down the escalator stairs, Nathaniel could hear the heavy-footed chase of the guard after him. All he had to do was make it outside the front door, make it onto the street, and he was safe. But it was Saturday and the first floor teemed with people that from the escalator steps looked like thousands of tiny doll-like figures amassed for the sole purpose of preventing his escape. Clamoring down the escalator, Nathaniel suddenly felt a warm wet trickle slide down his thigh. The realization that he had peed on himself unnerved him even more than the guard closing in on him. And suddenly Nathaniel wanted to cry because of his pants now sticking to his leg.

Still, he jumped from the last step of the escalator and plowed through the dense, intractable wall of shoppers. He punched, kicked and cursed his way through the crowd, eyes closed, teeth clenched, waiting, as he did, for the feel of the guard's hand on his collar. When the hand arrived again, it landed on his elbow and spun him around with such force that he ended up sprawled on the marble floor, the shimmering glitter and tinsel of the store's chandelier overhead staring down at him in glorious mockery. He felt as small as an ant. And as if in response to this thought, the security guard placed a booted foot on Nathaniel's thigh as he summoned another guard on his walkie-talkie.

He was put on probation for a year. And Esther took his actions as a personal affront. Logan had asked him why he'd been stealing. But Nathaniel looked at his older brother and sensed in a glance the extent of his possible understanding, shrugged and said nothing. How could he tell his mother and brother that in a period of a year he had stolen fifteen hundred dollars' worth of merchandise because he felt, by those acts, confirmed? He might have said that he was bored, impatient and felt most days as though no one, save his friends, really saw him. But he did not. Nathaniel would risk probation or jail. But he would never risk having the knowlege of who he was slaughtered by the judgment of an adult.

He inherited the trade from an older guy he had become friendly with during the two years he had attended the University of Maryland. The university had struck him as even more irrelevant to real life than high school had been. And Nathaniel failed, with studious, purposeful intent, because he would have been happier as a mechanic or a construction worker, anything using his hands. But Esther had nearly promised to have a stroke or nervous breakdown if he didn't go, as she said, "to some college somewhere." The size of the campus anointed Nathaniel with a numbing sense of anonymity that he eased by getting high, smoking marijuana a couple of times a week, floating through his classes in a mellow, indifferent haze. Assuming that his professors could not impart any knowledge worthy of his attention, Nathaniel sat in the back row of his classes, his eyes flat and dull with disinterest and inattention, gazing out the window or checking the time on his watch. As a freshman, the girls in his classes looked staunchly through him. And in the moments when he found himself, out of boredom or a latent curiosity, surveying the young women around him, Nathaniel imagined blueprints for the rest of their lives sputtering inside their heads like a computer printout. The girls' thirst for life, radiant as a force field around them, frightened Nathaniel so much that often he was nearly speechless in their presence.

This was how Jason Whitfield found him. Yet it had not really surprised Nathaniel that Jason, a graduate student majoring in engineering, sought out his friendship, looked around the cafeteria and, spotting Nathaniel at a table alone, chose to sit with him or stopped to shoot the breeze when they saw each other on the way to classes. Tall and big for his age, Nathaniel knew that many people often thought he was older than he was. And his face, like his father's, was so uncomplicated that some gazed upon it and were drawn to reveal themselves as if on their knees in a confessional. Only the Jasons of the world could look at Nathaniel, however, and fathom, behind the serenity of his gaze, his talent for the duplicitous or his smoldering need to brand his name across the sky of his small world in hot neon lights.

It wasn't until Jason had married, left the city and moved as easily out of his life as he moved into it that Nathaniel looked back and traced the method by which he was chosen and nurtured by Jason to take over the trade. He and Jason shot pool once a week at a pool hall in Silver Spring, a large room pulsing with the sound and scent of masculinity, sparked by men who played the game for a living or who hung out in the hall rather than go home and men who basked on imagined center stages as they regaled those present with raucous, earthy fabrications and exaggerations, embellishing their prowess with women and fate as they strode, rooster proud, around the felt-covered tables. Nathaniel measured the promises the men offered in this profane yet sacred setting and reached unhesitatingly for each one. Jason introduced Nathaniel to girls who, while schooling him in the proficiencies of lust, made him think they were the ones taking notes, girls who melted his muteness and shaped it into surprising soliloquies that astonished Nathaniel and set him nearly shivering with confidence.

Smoothly handsome, with a tall, sinewy frame that he draped in tailored, expensive clothing, Jason possessed a gleaming seductiveness that was asexual yet strongly potent. He made Nathaniel feel honored and revived by his friendship. Jason had descended upon Nathaniel with the precision of an eagle, yet his overture had been as endearing as a lark's. Jason waited nearly a year before telling Nathaniel he was dealing cocaine. In response, Nate said very little and that impressed Jason. "So you're what a pusher looks like." Nathaniel smiled. "And so are you," Jason answered.

Nate had dropped out by then and was working as a courier for a delivery company. Jason's fiancée had told him to get out of the business or lose her. With his M.Sc. in engineering, Jason decided to move to Chicago and offered his trade to Nathaniel, saying, "You're not a user. You've got your head on straight. And you know how to hustle. I've been watching you ever since we started hanging out and I can't think of anybody better qualified to fill my shoes."

Nathaniel said yes to Jason's offer because the classroom had suffocated him, made him feel like everybody else. The illicit, undercover nature of the endeavor appealed to him as much as the money. The thought of being both pusher and dutiful son inflamed Nathaniel's imagination as had no other prospect until then. He had spent his life, it seemed, improvising an identity, burdened and overshadowed by a legacy he felt no loyalty to—and so, Nathaniel sought no one's approval, only vindication of his control over his particular fate. Yet he loved his family—and so, he would make sure they never found out. This would be his, beholden to, springing from no one else and, though his actions were illegal, he would define himself as a freelance entrepreneur, a businessman—and so, exempt whatever he did from the fuzzy, negotiable world of ethics and morality.

At twelve, he and Esther had discussed the meaning of *covert operations*, the work of the CIA, nuclear plants that the government knew emitted radiation into well-populated communities. While they sat on the carpet, playing Monopoly, or prepared dinner, the television, as insistent as another member of the family, beamed glittering, sanctified visions into their home—the blank, dangerous faces of presidents no one trusted, random, final violence everybody took for granted and the two meshed in a jarring symphony that had come, ironically, to soothe and satisfy all who heard it. Nathaniel didn't even want to inherit the world his mother and brother longed to bequeath him, for he was neither meek nor innocent enough to accept the world with a heart rimmed with hope. Tomorrow might not come, there was a good chance of that. And that meant everybody was free.

Nathaniel quickly integrated the trade into his job as a courier. And, now he had two runners who gave him a cut of their take. He had taken the job of courier because it gave him the illusion that he was free. When he delivered packages and letters to office buildings around the city, Nathaniel checked out the folks there and whether they were secretaries or the chairman of the board, they were all chained to a desk. Seemed like if they didn't have a desk they wouldn't have a job. But he'd be damned if he was gonna carry a desk on his back, be a slave to a square piece of metal. And the vibes in some of the offices was murderous. He could tell in a few minutes whether or not the people working there were happy, thought their boss was an idiot or felt underpaid for too much work. The fancy sofas in the waiting area, the expensive artwork on the walls, the high-tech office computers he sometimes spied the secretaries pounding away on, none of that could conceal low morale. It got into the air. And it would seem like everybody was choking on it. You couldn't even open the windows in most of those buildings. Everybody locked in, sealed up tight. Most of the folks he supplied worked in offices and he was pretty sure that if he had to work cooped up like that all day, he'd start and end his day coked up too.

When he drove to the home of James Burroughs, Nathaniel saw him raking leaves in his front yard. His three-story house was located a block away from Rock Creek Park. And all the homes along the street were endowed with a stately confidence that informed those who looked upon them of their value in correct, perfectly modulated tones.

Locking the door and waving to Burroughs, Nathaniel wondered if any other criminals lived on the street. Burroughs, who owned a chain of computer software stores in Maryland and Virginia, which made him one of the most successful Black businessmen in the area, was also one of three suppliers that Nathaniel regularly dealt with.

"You're a good man, Nathaniel. If you say two o'clock, it's two o'clock," Burroughs said, glancing at his watch as he filled a plastic bag with leaves. "Most young men your age don't appreciate the value of time."

"I try to control it so it doesn't control me," Nate said, slipping into the slightly deferential tones that somehow characterized his voice during their meetings.

"That's an admirable philosophy and you seem to be able to live up to it."

"Can I give you a hand?"

"No no, don't bother. This is the last bag," Burroughs told him, stuffing the leaves into a nearly full plastic bag. Nodding towards a row of bags near the steps, he said, "I've been out here since twelve-thirty." Tying a plastic string around the bag, Burroughs asked, "How've you been?"

"Not bad."

"You look good. You ready to do business?"

"I am."

Nathaniel helped him take the bags through the house and they deposited them in the back near the metal garbage cans. Then they went into the house.

"Would you like a beer?"

"No thanks," Nathaniel said. "So you've got the house all to yourself today?"

"Sure have," Burroughs bellowed jovially, reaching into the well-stocked refrigerator for a beer.

The jogging suit Burroughs wore was slightly odorous with sweat and he reached over the sink and tore off a paper towel and wiped his forehead. Burroughs was a tall, broadly built man and his face wore a perpetual gaze of wonder. Behind his horn-rimmed glasses he seemed to peer at Nathaniel as though gazing at a tiny insect.

"Come on downstairs."

They descended the steps into the wood-paneled basement, its walls lined with hundreds of X-rated and pornographic cassettes. A pool table, which looked as though it had never been used, took up a portion of the basement. A giant fifty-six-inch screen loomed from an elevated stand, a huge omniscient eye filling the room with its presence. Nathaniel had never met Mrs. Burroughs, but he often wondered what kind of woman she was to put up with a guy like James Burroughs.

Once, shortly after he had taken over from Jason, Burroughs had pressured Nathaniel into watching a movie with him, a movie about three women and a man. He had been so new at it then that Nathaniel had not known how to tell Burroughs that he just wanted to make a buy and split. So they sat in the darkened basement that day, watching these three white chicks, all sleazy, dumb-looking types, lick this guy's balls, his ass, sit on his face. All while inspiring about as much excitement in Nathaniel as watching grass grow. But beside him Burroughs sat, his hands lodged between his legs, moving up and down, his breathing growing raspy and heavy. Nate could almost smell the old guy's come filling the suddenly tiny basement. And, when he could bear it no longer, Nate grabbed the remote control from the coffee table and flicked the screen off. At that moment Burroughs emitted a soft kittenlike sigh and slumped against the sofa for thirty seconds and then, without saying a word, scurried to the bathroom, where he stayed for ten minutes, and came out wearing a new pair of slacks.

Now Borroughs sat down next to Nathaniel, letting his hand rest on Nate's knee, and asked, "So how much are you in the market for today?" Nathaniel had tried to avoid Burroughs because he gave him the creeps, but Burroughs consistently had the highest-quality coke and he seemed never to run dry. But Nathaniel had told him to keep his hobbies to himself.

Nathaniel curtly told Burroughs, "I want two ounces." He said this, feeling the walls almost close in on him as they often seemed to do in that basement. "Business must be booming," Burroughs said, opening a safe hidden behind a knee-high stack of *Playboy* and *Hustler* magazines.

"It's not bad."

Burroughs reached into the safe and brought out two one-ounce plastic bags of cocaine and tossed them to Nathaniel. Nathaniel placed an envelope with two thousand dollars in it on the table in front of the sofa.

"You expanding?" Burroughs asked.

"Naw. I've got a coupla parties coming up this weekend I've got to supply."

"Somebody tried to break in here last week," Burroughs said significantly.

"You got any suspects?"

"A few. You're not one of them."

"Why should I be?"

"That's what I thought. Anyway, I'm getting a Doberman next week. And I've got a couple of .22's in strategic locations around the house. I'll be prepared if the bastards come back."

"It's getting pretty hot out there," Nathaniel observed almost casually.

"You carry a piece?" Burroughs asked.

"Sometimes."

"You better consider carrying one *all* the time."

"I'll think about that," Nathaniel told Burroughs as he stood up. Then he asked, "Were you for real when you told me last time that you'd never snorted, not even once?"

"That was the truth. My vices are more old-fashioned, less harmful," he said with a cold smile that he quickly erased as he turned to lead Nathaniel out by the hidden exit that led to the street.

Chapter Twenty-Nine

N A O M I

Trying to hold on to Nathaniel was like holding on to lightning. The boy would just slip right through your hands. And I never felt like I knew him. Not like I knew Logan. I don't think the boy was bad. Maybe I'm just saying that 'cause I'm his grandma, but I never saw no meanness in him. No, he wasn't mean, he was just selfish, didn't think about how what he did was gonna affect other people. And he always acted like there wasn't gonna be no tomorrow, like the world was moving too fast and he was moving too slow to catch it.

Just like with Logan, I helped Esther with Nate. Course I was considerably older then, but there wasn't no way I could see Esther hiring no sitter when I still had my health. I remember one day I'd gone next door to visit a neighbor and left Nathaniel and another little boy playing in the basement. Well, I come back and found the basement full of cigarette smoke. Nate and the other boy had smoked up half a pack of Kools Esther had bought the day before. Well, now I had to beat him. I sent the other boy home and went to my room and got my strap. And all the time I'm beating him, Nathaniel refuses to cry. I knew that strap was hurting him, but he just folded up on himself, his eyes hard and blank, staring past me. I'd made him take his clothes off so he was naked. And I was holding him with one hand and beating him with the other. He'd scramble around, trying to get out the way of the strap, but he'd done decided wasn't nothing gonna make him cry. I got wore out and I guess you could say Nathaniel won. 'Cause he didn't shed a tear. And I left him in the bedroom on the floor, his body trembling, breathing hard, as if he'd been chased by demons. And if he cried later on that day, I never heard nothing about it. Now I don't know what the boy got outta acting like that, but it was something he thought he had to do.

And I don't think I ever heard Nate say, "I'm sorry" more than two or three times in his life. My preaching, Esther's lectures didn't make a dent. It just never occurred to him to ask nobody's pardon. I think he thought being humble, even for a minute, made him less than he wanted to be. And the older he got, the more he liked to act like he wasn't scared of nothing. I'm no psychiatrist, but I know people like that, they're usually scared of more than the rest of us.

But when I think of what happened, and try to figure out why, I remember how I always thought he had time, and plenty of it, to leave all that behind him. To grow up. He was so young. He was still a boy and that's why I wasn't so worried. He was still a boy and so had time. But Nathaniel had other ideas. He was determined, even though he wasn't ready yet, to be a man. And 'cause he was so young, he got it all wrong, what a man is and what he's supposed to do. The boy got it all wrong.

They all thought he was a fool. All of them. And he'd learned to let them think that, while checking them out, scoping their weaknesses, then pulling a fast one that left him standing over them with his boot on their neck. Yeah, they all thought he was a fool. Lots of it was because of his name —Snookie. His real name was Samuel, but he couldn't remember anybody close to him calling him *Samuel* since he was three or four. And he didn't know which name he hated more. *Snookie* made him sound like a fool. But Samuel, hell, Samuel was somebody he didn't know and he'd probably never be. And even on jobs, after a while he'd usually tell his coworkers to cut the Samuel shit and just call him Snookie. Yeah, he knew part of it was his name. Part of it too was how he looked. He looked like a dummy, a black Howdy Doody, the name he'd been called more often in school than Snookie. His high, protruding forehead shaded small, deeply inset eyes as piercing as some tiny forest animal's. Few people noticed how the eyes, small as they were, sparkled with intelligence. They looked at his eyes and saw defiance, which, Snookie knew, was just a breath away from being smart. You couldn't defy what you didn't understand and he'd always understood more than anybody thought. His mama had thought he was smart, had called him Snookie like it was a word full of magic and love, but what did she know? She was just a dumb bitch who let men come around for pussy and nothing more. It was in school that he had learned how to strike back with his fists, to use his hands to bludgeon if not silence the contempt he inspired. That was when he learned too how the pain of others could eradicate, at least for a while, his own hurt, secret, dark and eternal. He'd had trouble reading, but that could've been fixed when he was in elementary school. They tested his eyes and found that he needed glasses his mama couldn't afford, so they put him in the class with the slow learners, put him there, he knew, because of the way he looked and the stocking cap he wore because he had ringworms and because he had seven brothers and sisters smelled of urine since they slept together on a mattress on the floor at night and Petey at five still couldn't control his bladder.

That was then, but as he tied the floral silk tie under his collar, a tie he had bought in Georgetown yesterday, Snookie thought as he had thought all his life about *them* and about the world: "Fuck you." His ability to salvage himself through this curse had saved and ruined him. Since he couldn't read words too well (he still refused to wear glasses, even though he could afford them), afraid they'd make him look like a punk, he had gotten good at reading people. He could look at somebody and they'd feel like he was staring right through them, feel faint in the presence of his power and vision. He could read women who took one look at him and didn't want to be around him. When he was fifteen, he had raped a girl in his homeroom in the basement of the school. She was small and brown-skinned and she had shoulder-length long hair, just like a white girl. She even had dimples in her cheeks and Snookie had noticed her nervously lick her lips when she had to sit next to him. And all the way through it, while holding a switchblade to her throat, he had made her whisper that he was handsome and that she loved him. The girl's parents withdrew her from the school and nobody ever found out that he did it. No, he hadn't gotten caught that time, but he did do time at Oak Hill for gun possession and by the time he got out at seventeen he'd learned all the lessons that really counted. And now that he was pulling in long bread, pushing coke, he could even read his lady Evelyn. She was just there till the money ran out and she secretly thought she was better than him. But he could replace her anytime. Snookie stood back from the mirror and assessed himself in the six-hundred-dollar suit. Nobody looked at his face anymore. Hell, not even him. And as ugly as his face was, nobody would look at it and imagine half the things he had done, half the things he had seen. They looked at his face and trusted it because it looked so dumb and that's what Snookie counted on every time.

Like Nathaniel, with his smooth, easy style. Nate reminded Snookie of all the boys and men who all his life had thought he was nothing. The boogie niggers in high school who laughed at his face and the holes in his socks and his too small jackets. And yet it was those pussies who grew up and became his customers and who, even when they met him in some stinking alley to make a buy, still talked to him like he was something slimy and slithery under the soles of their imported shoes. Snookie never really trusted Nate. And he didn't even like him. He couldn't figure the dude out. What was in it for him? The money? He knew Nate's brother was a doctor. And out of curiosity, Snookie had checked out where Nathaniel lived one evening and found a closed, tight little enclave of comfort and affluence. So what was he trying to prove? That he was a *bad* nigger? Hell, he was a chump. All the time telling him and Ulysses to be *cool*, to hold on to their regular jobs as a cover. Hell, maybe Nate and Ulysses was satisfied using their jobs as a cover. But he was a janitor and he was ready to bust out. He'd already started getting stuff from another supplier to sell to his customers. A seller's market and Nate kept telling them to be cool. Hell, the kid was scared, that's all it could be. Scared to move into the big time. It was one thing for Nate to tell them to be cool, he'd never wanted for a thing in his life. You could see that just by looking at his pampered face. Snookie looked at Nate and knew without asking that he had a mother who loved him too much, that because of how he looked he never even bothered to count his blessings. If he hadn't started pushing cocaine, he'd have made it just as big at something legit. Nathaniel nearly preened with confidence that came from being given half a chance by the world. Feeling his heart pump jaggedly in outrage, Snookie put on his jacket and slid his piece into his side pocket.

Dante's sat on a dead-end street in Southeast Washington, a squat three-story brick building, formerly a warehouse that had been turned into a nightclub. The streets around the club were lined with rows of barracklike low-income apartments. Block after block was claimed by dry, tufted weeds where lawns had once sprouted, boarded-up apartment windows and doors or yawning gashes where windowpanes had once sheltered occupants from the night. Of the five hundred units surrounding the club, over half were unoccupied and were home to rats, drug users and homeless men and women. At night the street was lit faintly by a dull sputtering streetlight that seemed to heighten rather than defeat the darkness. There were few trees and the flat, wide street possessed the eerie, unchartered atmosphere of a newly discovered planet.

Yet every night that Dante's was open for business young people surrounded the fire engine red structure, whose blazing neon sign seemed to verify the screaming, manic presence of life lived where it was too often denied. The young people swarmed to Dante's from the stifling, ragged confines of the apartments on adjacent streets. They gathered at Dante's to break the steely grip of boredom that flowed through their veins, numbed their senses, and which they fought best at night, beneath skies strewn with stars that made them think of silver dollars lining their pockets. On nights like this still balmy December evening, those too young to enter Dante's huddled in groups across the street from the club, leaned and lounged atop and in cars of friends, unleashed laughter and knowledge saved to be stripped and offered up on streets like these, gritty and thunderous as the pulsing drum-based music filtering through the windows of Dante's onto the street. They came wearing gold chains, glittering and monstrous around their necks, chains as corrupt as those that shackled ancestors they cared nothing about. Their clothes were studded with emblems that designers had turned into talismans ensuring self-worth. And they stood, pranced and preened, each move a small explosion lighting up the night.

Inside the club were the players—the off-duty policemen and government workers, lined up before sinks in the always crowded men's room, marveling at God's invention of the nose; the young girls and women who clung to the pushers with greedy, obsequious desire sparked by the thought of how much money the dealer carried at that moment and how much they would spend on them; the dealers, cellular phones in hand, beepers on their hip, treating whole tables of friends to Dom Pérignon.

Nathaniel had come to Dante's to do business, to watch the women, to scope and study his competitors. But he came to Dante's as well to be bathed in the coherent, hypnotic mingling of music that taunted the brain with its thudding, militant beat and verbal warnings, the hint of sex buttressed by the unveiled glances of women whose price he could afford and the dangerous combustion of drugs passed beneath tables and car trunks filled to bursting with guns for sale. Nathaniel sat at a table alone, every pore of his body electrified by what he saw, all of his senses taut, poised for action. The club itself was a narcotic, all of its components activating or slurring vital life signs, challenging and egging on every forbidden, stifled fantasy, setting desire of any kind to music.

A strobe light whirled from the ceiling, casting tiny slivers of light around the hall beneath the pale blue darkness tinted with red. The strobe light made the dance floor look like a movie cut by somebody on Quaaludes, the dancers' movements made swift incisions in the semi-darkness, their faces inert yet glowing.

Earlier that evening Nathaniel had seen Ulysses and collected his share of the take. He had recruited Ulysses right here in Dante's one evening after they all finished work. Like Nathaniel, Ulysses was a courier and Nate felt comfortable with him. Like Nate, he had had something to lose, something he valued more than the dealing. Ulysses had been married since he was eighteen, six years, and he was a settled, inconspicuous kind of guy. He had two kids and his wife was a secretary. On the side, Ulysses was a musician who hoped to make it big one day and he was building a stash to buy a club where *he* would be the main attraction every night. Still, Snookie was the best of the three of them—he sold more cocaine faster than Nate could supply him with. And everybody in town knew Snookie. Snookie knew when a major bust was coming before anybody else. If the shit was bad or tainted, Snookie would warn them to look out. Snookie beat them at their own game because he had nothing to lose and everything to gain. He was hungrier than Nathaniel or Ulysses could ever imagine being. But the nigger was crazy. Right here, Nathaniel and Ulysses had watched Snookie beat the shit out of a dude at the bar who he heard call him an ugly motherfucker. Snookie beat the guy so badly the guy was unconscious for three days. And Snookie had done it so methodically, so dispassionately, that he might have been sawing a piece of wood rather than bashing in a man's head. Nathaniel had taken him on as a runner because he looked at Snookie's face and figured he could control him. But by the time Nathaniel realized how indispensable and dangerous Snookie was, he didn't know how to tell him to get lost. Ulysses had been telling him for months to let Snookie go, had told him how he was always grumbling about wanting to widen their network. Yet until recently, Nathaniel had counted Snookie's intimate knowledge of the streets and the whole drug scene as worth more than any aggravation he might cause. Besides, he knew, they all knew, you didn't just "fire" Snookie. If and when Snookie split, there would be a price to pay and Nathaniel wasn't sure who would pay it.

Nathaniel took a sip of Courvoisier and as he set the glass back on the table, he saw Snookie walk out of the press of bodies on the dance floor. Smoothing his suit, Snookie gazed around him with a carefully honed paranoia and then walked over to Nathaniel.

"How's it going?" Snookie smiled, his small skeptical eyes assessing Nathaniel as he sat across from him.

"OK, OK," Nathaniel answered smoothly, his voice belying the quivering nervousness Snookie's presence nearly always invoked.

Snookie slid a brown envelope across the laminated tabletop.

"You look good," Nate said generously, slipping the envelope into his pocket. "New suit?"

"Yeah. You like it?"

"I might get one myself." They both knew that was a lie, for the suit advertised its wearer's quest for the least easily attainable attributes—style and confidence. On another body the suit could have been an enhancement, but on Snookie what the suit attempted to portray was incongruous and so unexpected it became fraudulent.

"I was thinking of getting a couple of these," Snookie said absently, then said urgently, "I been waiting to talk to you for a while."

"I know. And I know what about."

"Now's the time, Nate. If we don't move to expand, cover more turf, somebody else will. Hell, I got folks at GPO I can't even supply. The other government agencies are just sitting there, waiting."

"Look, we agreed."

"Yeah, we agreed back then. Hell, that was over a year ago. The stakes are higher now. You can't *sorta* push cocaine, either you in it all the way or you get run over by the competition."

"We agreed to be cool. To get in and get out with our skins and Ulysses still goes along with that. And if you don't . . ."

"When was the last time you was on the streets? Y'all push in them office buildings and high-rises. Hell, my customers are all over—in the clubs, on the block. And out there it's hot. So many new young punks are moving in it makes your head spin. I almost got ripped off last week."

"Where was your piece?"

"Hell, that's what saved my life and my money. But the dude couldn't have been more than fifteen. That's the shit that blew my mind."

"What's your proposal?"

"That we jump in full-steam ahead. Recruit some more runners, get the word out that our turf is ours. Send out some messages. Kick some ass if necessary." Snookie sat before Nathaniel, his face gleaming with sweat. The actions he had outlined so excited Snookie that Nathaniel imagined if he gave the word Snookie would charge out the door and off somebody that second. "And we got to expand or be moved on, that's the reality."

"Let me think about it, you don't just pull runners off the street," Nate said, his stomach rumbling in discontent, feeling the neat, ordered world he had erected crumbling in the wake of Snookie's words.

"But you don't just sit still when everybody around you is moving either."

"Let me think about it, I'll call you in a few days," Nathaniel said, dismissing Snookie with a worried, agitated nod of his head. And at that moment Snookie knew what he would have to do and knew he could do it easier than he'd once thought. This knowledge arrived almost as a blessing and calmed the jittery impatience that had racked him as he listened to Nathaniel, hedging and, he could tell, afraid.

"OK, man, whenever you ready," Snookie said, rising, imagining that he sounded as suave as a diplomat. Standing up, he caught of glimpse of himself in the mirror. Slicking back his hair, he said, patting the .22 bulging in his side pocket, "Yeah, I think I'll pick up a few more of these suits. Clothes *do* make the man."

hen Nathaniel placed his key in the lock of the front door, he knew that Esther would be awake. It was 2:00 A.M., Sunday morning. And he had not seen his mother since he left for work Friday morning at 7:30. Even then he had not seen her, but rather heard her, her voice, stretched prying and determined into the second-floor hallway as he left the bathroom. Es-

ther had asked in an interrogative tone that belied the early hour, "Will you be home for dinner, Nate?"

"Maybe. I don't know," he called back, hurrying down the hall, not because he was going to be late, which was guaranteed, but to place his bedroom door between himself and his mother. And wrapped only in a towel below his torso, leaning against the bedroom door and clutching the doorknob tightly as if to bar any sudden attempted entry, Nathaniel wondered why, more and more, he was filled to overflowing with rage by the insistence of Esther's concern. Sometimes with his mother it was just like with Trudy, he couldn't stand for her to touch him. Rarely could he look Esther in the face now. And his reluctance to do so inspired her to grab his chin in her sturdy fingers and force his face into full view. Nathaniel knew that Esther saw the bloodshot eyes and the bags from too little sleep. And she saw his lips pursed in defiance, prepared to offer nothing in answer to her questions, the who, what, when, where, why she demanded as if he was still a child. Her love had always threatened to extinguish him, for he had been her child, the son, confessor, friend during all the years Logan was away. Once, when he was twelve and Esther broke up with some guy she'd been seeing, it was on his narrow shoulder that she had cried, the mascara she wore bleeding onto his shirt, the snot from her nose dripping from the too dainty handkerchief onto his neck. And it was he who, as Esther begged him, prepared a gin and tonic (he made them better than she) and gave it to her, then at her request put on his pajamas and watched Cary Grant on the late show with her, stretched out on her bed, back against one of her overstuffed pillows, and let Esther hold his hand until she feel asleep. It was he who did all this and was late for school the next morning because of too little sleep.

She was as persistent a presence in his life as she had been sporadic in Logan's. When he left for school in the mornings, even in high school, Esther's gaze padded behind him like an eager puppy as she stood at the front window of their house. She had never liked any of his girlfriends and, in exasperation with his choices, took to bringing home the daughters of friends for him to meet over dinner. And they were nearly always timid, plain young girls who Esther thought would be grateful to be desired by her son. Their dull pallor would absorb and mute the volatility that made Nathaniel so alluring and that also promised disaster. In time, since Esther did not like the girls he brought home, he chose only the girls he would not have wanted to bring home anyway, girls whose appetite for danger was even greater than his own, girls who had babies but no husbands, dead-end jobs and no desire for anything more, girls who thought fucking was the highest form of human communication, girls he even hid from his friends.

"That you, Nate?" he heard Esther ask.

"Yes, ma'am."

"What time is it, son?"

"Two o'clock."

He found her in the living room, huddled on the sofa in socks and a terry-cloth robe, her hair in rollers. Barren of makeup, Esther's face was that of a woman who was simply getting old and who had chosen to resist the onslaught of age with a well-stocked arsenal of denial and retreat. As he sat down across from Esther, Nathaniel noticed the Bible that she clutched in her lap. It was a small white leatherbound Bible with gold lettering.

"What are you doing up so late?" he asked.

"I wanted to be sure I saw my son."

"I called earlier this evening," he lied.

"I haven't stepped out of the house once today," she told him coldly. "If you want to live like people do in a rooming house, move into one."

"What did I do wrong? What is it you want?"

"You still owe me some respect," Esther fumed.

"What about me? Don't you owe me some freedom?"

"Freedom? Seems to me that's all you've got. Freedom to run the streets. You think freedom's nothing but doing what you want."

"Shut up!" Nathaniel shouted, clamping his palms over his ears. "Shut up, just shut up," he roared, looking down at the floor.

Esther bounded from the sofa as resolutely as a panther and stood before Nathaniel, slapping him on his cheeks and on the side of his head in rage. She grabbed the collar of his jacket and hauled him onto his feet. Staring up at him, tiny petals of sweat blossoming around her brows, stationed on the skin of her forehead, she said, "Damn you for your pride and arrogance. Damn you, I say, even if you are my child."

The words sapped the strength from Nathaniel's legs and brought him nearly crashing to his knees. "Just tell me what you want, Mama. Tell me what you want," he sobbed breathlessly into the folds of Esther's robe. Her hand rested on his head and she whispered, "Nate, I want you to be good. That's all. Just be good."

"Mama, I'm sorry."

"I know you are, Nate. I'm sorry too. And for more than you know." Esther gently slumped on the floor beside Nathaniel and asked, "Will you pray with me?"

"I don't know how."

"Well, you let me pray for us both."

And Nathaniel sat bowed on the floor, listening to his mother's voice, pleading, triumphant, shamed, ask for his deliverance. He had thought the words would evoke some power that would wash over him, rivet him with fear, and Nathaniel sat on his knees and waited to feel forgiveness, waited to know transcendence. But he only heard his mother's voice and it sounded, the longer the prayer lasted, as it always did, as confused and longing as his own. And so, without even being aware of it, Nathaniel closed his ears and heart to Esther and her prayer for his redemption.

When she finished the prayer, Esther asked Nathaniel, "Will you be good?"

And Nathaniel promised her that he would. He promised this even as he knew it was already too late.

Chapter Thirty-Two

Nathaniel sat in his car, parked across the street from Trudy's apartment. He had finished up business for the night, made his last delivery two blocks away.

It had rained all afternoon, a slow, steady humid drizzle that contradicted the generous sunshine and balmy light winds of the previous day. Springtime had limped in, indecisive and unpredictable, unseating winter with a fickle, uneasy strategy. Trudy's apartment building was a massive four-hundred-unit structure across the street from Meridian Hill Park that had once been an elegant hotel. Faded art deco murals and tapestries unraveling at the edges lined the walls of the lobby. The building now reeked of past unretrievable glories and fear of the future. Young Black professionals, Hispanic couples and elderly men and women crossed paths in the carpeted halls, their worlds foreign, indecipherable, resisting forced entry by a smile or hello in the hallway.

Trudy lived in the building with her mother, who owned a small public relations firm. She was a brisk, extremely attractive woman whose abundant charisma had been passed to her daughter. They lived on the eighth floor and Nathaniel gazed at the upper windows, half-expecting to see Trudy at the window.

Although Nathaniel was older than Trudy, she always managed to make him feel like she was the one in charge. In fact, she'd asked him out the first time. She was a secretary-receptionist at a law firm he made deliveries to several times a week. That's how they met. Trudy was the first person he saw through the glass panels on either side of the mahogany door leading to Baker, Nash and Perry when he stepped off the elevator on the tenth floor. Nathaniel liked to watch Trudy handle several calls and visitors arriving at the same time—brisk and confident, ever polite and friendly. And if there was a secret, it was her voice—slightly gruff, almost masculine at its base, evolving into a recital of lighter yet no less vibrant tones. After she'd signed for a package, chatting with him about the weather outside or his weekend or something in the news, she'd look at him standing before the desk, just waiting for him to ask her a question that would change her life. Then she'd laugh a heartfelt, glowing laugh and hours later he would flash back to the flavor of her voice. Sometimes

Nathaniel would call Trudy's office, just to hear her speak. He didn't say a word and, even mildly irritated, asking "Who's calling, may I help you?", Trudy's voice shivered with the same secret yet persuasive unspoken pledge. After a while she knew he was making the calls. She didn't say anything, but the reluctant way she handed him back the forms and the clipboard she had to sign for the packages he delivered revealed her knowledge.

The same day he had decided to ask her out she slipped him a note on a sheet of pink stationery in return for the package he delivered that told him to meet her at one o'clock at the Post Pub across the street. Nathaniel did as he was told.

Over lunch, Trudy unfurled her desire for Nathaniel through a meticulous, unwavering interest in everything about him. She was calculating and spontaneous, rapt with attention and playful. She told Nathaniel very little about herself, plying him instead with questions that she had rehearsed to ask with just the right amount of ease. Nathaniel had never met a woman so unflinchingly interested in the details of his life and thoughts. Sitting across from Trudy, Nathaniel felt naked and yet strangely fulfilled, heard himself revealing beliefs, attitudes and opinions he had been only vaguely aware that he possessed. His conversations with his family throbbed with the weight of their disappointment in him and their breathless vigil as they waited for him to fit into the mold they had cast for him. And with his friends, conversation was studded with competitiveness, an edgy sense of incompleteness that inspired bouts of outrageous boasting or bravado but rarely an unplanned moment of revelation.

Trudy asked Nathaniel what few others had—"Who are you?" And when she heard his answer, Trudy watched it take shape before her eyes, refused to trample over or embellish Nathaniel's reply, but with him, respected the quest that the answer revealed.

She had not told him that first day, but soon Nathaniel discovered who Trudy was. They started dating and Trudy fell in love with him—and she fell in love the only way she knew how—rapturously, afire with the desire to lose herself completly. The deeper her love grew, after a year, the steadier and more blatant was Nathaniel's retreat. But Nathaniel's flight merely confirmed what love songs, soap operas, old wives' tales and movies had all taught Trudy—love was a psychic battleground, an emotional volcanic eruption that terrified men and obsessed women. In the script spewed forth by culture and conditioning, Trudy's role was to suffer as long as she recognized a sign of devotion from Nathaniel.

And yet they stayed together, bound more by their inability to create a new dance than real desire. Neither could say goodbye or that they had had enough. And so they spun like a top—ruthless and fast, the movement itself the only reason for being.

Even now Nathaniel didn't know what had happened. He did know that, in the end, Trudy had wanted too much, just like everybody else. The day before Christmas she told him she was pregnant.

"Pregnant?" he whispered, almost as though he didn't know what the word meant. They sat in his car and, as Trudy told him, it had started to snow, huge fluffy flakes that landed against the windshield and melted, sliding easily down the glass, as if, in the brief seconds of their existence, they had discovered that life was simply too much to bear. He had never asked Trudy about birth control, he had just assumed.

"I thought you were on the pill."

"I was for a while, but I started bleeding between my

periods and the doctor took me off of them and I was using the diaphragm and once or twice I didn't put it in. I didn't think anything would happen."

She was a woman, Nathaniel thought to himself, and, as a woman, she bore it all, the pleasure they shared and the responsibility to see that neither of them paid too high a price for that pleasure. She was a woman and she had failed them.

"Great," Nathaniel sighed bitterly, slumping in his seat. "Just fucking great."

"I'm sorry," Trudy said, as if she had stepped on his toe or knocked something out of his hand. "I'm so sorry."

Nathaniel turned on the radio and Nat King Cole, crooning "The Christmas Song," filled the car with a lush melodic comfort that almost made him relax.

"We'll have to get rid of it."

"I can't do that."

"Why not?"

"I don't believe in abortions. It's murder."

"This is a great time for political convictions."

"You mean *moral* convictions. I'm not surprised you want me to get an abortion. You don't know morality from politics."

"Maybe I don't know that," Nathaniel shouted, punching Trudy's shoulder and pushing her against the seat, "but I know the difference between a good life and a lousy one and me being a father right now is a recipe for a life I don't want." Pressing Trudy against the seat, straddling her, his heart pumping, so full of anger, Nathaniel thought how easy it would be to let his hands slide upward from her shoulders to her neck and . . .

"Get off of me!" Trudy screamed, her voice careening and hysterical. "Get off of me."

Nathaniel slid over to the steering wheel, breathless with disappointment.

"OK, go on, bail out, just like a man," Trudy screamed, fighting back tears. "I'll have my baby anyway. I don't care if you don't give me a dime. I don't need you," she blustered, fumbling with the door.

The snow was falling harder now, the flakes had evolved, become sturdier, stronger, able now to survive the fall, and they glazed the windshield with a thin slick coat that was turning, in the cold, to ice.

"Wait, hold on," Nathaniel said, pulling Trudy towards him. "I didn't say I wouldn't help. I said I'm scared. For Chrissake, you tell me I'm gonna be a father and act surprised because I lose it! Shit, give me a break, Trudy. That's the least I expect from you."

She lay snuggled against him, the car filling with the sound of one Christmas song after another, "White Christmas," "I Saw Mommy Kissing Santa Claus." The songs numbed them, temporarily diffused their anger and fear. Nathaniel knew he would not be able to change her mind. When she wanted something, Trudy pursued or clung to it with everything she had. Like the way she had held on to him. Just for the hell of it, he'd started seeing this other girl, just to get some space, some breathing room. And he had even let Trudy know it, had suggested that maybe she should go out sometimes with somebody else. But she hadn't. She had acted just like she had when he was hers exclusively and that impressed Nathaniel so much that he had dropped the other girl. A baby, what the fuck would that mean? Esther would croak at the news. Logan would shake his head, like he had expected it all along. He heard Trudy's gentle snores and shook her awake. He heard the ten-year-old voice of Michael Jackson, singing "Rudolph, the Red-Nosed Reindeer," and remembered how, as a child, he had wished that he would never have to grow up. The adults he witnessed seemed locked in a land of obligation and regret. To Nathaiel, it appeared that they could do anything they wanted and still they remained unhappy. Even then he had suspected that being an adult was a drag. Now he knew.

And so this night, as on so many others since Trudy's pregnancy derailed the certainty of what they thought they felt, they ended up in bed. Sex was now a refuge, blurring the pain and confusion that sprang, vivid and mocking, when they faced one another. Within half an hour of his arrival in Trudy's apartment, they lay next to each other in her bed. Her mother had gone out of town for the weekend and, as they had sat on the sofa, Nathaniel sipping a beer, their voices stumbled clumsily toward one another in tiny frightened steps, their words dazed and imprecise, hollow and lonely, offering questionable comfort neither was sure they could use.

When Nathaniel could no longer bear the sound of the silences drenching even their muted laughter, he reached for Trudy, pulling her close to him, as though this action was what all the mangled words were meant to lead up to anyway. Nathaniel's hands caressed Trudy's stomach, lifted the loose blouse she wore over a pair of slacks and found a comfort in the touch of her flesh that nothing she had said to him had offered.

And when it was over he felt like he had when they had sat on the sofa, terrorized by a vague yet utterly complete emptiness. Trudy turned on a small light next to her bed and the bedroom was colored by a soft glowing haze that hid the most important things about them. Nathaniel lay against his pillow, smoking, Trudy snuggled against him, her legs, beneath the sheets, entwined in his. Anyone looking at them for the first time would have thought they were in love.

"You'll come around to see me after the baby comes, won't you?" Trudy asked, as though Nathaniel was already preparing to leave.

"Sure. Why'd you ask that?"

"I just wanted to make sure."

All she could talk about now was the baby. And he hated that subject, grew tense, distant, longed to flee at the mention of the child.

"If you're really asking if I'll give you money for the baby, of course I will, and I wish you'd just say what you mean," Nathaniel said, taking a last long drag on his cigarette and mashing it out in an ashtray on the floor.

"I didn't mean that." Trudy's voice rose in indignation. "If I had, I'd have just said it."

"OK. OK," he apologized, irritable and impatient.

"What's the matter with you?"

"Nothing." Nathaniel shrugged. Then he said, "I've been having some trouble with my business, that's all." He was surprised to hear his voice, revelatory and seeking. Trudy leaned up on her elbow and gazed at him seriously. The lamplight glazed her caramel-colored skin with a sensuous sheen and her breasts hung heavy and promising, grazing his chest. Nathaniel saw Trudy's face—already detecting some part of his anguish—and was shamed by the love for him he saw mirrored there.

"What kind of trouble?"

"Snookie's not running for me anymore."

"Good riddance," Trudy said with a shiver. "He always gave me the creeps."

"It's not that simple."

"What do you mean?"

"Now he's my competitor. And one of us has got to go."

He was not surprised when it happened, when Snookie finally drew the line he had to cross. Nathaniel had awaited the arrival of this feared, awful place as one watched a rain-sodden sky for thunder. Violence was the sinewy undercurrent of the world he and Snookie inhabited. Nathaniel had witnessed young men shot over a glance raging with subtle misread implications, over indecipherable yet incriminating smiles exchanged with women or a tone of voice that brushed against hard-won self-respect like an arctic blast. Everpresent, thrusting itself around their necks with the skill of a mugger, violence hovered, its heart pumping silent and deep with the promise of a hammer blow. The drugs they sold were worth a fortune. But their lives were cheap as plastic trinkets and discarded with even less concern. And survival required that Nathaniel swear allegiance to this devastating equation. Until now he had not known that he had done so. Until now Nathaniel had chosen not to hear the sound of his own life.

Several weeks earlier Snookie had met him at Dante's and told him, "I'm tired of fucking around, man. As from today, I'm on my own. I run my own thing. and I run for nobody but me."

"When did you decide all this?" Nathaniel asked with a false yet studied aplomb.

"I been thinking about it a long time. A real long time," Snookie sneered. "Ever since I found out what a chump you are."

"And just what makes you think I'm a chump?" Nathaniel asked, flinching, yet feeling his body relax with a remarkable patience in the presence of someone he totally despised.

" 'Cause you scared, motherfuckah, you scared. And always will be, to go for the prize, to expand and take over."

"And you think you can do that?" Nathaniel asked, his eyes bulging with a withering incredulity that sparked the eruption of a brush fire of anger on Snookie's face. "You must know something nobody else does, man, you must have something I haven't seen since I met you. You're a loser and a punk. And don't come in my face with another word about nothing," Nathaniel said, rising from the table.

And as he stood gazing at Snookie, leaning on the table, Nathaniel broke into a lethal tremor of laughter, so brittle and mocking, dredged from so deep within him, laughter billowing like steam from his mouth and rising in clouds over Snookie's head, that people at other tables turned to look. And in the midst of this laughter that had set Nathaniel to trembling with smug mirth, Snookie jammed a switchblade into the tabletop a quarter inch from Nathaniel's hand, slicing the laughter, gutting its voice and surprising Nathaniel so that he quickly removed his hand and rubbed it, although it was not touched by the knife.

Staring at Nathaniel, Snookie dislodged the knife and warned, "Watch your back, man, watch your back. We'll see just *who* is *what*." And he stood up, ramrod-straight, his countenance oddly courageous as he buttoned his mohair coat and winked at Nathaniel, promising, "We gonna see. We gonna see."

"You're smarter than him," Trudy said when Nathaniel finished the story.

"That's not the point, that's got nothing to do with it. He's angrier, crazier than me, with less to lose."

"Didn't you know you were risking everything when you started?"

"Do you think I'd have gotten into this if I'd thought I could lose everything? Hell, I don't know. Maybe back then it didn't matter."

"It matters now. What're you gonna do? You'll have to defend yourself."

"Like you said," Nathaniel told her, "I'm smarter than him. That'll count for something."

The knowledge of what he had to do invested Nathaniel's days with an urgency that made each act he performed a reenactment of hope now permanently dashed. He managed in the days following his talk with Trudy to approach, in his imagination, the implications of the act that fate and survival required and, with a stunning dispassion, he gazed into the sunken hollow eyes of his future. No longer was he afraid. Fear would only hamper the execution of what he had convinced himself was nearly a civic duty. Taking Snookie out would leave the world with one less walking, talking nightmare, one less mutation of human potential, one less scar on the flesh of the city. And some mornings he managed to wake up flushed not with fatigue but pride at the thought of what he was going to do. And when it was over he would get out, just like he'd planned, get out and go straight, maybe try to make things right with Trudy, go back to school. Nothing in his life after this would fill him with the same tightrope-walking, on-the-edge, in-control, maniacal, dreadful sense of power. Nothing. Not sex. Not love. Not living. Not death. But he would get out, there'd be nothing else he could do.

And it was in these days that were, unbeknownst to him, his last days that Nathaniel discovered his love for his mother. He had promised to be good, made the oath to both Esther and Logan, and so, as a counterpoint poised in obscene juxtaposition to what else lurked in his heart, Nathaniel tried to become the son his mother wanted. She was a beautiful woman. He had always thought that. So precise and careful now, her countenance a stark reprisal against the despair-drenched, madness-haunted, courage-filled days of her youth. When he looked at his mother's face, Nathaniel could not believe the stories Naomi and Logan hinted at, the tales dropped carelessly in conversations, that in the wake of revelation were censored, checked, closed against Nathaniel's eager questions. Families created mythologies to serve and protect the illusions they needed most, this is what Nathaniel now knew. And truth, more often than not, simply got in the way.

He spent more time at home now and, in the mundane extraordinary passage of time with Esther, Nathaniel profoundly regretted the possibility that everything he discovered now was a postscript to his existence, scribbled too late. One evening after Nathaniel had beaten Esther at two games of Monopoly and the card table was littered with popcorn and cans of Diet Pepsi, as they gathered up the play money, the deeds and other miscellany of the game, Esther said, "It's important that you are good to Trudy." She told him this slowly, the words breathless and weighty, her eyes assessing him with resolute concentration.

"What do you mean?" Nathaniel asked, placing the top on the Monopoly box, shoving the game to the center of the table.

"I know you don't love her. But she's going to have your child. So if you forsake her, you forsake that baby too."

"But you were the one who told me to tell her to get rid of it."

"That was my disappointment talking," Esther said with a shake of her head. "I had no right to tell her what to do."

"Did you ever think of getting rid of Logan or me?" Nathaniel stretched his legs out beneath the table, laced his fingers together behind his head and nestled against the caress of these unexpected moments of intimacy.

"It never crossed my mind. And I wasn't married either. And I want you to tell Trudy that if she needs anything— anything at all—to get in touch with me."

"I will," Nathaniel said quietly. "Now I'll always be a father and I was hoping . . ."

"Now you'll always be a man—if you handle this right."

"It takes more than a baby to make somebody a man," Nathaniel countered with a nervous laugh that made him sit up straight.

"All your life, Nate, everything you do in it really is about how you treat other people, what you give to them, do for them, ask from them. A baby makes you deal with that in more ways than you thought possible."

"What have I got to give a baby?" he asked, shrugging indifferently, looking away in shame.

"You're my child, you're your father's child. So you've got plenty."

"He'd be disappointed if he saw me caught up in all this."

"Not really, he'd just see it as a test. He'd watch to see what you did. Which way you took, the easy way or the hard way. In the end, Nate, the hard way is all there is."

"I'm thinking about going back to school in the fall."

"Thinking about? Or planning to?"

"Thinking about."

"Well, that's a start."

"Was it all as easy for Logan as it looked?"

"You just don't know how hard it was. I wasn't there for him, like I was for you. Randolph and Mama mostly raised him. They did a better job than I could've back then. And he was real close to Randolph. But a child needs both parents. I say that, even though I've been able to give you all the material things you needed. You need a father to trust and a mother so you'll have somebody to please. You and Logan both got cheated. But then, there's a way we all get less than we're owed somewhere along the line. You got cheated. But me and Mama gave you all we had. Sometimes it works out to be enough. Was it enough, Nathaniel, was it enough?"

"I wish my father had been here," Nathaniel said.

"So do I, Nate, so do I."

Chapter Thirty-Three

Nathaniel watched his back, while shaping and trying to discover a way to strike. Then Ulysses was beaten and robbed by one of Snookie's runners and he told Nathaniel to count him out. Nathaniel recruited two new runners, certain he could start over, and within two weeks they too were beaten and robbed by Snookie's men. Nathaniel had not seen Snookie since the night at Dante's, yet he had felt him, sensed him like a radioactive force field erected around all his future plans. Now that his men were being routed, nobody took Nathaniel seriously. His customers played around with money they owed him, suppliers tried to sell him stuff so impure Nathaniel refused to buy it. And now the fear returned, for he had not anticipated the subtlety of Snookie's mind, that he would launch an attack that was psychological rather than physical. Snookie put out the word and Nathaniel found it impossible to get runners. And everywhere in "the world" he went—the clubs, the streets, the bars—Snookie's name was on everyone's lips. He had put not just Nathaniel but a dozen others out of business and it was rumored that Snookie and his men were behind a turf war raging in Northeast that had killed five young men in ten days. The buyers, the sellers, the runners, the lieutenants, the suppliers all performed now in an atmosphere not unlike that which precedes a revolution or a coup—each moment fraught and unreliable, all attention riveted to a tomorrow so jealously sought, few cared what it would bring. Snookie had won, that's what everybody would think. That's what they'd think until they heard how Snookie had got his. Nathaniel knew that half a dozen crushed former dealers were gunning for Snookie, but he wanted to be the one to do it. He had decided what to do when one of Snookie's runners met him as he came out of the courier office one afternoon and told him that Snookie wanted to have a peace conference with him, wanted to discuss ways that maybe they could work together. Nathaniel told the thirteen-year-old boy to tell Snookie to meet him in the parking lot behind Dante's, Monday at ten o'clock. Three days away.

The next day Trudy had the baby and Nathaniel sat and talked to Logan about everything except that which mattered most. Logan had convinced him to talk to Trudy, to make peace with her, and he had tried, entering Trudy's room after Logan left, only to find Trudy asleep. Nathaniel sat in the chair beside her bed and watched Trudy sleep, lying on her side, her palms balled into fists, her face unsettled and agitated, as though the tail end of a disturbing dream or premonition had rumbled across her mind. Nathaniel sat in a dark green slant-backed chair, as darkness filtered into the room, its arrival a relief. He closed his eyes and a jumbled static-filled image of Snookie and Esther and Trudy, his new baby daughter, all superimposed over one another, fading in and out, looming, laughing, the baby crying, Esther gazing at him like a stranger plumbed the depths behind his closed eyes. When he opened his eyes, the images, regurgitated from the tangled web of fear tightening across his stomach, stoking the perspiration soaking his skin, disappeared. But when he closed his eyes for longer than the time it took to blink, Nathaniel heard the scrambled, squealing return of the images, too close to his heart to ignore, too incriminating to watch.

When he left the hospital, Nathaniel drove to Logan's house, running red lights, jamming on the brakes, gazing in his rear- and sideview mirrors to see the startling dream trailing him like smoke from the exhaust. He parked before Logan's house and only as he reached for the keys did Nathaniel see that the house was dark, its shutters drawn, sitting closed against the entry he needed at that moment more than anything else. And the sight of the darkened house so saddened Nathaniel that he sat in his car and wept as he had never done before. And the tears, drained from behind his lids, cleansed him of the dream, washed away the loved/ feared faces. The tears had set him free. Then Nathaniel reached in the glove compartment and retrieved his gun. He held the .22 in his lap, watched his brother's house, and the cold, resistant feel of the weapon assured Nathaniel that by Monday night everything would be all right.

let the issue lay for a while, almost all summer
long. I knew where the nigger lived, where he
was half the time, who was his customers, the
whole bit. I could've done it anytime. But I
wanted to catch him off-guard. Let him think
I'd forgot about his smart-assed remark. Let
him think I was so busy building me a empire
I didn't have time for punks like him. I'd spotted his weakness way back. Way back. He
liked to act tough, but that's really all it was.

A act. He'd never had to *be* tough. So all the acting in the world couldn't save his ass on the streets I be walking. Nigger had a heart. And ain't no room for nothing like that in this scene. Don't nobody care how big your heart is. Anybody I ever saw with a heart got it tore out or broken. And I decided, early on, that wasn't for me. How big is your wad of bills? How big is your Benz? How big is your bank account? Don't nobody give a damn how big your heart is.

When I was a little kid, I used to have these fantasies about me growing up and becoming a lawyer. You know—the suit, the briefcase, the whole bit. I got that from watching TV all day long. Then when I'd go to sleep at night, got so I was having these dreams about me as a lawyer. But no matter how hard I tried, in them dreams, I always turned out white. I'd try and try to make the man in the dream Black, but only now and then could I do it. And then he was real fuzzy. But I could see him like he was standing next to me when he was white. Well, I sure didn't want to be no white man so I forgot all about wanting to be a lawyer and did what I was good at.

I felt kinda sorry for him almost. I mean, he'd set his own self up and he didn't know it. Thinking he could be a shark when he was raised to be a guppy. And, I figgered, even if I did some time, so what? I'd been doing time since the day I come from between my mama's legs. I'd done time before and it just made me tougher, prepared me even more for the world outside the joint. Doing time ain't no big thing. But got so he was like a fly bothering me. And I wanted his trade. I couldn't stand knowing he was out there selling. I'd muscled some other folks out the way, carved out my turf and took over theirs. He was the last one left.

I got a coupla my runners to jump Ulysses and kick his ass as a warning. Told them to tell him next time it was gonna be Nathaniel. And then one night I saw the punk at Celebrity Hall. The place was packed, teenagers, the go-go music pounding like some jungle beat. He was there by himself. And I'll say this, he looked good, the chump did. Looked good, like he always did. Dressed like he'd just stepped out of some magazine. Looking sure of himself and proud. You'd have never thought by looking at him that he'd lost half his trade, that he was scrambling for customers. Ulysses wasn't running for him no more. In fact, Ulysses wasn't running for nobody, not even himself. I saw to that. So it was just Nathaniel now, hustling all by his lonesome. I watched him go out in the parking lot with a young girl who made a buy. I coulda walked up to him then and did it. Bumped into him. Said something to him, shit, just got up in his face and did it, but I wanted to catch him off-guard and I wanted to invade his turf.

And then, after that night, seemed like I couldn't stop thinking about him. And then I realized the real reason I wanted to do it. It wasn't 'cause of what he said in that bar. I'd bashed niggers' heads for less than that. It was 'cause I wasn't never gonna have what he had or be what he was. Way back when it counted, somebody had made him feel like he was something special. Naïve as he was, you could see that, by the way he talked and walked and dealt with people. Other dudes liked him. Bitches wanted to give him some play. And the more I thought about it, the more I realized I wasn't never gonna be able to be *me* till he was off the scene.

And that peace conference number, well, I coulda done it at Dante's just as well as anyplace else. But I got impatient.

Didn't want to wait three days and I drove over to where he lived that Sunday morning. He lived in one of them neighborhoods where people was all the time cutting their grass or sweeping the street or washing their cars. Like the cleaner they were, the safer they were. Looking at those houses, you'd think the people that lived in them didn't know what sin or misery was. Nathaniel lived on the kind of street everybody wants to live on.

Well, I parked across the street from his house and just

waited. I didn't know what I was waiting for. I just knew what I was gonna do. But a hour later, his momma comes out the house and I could tell by the way she was dressed she was headed for church. She drove off and, although Nathaniel's car was parked at the corner, I couldn't see no movement in the house.

I took the gun out of my briefcase. And for nearly half an hour I just sat there, thinking how good I'd feel when it was done. When he wasn't around no more and I could go on and be me. Like when I got rid of that girl in junior high school. The one I raped 'cause I knew there was no other way somebody like me could ever have somebody like her. I felt good for a while after she left the school. Felt almost like a real person, like I was as good as everybody else. But then that bad feeling, the one that makes me feel like I'm nothing, it come back, just like clockwork. Maybe this time, I figured, it'll go away for good. Go away and stay away. And thinking about making the feeling go away made me get out of the car. The street was still quiet, hardly nobody stirring. And I walked up the steps to Nathaniel's house and rang the bell. I rang it three times and finally I heard him coming down the steps, hollering, "Who is it? Who is it?" And with no reason to be scared, living on a street like this, the chump just opens the door. He's got on a undershirt and a pair of BVD's, he standing there scratching his balls, his eyes ain't even all the way open. And just as they open all the way, I unloaded my .22 in his stomach. And his eyes filled with so much surprise, just before they closed the last time, I almost wanted to explain to him why I had to do it. But there wasn't no time for that. Besides, I was beginning to feel better already. And by the time I got to the car and saw the man next door to Nathaniel's house open his door and look out to see what was happening, I felt pretty good indeed.

ogan sat in the kitchen of his house, the sound of Naomi's voice peeling like skin from his memory. It was 2 A.M. He had sat the entire evening at his grandmother's side as she unearthed and recalled family history, private pain. Logan had sat enraptured by Naomi's griot-like rendering of all that had made them a family. Much of it he knew and yet the retelling, time and again, surprised and redeemed him, reaffirmed him as inheritor and link in a family he did not know how to deny.

Upstairs Felicia and Mugabe slept and the house was still, blessed and certain, seeming to assure Logan that it would always shelter and protect. He liked the feel of his house around him. At that moment the house—inanimate yet alive—reminded Logan of the things that transcend disaster, overcome despair. He took a sip from a can of beer, seeking to erase the sight of Esther from his mind. When he left Naomi gently falling into slumber, her voice hoarse, stubborn, tired yet not depleted, Logan walked downstairs to the living room and lifted Esther from the sofa and carried her to her bedroom, where, as she lay nearly entombed in a pill-induced sleep, he removed her shoes, her dress and covered her with a thin blanket. Esther's face was clenched, frozen into a permanent mask of disbelief that even sleep could not subdue.

In the living room Logan began to gather the photos of Nathaniel that Esther had removed from the photo album and that lay scattered on the sofa and the coffee table like clues left to find the way home. Logan picked up the photos and saw Nathaniel's face as he always thought of it now— the face he used to blot out the memory of death. And what Logan saw on his brother's face made him leave the photos as Esther had left them—cluttered, disruptive, now all she had.

And now, sitting in his kitchen, Logan felt Nathaniel all around him, as he had felt him the day of the funeral, insistent, persistent, as he could not have felt him in life. He drained the can of beer and, as though running from the shadow of a ghost, Logan turned out the light in the kitchen and climbed the stairs to his bedroom. In the darkness he stripped quickly, quietly and fell heavily into bed beside his wife. Logan reached for Felicia, pulling her to him, she resisting him in sleep, and as she slept, he took her, with serious, grateful intent that still did not erase the presence of his brother. And when he was through, Logan kissed Felicia, still asleep in his arms, watched her startled eyes open in the darkness and then he held her, held her tight and everlasting, so that he would never die.

Chapter Thirty-Six

N A O M I

don't have much longer, but I'm not ready to go just yet. Of course, there's days when I think of Nathaniel, I wish it had been me instead of him. I'd have been missed, but not like we miss him. I'd have been missed, but not with this anger and shame and confusion we all feel. I wish it had been me. And this is one time I'm not going to try to pacify myself by talking about the Lord's will. 'Cause this time the Lord's will, to me, makes no sense. Esther driving herself crazy asking what she did wrong and Logan feeling things too deep to even speak.

And yet I'm proud of my family, every last one of us, from Rayford right on through Nathaniel. We each had a destiny and for some of us God and the devil both had shaped it. Nathaniel got caught up in all that ugliness, not because he didn't know better but because he didn't know. He didn't know how to be afraid. How to fear God. That's what's killing everybody now. And the answer is so simple nobody can see it. He didn't belong to Esther anymore. Whether he liked it or not, manhood was trailing him, hot after him. And so he took on all the tests, made up answers that were loud but made no sense. We did all we could, but we couldn't do no more than our hearts would let us. And in every family there's pitiful few pure hearts.

All the things I've seen in eighty years! Much of it made me cry. But I wouldn't have missed none of it—my mama and my daddy, marrying Rayford, having Esther, raising Logan, seeing the progress my people have made, the distance we've come. And Nathaniel—we didn't have him long, but for the time we had him, he was a miracle. And it's not over. We got Amir and Tiambe and Mugabe. Even got the baby Trudy had. Still, just like I told Logan, I'm not going to miss this life. People laugh at me when I say it, but this thing called living has been the rough part, the part that hurts but we hold on to with everything we've got. I'm just biding my time. And I pray to go peaceful, right where I am now, in my bed. And, you know, there's days I almost can't wait? Love is going to replace life and from then on it's all smooth sailing. Love will replace life. Lord have mercy! I wonder how that feels?